Fr & Kai

Kyle T. Davis

Frostt & Kai Book One

DEDICATION

First and foremost, this book is dedicated to Jesus Christ, my Lord and Savior. Without Him I would be nothing and nowhere. Thank you, Lord, for all the blessings you have given me.

To my father for teaching me how to stand tall and have the courage to do what is right even when the world is against me. Thank you for showing me that hard work is nothing to be afraid of and making sure that even when I complained to kick my butt into gear.

To Mike, my father-in-law, thank you for trusting me with your daughter's heart and security, especially when I haven't deserved it. Thank for showing me how to grow a generous heart. You are a steadfast oak among men.

To Ben, my brother in all but blood, thank you for walking this life with me. For showing me what a true friend is and challenging me to see the world in new and different ways.

To these and all the countless men in my life, the teachers, friends, and mentors, who have helped shape me into the man I am today. Thank you for supporting me and giving me hope in my darkest times.

CHAPTER 1

Fumes wafted off brackish water outside the dive bar's open door. Inside, the softly lapping waves added to the low hum of muted conversation, battered lottery machines, and the clinking of half empty bottles attempting to fill the empty holes in people's lives. Shelves along the back of the bar held a barren variety of liquors and watered-down beer, a background to the old bartender wiping the counter.

Among the few occupying the lonely bar stools, Malcolm Frostt's agile frame hunched over his half-finished limp burger and greasy fries. Lean, hard-earned muscles rippled along his arm as he threw back the rest of his Maker's Mark bourbon, the best from the dusty shelves, and motioned to the bartender for another.

The aged bartender ambled over and poured another healthy measure of the amber drink. "Anything else from the kitchen, son? It be closin' shortly."

"No, thanks," Malcolm shook his head, his shoulder length black hair moving languidly, "I'm still picking away at this." He motioned to the half-eaten plate, "Bourbon will be more than good."

"Did you know bourbon got its name from Bourbon Street here in New Orleans?" said the bartender.

"I thought it was from Bourbon County in Kentucky. Or from the French," Frostt saluted with the dingy glass and downed it, "In the end I don't think it matters much. It's good and gets the job done." The bartender chuckled, filled his cup once again, and moved away to help the few other patrons at the bar.

Malcolm sipped at this cup, picking out the least greasy fries. An old tube TV glared over the far corner of the bar. The late-night news muted, but words scrolled along the bottom of the screen: *Historical swearing in of President Kai drew hundreds of thousands to the capital. First time in recent history a political event drew higher TV ratings than the Super Bowl---The Dow closed down 452 points, worries of...* Malcolm turned away from the TV and caught the barkeep's eye.

"New president today?" he let the word drop into a question.

"You been living under a rock, boy?" smiled the old man in genuine confusion, "Yeah, it's been all over the news and only thing on people's lips for the last fortnight."

"I don't get out much," replied Malcolm.

"What's your name, son?"

"Friends call me Mal."

"Okay, Mal. We got ourselves a historic day today." The bartender shook his head in good humor. "In all my life I never thought I would be seeing a black man as president, but I hoped. And it happened. But I would've laughed a good one if someone told me a woman would be president. We ain't that open of a country." Mal raised an eyebrow at that. "Yep, that's right. A woman president. But that ain't all. They say she is also the youngest president ever. Damn near a kid." He shrugged his shoulders, "But I am an old croon, so that could just be me."

"Youngest ever, ey?" chewed Mal.

The old man shook his head again, "Yep, but that's not the best part." He smiled large, "She is no Democrat or Republican. She's third party. An Independent."

"You're pulling my leg old man," Mal smirked. "No independent has been in office since John Tyler in 1790, and that was only cause the Wigs kicked him out after he became president."

"Wow, son, you're just a walking, drinking wealth of facts, but you don't know what president we voted in?" he chuckled.

Mal simply shrugged one shoulder dismissively.

"Yeah, it's something else, that's for sure. I voted for her. Why not? Didn't think it was going to do much, but I'm just tired of them two old parties bickering all the time. It's about time for some new blood. Shake things up I say."

Mal ran his hands down his long unkempt beard, the same deep black as his hair. Dark gunmetal eyes picked up flickers of the bars half-light. "You don't say? That is something else."

"Yep, things are changing." He pointed to Mal's drink. "Another?"

"Nah, I'm good." He pushed the glass away, and asked with furrowed brow, half an idea forming in his mind, "You turn up the TV though?"

"You be good, son," said the barkeeper. He took up the wrinkled cash Mal put on the counter and went to the TV to give a few good smacks before the volume worked.

The news anchor droned on, something about drugs and guns. A few moments later the news anchor faded away to what Mal was waiting for. The camera revealed a woman standing in front of the Capital Building in Washington D.C., in a pale fitted blue blouse and charcoal pants. Standing roughly 5'8", her raven hair brushed her collarbones as she spoke with a calm, collected poise, her voice clear and passionate. Her beauty resonated almost painfully, harsh, stone-cut. Strong.

Mal's idea changed from floating in the ether to something tangible as he stared at the woman on the screen. A plan formed at the fringe of his mind, the edges already bloody with violence.

Chapter 2

Michaela Kai smoothed her white blouse down once again, the clock mounted above the mirror reading ten minutes to six in the morning. She'd already been up for hours, a hard workout and cold shower having done little to ease her nerves. The tan slacks and white blouse fit her frame comfortably without crossing over to baggy. She had a lovely, strong figure, the result of good genetics, intense workout routines, discipline, and over a decade of military training, but she had no wish to show it off. Her face showcased her Japanese heritage beautifully, but her crowning feature was her eyes, a gift from her Irish grandmother. The intense and intelligent blue contrasted her midnight hair and angular face dramatically. Those almond shaped eyes now examined her outfit in the mirror critically. She was by no means a vain woman, but the momentous day weighed on her mind.

"What have I gotten myself into?" she whispered to the mirror. *I feel like a raw recruit just stepping off the bus, but in more danger,* she thought. A knock at the bedroom door interrupted her quiet reflections. Before she could respond or even step out of the massive walk-in closet, the bedroom door opened.

Anna Williams strode in on dangerously tall heels. "Good morning, Madam President." Her long blond hair pulled into a tight but stylishly frayed bun. "You sleep well?"

"Not really," replied Michaela. She moved over to the small sitting table in the far corner of her room. Her dress jacket hung off one of the chair backs.

"You are not really wearing *that* on your first full day," Anna gestured with her leather notebook up and down Michaela, "are you?"

"What? What's wrong with it?" Michaela scrutinized her outfit again, seeing nothing amiss.

"Oh, nothing, of course. *If* you want to make it obvious you're young and trying to appear older."

"I wore this all the time in the House, and you never had an issue with it before."

"Girl, your boobs disappear in that tent of a shirt," grimaced Anna, tapping her foot.

"I don't think the nation is going to be too worried about my boobs on my first full day as President."

Anna laughed a high chirping noise. "Yeah, honey, they will. They are going to care about everything. Now I am not telling you to show flesh, but you've got a good set of curves, girl, and it wouldn't hurt to see that bubble butt

"I do not have a bubble butt," snapped Michaela back with a laugh. Anna was not listening.

She had already put down her notebook and now searched around the walk-in closet.

Michaela had known Anna Williams for a little over eleven years. They first met at the Farm, the CIA training facility in northern Virginia. Michaela, known to Anna only then as MK, was on a stint of instructor duty after several major combat wounds. A result of her Special Operation Group team getting into a little unforeseen trouble on an operation. The SOG was a key part of the CIA's Special Activities Division, since renamed after Michaela's retirement to SAC, Special Activities Center. The SOG's mission was to deal with high threats and direct combat operations; missions and deep reconnaissance that the US government disavowed all knowledge of

By the time MK met Anna, she had a well-earned reputation among the CIA's clandestine services for being one of the best. MK drove Anna, the green recruit, into the ground. It was also MK though that recommended Anna for the Political Action Group. The other side of the coin to SAC, PAG went beyond manipulating foreign governments to handle psychological operations further out than even the US military could take credit for. Anna showed a keen knack for political games and cunningness that had been unmatched by any recruit in recent memory.

The women ended up working together several times over the next few years and after an extremely bloody and successful mission (and copious amounts of whiskey), the two became fast friends, sisters forged in blood. They kept in touch over the years, and when Michaela decided to retire to civilian life and then later run for the House of Representatives, Anna was the first person to join her team. Four years later, Anna continued to put her PAG skills to use, now as Chief of Staff to the newly appointed President Kai.

Anna emerged from the closet, the morning sun dusting her pale skin. "Here you go." She laid the new outfit on the bed: straight-legged charcoal pants Michaela knew would hug her backside, a turquoise button-down blouse with flattering neckline, and a black jacket with a tailored waist.

"I am not wearing that." Michaela folded her arms.

"MK," Anna set one of her famous eye-locking gazes on her. "Yes, you are. You are not leaving this room for your first day as badass Missy Prez looking like that."

"You do know you work for me, right?," stated Michaela, crossing her arms and raising an eyebrow.

Anna laughed again, "Me fashionista. You grease monkey. So, trust me. I am saving you from yourself."

"I don't want to come across as some flaunting bimbo, I need to look like a president!" Michaela let her anxiety peak through her words ever so slightly.

Anna's face softened. "MK, the world is changing. Come look at you. First female president, not to mention youngest ever." She sighed and leveled an earnest stare at Michaela. "What I am saying is you need to be conservative in your dress, but you also must not to shy away from your womanhood. It is important that you play both: Don't be a woman pretending to fill an old man's shoes, make them a *woman's* shoes." She pointed firmly at the clothes she'd selected, "This outfit screams first woman president: Strong leader, stylish and modest, proud and unashamed."

"Okay, okay," Michaela raised her arms up in defeat, "You are right, okay." She moved to collect the clothes and shoes and head back to the closet. "I need to stop arguing with you."

"True," said Anna as she snatched up her notebook again, the leather smoothed from years of handling. She opened it up, all business once again. "You've got a busy day today… well, a busy next four years, but that is beside the point." She flipped a few more pages. "We are breakfasting with CIA and Homeland Directors, then we need to review your State of the Union speech, then a meeting with the Joint Chiefs about North Korea's latest posturing. Then it's lunch, maybe," she shrugged, "then off to a Cabinet meeting. That is going to be a long one. After that, you have a debrief on the latest out of Iran. Lastly, you have a late meeting with Senate party heads and Conrad… the dickhead." A rueful chuckle escaped the closet at the last comment. Conrad Crane was the Speaker of the House of Representatives. An extreme left-leaning Democrat, he and Kai had sparred many times on the House floor. Not to mention he was the democratic candidate that Michaela wiped the floor with during the Presidential election. Anna looked up from her notebook, "Then we need to find some time to go over our platform. We need to strike while the iron is hot on some of the commitments you made during the campaign."

Michaela strode out of the closet, grudgingly admitting she felt more herself and more confident in the outfit Anna had picked. "The vets are first. We are changing it."

"Damn girl, you fill that out." Michaela ignored her.

"I am serious, Anna," glared Michaela. "We are going to address veterans' health first. I will not stand and watch more of them fall apart after what they have sacrificed for this country."

"Yes," Anna waved her hand. "I know. It's not going to be easy." At a well-known look on Michaela's face, Anna rushed on, "but we will make it happen. It will show your dedication and commitment."

Anna cleared her throat and stretched her already tall height of 5' 11", not counting the heels.

"President Kai are you ready to start your day?"

"Yes, Madam Chief of Staff."

The two grinned.

∘ ∘ ∘

Light spilled through the muddy portholes into the makeshift office/bedroom. Mal's fingers flew over the keyboard, the printer next to him grinding away on a set of documents.

The room smelled of whiskey and microwave dinners. The old fishing trawler swayed unnoticed by Mal. The bustle of the New Orleans Marina was in full swing in the early hours of the morning. The fishing trawler did little to stand out, not the worst boat in the slips nor close to the best. Pale beige paint peeled at dozens of spots, rust showing through in many, the outriggers were a rusted mess, and the windows of the top cabin cracked and spider-webbed.

Inside was not a sight much better. Engine grease and oil-stained the floor, the small galley piled with dirty dishes, and the smell of dead fish that never seemed to leave the once-proud, but now nearly derelict, fishing vessel. Unseen by anyone was the array of hidden cameras and motion sensors.

Malcolm moved about the main cabin, picking up a few books and heading back to his computer, then to the printer to read over the latest spewed-out text. He pinned several of them to the hull of the boat, the entire bow wall of the craft covered in newspaper clippings, printouts, and handwritten notes, with both multicolored string and large, red Sharpie lines connecting the wall of madness into a nut house. It would've been the envy of any tinfoil-hatted man.

A cleared section of the wall held a new set of photos, text, and strings. A magazine photo sat at the center of it all. A black-haired, vibrantly beautiful woman. The bold print of the magazine read, 'President-Elect Kai: A look into the life of the soon-to-be most powerful woman on the planet.' Her face was circled in thick red Sharpie. Mal paused for a moment, a foldout map of Washington D.C. clasped in his hands, and stared at the photo of the woman. Only a few years older than himself.

An old 1980s TV, its glass cracked in the corner, showed the morning news rambling on about the stunning and powerful outfit of President Kai on her first full day in office, modest and feminine in the same stroke. Mal spread the map out on the kitchen table, downed a day-old cup of coffee, and started to trace outlines with a pencil and ruler.

Several minutes later, he tossed both aside. "Dammit! Just piss an' half." He looked at the map with disgust. "It will never happen in D.C. Just too many variables," he let out a heavy sigh, "it will have to be somewhere else."

He looked at the map for another minute and then proceeded to fold it up when a new voice on the news caught his attention.

"Yes, Julie. I don't agree with the new President on the veterans' health plan. There I said it," the male voice finished with a chuckle. Mal turned to look at the TV. The news anchor, Julie, was interviewing a man that Mal recognized immediately. His photo hung in several spots on his crackpot wall: Senator Andrew Otts from New York State.

Julie, looking unconvincingly concerned, asked, "What do you mean by that Senator? Are the veterans' not deserving of better care?"

Otts waved his hand in mock protest. "Now, don't put words into my mouth." His perfect teeth flashed, and his thick golden hair lay stylish above his well-tanned face. "What I am saying is, why just veterans. The health crisis affects everyone. I completely understand the sacrifice, having served in the Navy myself." Mal snickered at the comment. He knew from his research what Otts meant by "serving". He was a paper-pusher in the Navy, and never once step on a boat outside of basic training, much less saw any combat. He served his single enlistment with no major merit or even gaining a new rank as an office rat in D.C.

The TV went on, crackling with a lack of reception on the antenna, "Why not the single mom? Why not the senior who can't afford the medical care they need?" He did another perfect smile and split his attention between the camera and Julie. "What we need is no more half fixes nor false promises for one particular group, but a full comprehensive fix to the health crisis."

"That is a great point Senator. And with Congress split across party lines that may be a larger challenge than this young President can take on. Especially with no party of her own."

"Yes, but this also may be the perfect time. The one thing President Kai has done well is fill out her new administration with a great mix from both sides," replied Otts. "It is my hope that we can put aside party lines and with the help of a neutral president, make real progress. Progress that helps the American people."

Mal zoned out as the news show moved onto new topics. He looked over the section of the wall dedicated to Senator Andrew Otts. He chewed his lower lip looking over the clippings and notes. The connections of chance and of design.

A few more hours of research, a half-dozen protein bars, and a few pots of coffee later, Mal closed for the day, the sun barely over its apex. He looked at the clock: twelve hours to his next task. A task that needed the cover of deep night. He fell asleep in his efficient way, a customized Heckler & Koch P30 sitting on the makeshift nightstand. Next to the pistol, a weathered and frayed photo of a young, red-haired woman and a small girl leaned against a half-finished bottle of Wild Turkey 101.

Chapter 3

The night still hung onto the humid heat of the day, damp, and cloying. Half the streetlights were out or flickering. A few people moved around the rundown neighborhood, no one paying attention to the limping homeless man working his way slowly up the street. A tattered oversized coat, dirty hair, and muttering sounds warned people off, not to mention the smell of spoiled meat wafting off the man.

The man turned a street corner. Two barely dressed young women standing by the streetlight moved a few paces away as he passed. He continued to move down the dead-end street, a cul-de-sac at the end, only one house with lights still on, the largest on the block. The man nearly fell over trying to walk over a section of broken sidewalk, his gait stuttering at best. He turned before reaching the large house and slipped into a short walking path that cut through the block and led out of the cul-de-sac. He quickly moved through the side gate into the yard of the large house. A row of trash cans greeted him, along with the rhythmic drum of music coming from the house easily loud enough to piss off the entire neighborhood. But no one brave enough to ask the inhabitants to turn it down.

With little care to be quiet, the homeless man pulled the lids off the trash cans and moved about searching for dinner. It only took a few minutes for a head to look out a side door window and then two young men, both holding large beer bottles, stepped out onto the raised patio.

"Yo, old shit," barked out one, a lit joint between his lips. "Piss off. Go find some other trash to eat."

The man in rags muttered in return. Digging deeper into the trash, he put his head into the can to search for buried treasure.

"Shit," said the same man again. The other one took a long draft of beer and laughed drunkenly. "Hey, beggar man!" The man said as he stepped down the three steps and grabbed the back of the dingy coat. "You gotta go before we beat your ass."

The beggar moved away from the pulling hand just enough to fully extend the man's arm. The man breathed out to say something new, but stopped seeing the beggar's eyes. Sharp and hard. The hand that came out of the folds of the beggar's coat struck him in the throat, the joint falling away and the bottle dropping to the ground. The beggar twisted the man to the side and a soft *thump* sounded out as a bullet flew from the end of the silenced custom H&K P30 pistol. The 9mm round punched a hole clean through the second man's head, still standing on the patio. The gun turned on the man closer, trying to pull in breath through a collapsed windpipe, two bullets to the head stopped his worrying. Mal grabbed the man in the dirt one-handed and pulled him up the stairs, dropping him on his friend, the gun never leaving the side door. In the next minute and eighteen seconds, he cleared the house, the H&K singing its soft thudding death song.

The tattered coat, pockets full of spoiled meat, had been dropped with his first step into the house. Mal stood on the second floor, a bulletproof tactical vest over his black shirt. A hidden room opened in the master bedroom, a dead man at his feet. Mal stepped in. A single lightbulb illuminated the unfinished space. Stacks of money filled the room, tucked in between the studs and any open spot. Along with a collection of AK-47 rifles and numerous other guns. Several shelves were packed full with plastic-wrapped bricks of marijuana, cocaine, and baggies of pink and blue pills. Mal guessed the street value of the drugs alone topped twenty-five million. He filled his pack neatly with stacks of money, making sure to get a mix of denominations.

He stepped out of the hidden room and went into the master closet. A few moments later, he walked out with a long, thin coat, only barely too small for him. He grabbed a clean ball cap off one of the three dead men on the floor. A cheap whiskey bottle sat on a coffee table next to several blood-sprayed lines of cocaine. He helped himself to a long pull, before tossing it into the hidden room. An echo of breaking glass came out of it. From the hard-case pack on his back he pulled out three water bottles, each one filled with a gelatinous, semi-opaque liquid. A digital watch and several wires wrapped each bottle. He pressed the side of the first watch twice and placed it in the drug vault. The second went into the kitchen, and the third in a blood soaked patch in the living room. He pulled the ball cap down low over his face. On his way out the side door, he grabbed two bottles of high-proof vodka and poured them over his first two victims hidden in the shadows of the side porch.

Mal soon disappeared down the alleyway leading to another street. He was too far away to hear the dull pop of the plastic bottle bombs lighting off; he only heard the wail of sirens. A smile crossed his lips as he thought over the evening. The rush of adrenaline always came with killing. The money held tightly to his body lent him another kind of feeling: hope and drive. It funded the next task. A much more dangerous one.

The most dangerous one he could take on.

Chapter 4

Michaela Kai leaned against the front of her Oval Office desk and stared out into the group of men before her, none within a decade of her age, all of them hard men. Men of war and politics, the latter typically being the more ruthless. *And they turn to me for a decision*, she thought to herself, *half of them hate that I am a woman in power, and the other half fawns over me to prove otherwise. And Roger needs to keep his eye on my face, not my chest.* She turned her stare into a glare for Roger Bliss, the Chief of Staff to the Vice President. She did like her new wardrobe, all hand-picked by Anna. It worked apparently; she had already started a few fashion trends Anna told her.

Turning from the ogler to the room at large, she cleared her mind with three quick breaths and slowed her heart rate down, an old sniper's trick she had learned.

"Gentlemen," she spoke clearly, "We will not in any way bow to North Korea's childish tantrums. If Kim Jong Un wants to strut his stuff and puff up his chest, let him. We will not give an inch, and we will damn sure take a mile if we please." She panned her look over the Joint Chiefs, the Vice President, and a half dozen others. "We should consider imposing another round of sanctions on them."

"I don't know if that is the most prudent course of actions," spoke up the Vice President, more to the whole room than in response to Michaela. Jonathan Cever had been a necessary evil in Michaela's mind when picking a running mate for the White House. A sixty-something career politician, he was middle-of-the-road on most topics and had jumped parties more than once. He had delivered the elderly vote and most of the South, though, coming himself from the great state of Alabama. He stood tall and strongly built, his body never seeing much fat. He had a good-humored look to him, with soft eyes and white-grey hair, masking the tactical and cunning politician that lurked at his core.

"Why would that be, Mr. Vice President?" asked Michaela. The two had never developed a close relationship. She could tell he had joined her bandwagon at the chance for major office, most likely hoping for the prime seat himself someday. She had tried a few times to start up a friendship with him, but it never amounted to much. He had a good head on his shoulders for the most part and they agreed on most points. *Mostly.* He did, however, have a way of treating her as a student needing to be schooled in the ways of the world instead of a superior, or even an equal.

"I mean, Madam President, it might come across as militaristic and rushed…or brash… for someone so…" he petered out on the last part letting the point hang in the air.

"You mean someone so young."

"No, not that."

"Anyone with two bits of sense and one eye can see it's a terrible idea to give any wiggle room to that madman in North Korea," spoke up a new voice. The group turned to look at General Patrick O'Connor, the Chairman of the Joint Chiefs of Staff. An old army dog, he had joined the army at the age of eighteen and never looked back. More ribbons than sense, some said, but one thing was true: he never backed down from a fight. He had been in the position before Michaela had taken office. They had met once in her brief stint as an Army MP before the CIA came recruiting.

"I am not saying we let him do whatever he wants but going too harsh too fast in our current position could lose any progress we have made in relations with them," replied Cever.

Well, aren't the boys having fun talking over the decision when it has already been made, she thought bitterly. She went on out loud, "Gentlemen let me say it again and for the last time: We will give no ground to North Korea and will investigate new sanctions. Until Kim is ready to start real and meaningful talks with South Korea, we will stand firm." The Vice President moved to interrupt, but Kai continued, ignoring him, "Now I want recommendations from all Chiefs of Staff and all department heads by the end of the week on what new sanctions we could impose." And with that final edict, the room broke apart, a half dozen conversions picking up at once. Cever and Rogers huddled together as they left the Oval Office.

Soon the room cleared but for General O'Connor. He took a few steps to the middle of the room and spoke. "You did the right thing, Madam President. Don't pay mind to old politicians like that. They spend more time looking out for themselves than for the country."

Michaela sighed, "I know, sir. Thank you for the vote of confidence, sir."

The General flinched almost imperceptibly, "You know, Madam President, you don't have to call me sir anymore."

"Old habits die hard. You know that...sir."

"Yes, yes, I do," nodded O'Connor. He turned to leave but paused after a few steps and looked at her seriously. "Madam President-," he hesitated, then continued in a more confidential tone, "Michaela..."

Michaela's attention fixed assuredly on the General with his drop in formality.

"You should have received the Medal of Honor, not the Silver Star, for that business in Kharlachi," Michaela opened her mouth to interrupt him, but he went on quickly, "It would have been given to a male soldier." He looked out of sorts, a rarity for him. "I was the commanding officer in CENTCOM at the time, and I knew the details of the mission when it happened, as it happened. It should have been yours, I...," his head dipped ever so slightly with an regretful nod, "I should have made sure of that."

"General, it's…"

He cut her off, "Madam President the sins of the past are not expunged with time, but only with action." Michaela held her tongue, and let the man go on. "I am sorry for what happened and more importantly, I am sorry for my lack of courage to stand up for you. To stand up for a woman who so bravely serves her country and her brothers and sisters in arms."

Michaela forced her eyes to stay clear as she responded, an old, sad bitterness creeping up from the past. "Thank you, General. I accept your apology."

The General simply nodded, gratitude etching his features, and moved to leave.

"And sir?" she called to him as he opened the door. She continued when he was once again looking her way. "Thank you. Thank you for still teaching me what it means to be a soldier."

He nodded once more, a thousand words held in that small motion, and left.

○ ○ ○

Michaela quickly found that most of her time, even dinners, were taken up by the needs of others. This evening's dinner was being held in the famed East Room. The walls were adorned with photos of past Presidents and historical figures. Anna had added a touch of modern décor and what she called "un-stodginess" to the room and to most of the White House. Nearly forty people filled the circle tables spread around the room. The clean and elegant noise of a grand piano filled the air.

Kai had made her circuit upon entering the room, shaking hands, and exchanging pleasantries. She once again thanked Anna silently for picking another amazing outfit. A black, well-fitted dress with a dusting of turquoise at the hem. An elegant and modest piece, it showed her feminine allure and firm authority at the same time. Her only piece of jewelry: a pair of jade and gold earrings.

The meet-and-greet soon turned into a murmur of separate conversations as the tables filled and waiters came to take orders. Kai's table held Vice President Cever, Roger Bliss, the White House Secretary Madeline Vento, Anna (though she would not join them always off working the next angle), and Conrad Crane. The latter was the one Kai trusted the least.

Conrad was one of the older men that ruled long and hard in Congress. Starting his career back in the middle of the 1970s, he worked his way around Congress and major committees ever since. He had held his health well into his early seventies. His full head of hair was pure white, and although his face was blocky and wrinkled from a life of stress, his eyes were as keen as knives. His grandparents on both sides were Russian, and those physical traits dominated his appearance. He also was one of the brightest people in Congress. He held two PhDs, one in political science and one in constitutional law, spoke a handful of languages, and had written a half dozen bestselling books. In Kai's opinion, he was a backstabbing political extremist who would sell out his own mother for personal power.

He wasted no time in landing the opening strike as the waiters laid down the first course. "So, President Kai," the word 'president' much too slick on his tongue, "you're ready for your State of the Union speech, right? I know that must be very nerve-racking for someone so inexperienced."

"Don't worry about me, Conrad. I have no problem speaking in front of people, as you well know," replied Kai. She was referring to two years earlier when they had gone toe-to-toe on the House floor and her rousing speech had gotten enough votes to slap down the heavily socialist bill he had sponsored.

The waiters returned a moment later with bottles of wine, asking each person which they would like. The waiter serving Kai's table skipped over Kai without asking, no doubt to Anna's orders. Kai secretly thanked Anna again. It was not a secret that Kai did not drink because of a heavy drinking issue before joining Congress; something Conrad had made sure to dredge up during the election. She preferred not to draw attention to it.

Kai could feel the sharks all around her, waiting for blood. She smiled inwardly. She was no shark; she was a shark hunter. "Conrad, when should I be expecting your official invitation to give my State of the Union? Or do you need more time to get approval from your corporate donors?"

Conrad did not respond to the jab, it hit too close to home from his recent donor issues in the presidential election. The conversation soon slipped into idle talk such as North Korea, Iran, the trade issues with China.

The main course arrived, a salmon filet with a lemon garlic butter for Kai. Roasted vegetables and rice pilaf for sides. The food was amazing.

"What about you, son? Are you going to make a run for office someday?" Conrad motioned to Roger as he spoke, giving his wine glass another swirl.

"Maybe one day, sir."

"Hell, you could be sitting in that seat someday if you play your cards right," Conrad added, clearly meaning Kai's seat.

"Oh, I'm not sure about that," said Roger with a darting, awkward, and undressing look at Kai. "Maybe an office in Congress someday, but as Vice President Cever has said before 'real power can only be found in the shadows.'"

At the mention of his name, Cever turned away from the engrossing conversation with Madeline. "Are you stealing my advice again, Roger," he chuckled.

"No of course not, sir."

"Power only in the shadows. I didn't take you Mr. Vice President as a cloak and daggers man," commented Conrad.

"The full saying my old man taught me when I was cutting my teeth in D.C., is 'Real power cannot stand fully in the light. The view of others steals it away and fragments it. The only real power can be held in the shadows.' He meant behind the scenes, of course."

Kai joined in the exchange of words, feeling something much deeper than what was being said, "Are you insinuating that positions such as ours are powerless? Such as the presidency?" She cocked one eyebrow, letting him know just what she thought of that opinion.

Cever waved the comment away. "No, of course not. It just means you are bound by the people who can see you. Your actions are on full display for the world. One reason I never want that seat, too much pressure."

"Fair enough," nodded Kai.

"It is a nasty business we play. The realities can be unpleasant to say the least," said Conrad bringing the conversation to a close.

The rest of the meal was filled with small talk, Conrad never missing a chance to goad Kai. Cever did little to back her on any policies her administration wanted to get pushed through, but Kai held her own comfortably.

The meal finished with a round of desserts, chocolate sorbet with mint, and mini cheesecakes with a black cherry sauce. Michaela felt it was the highlight of the trying evening.

Chapter 5

The last several weeks had passed in a rush of meetings, interviews, and briefings ranging from the mundane to the world changing. Of the half dozen clocks on the wall above the mantel, only one read local time, nearly half past 2200 hours. The living room on the second floor of the residence had been laid out to fit the taste of the new president and work was the rule.

Michaela sat at the large oak desk at the back-center of the room. Several empty armchairs sat in front of the desk, facing the flat screen on the wall, which was currently on low volume playing the late-night news. A dozen stacks of paper, folders, a laptop, and a tablet computer covered the desk. A half-read folder lay open in front of her, 'Top Secret' stamped on each page, and a forgotten cup of lukewarm green tea sat next to it.

The door opened, but before the newcomer could speak, Michaela said, "What are you doing here so late?" She didn't look up from the folder.

"Just wrapping up some work." Anna walked up and leaned up against the desk. "How did you know it was me? I barely opened the door before you spoke."

"I heard you walking. Those ridiculously high heels you are wearing clicked on the floor outside."

"Still always on, eh, Kai?"

"Old habits die hard."

"Yes, but you should take some down time at some point." Michaela didn't reply. Anna leaned forward and placed her hand over the current reading material. "I'm serious MK. You need to take a break. You have been going seven days a week for over three weeks straight." She looked concerned at her friend. "You were up before dawn and still working near midnight."

"I know, I got this..."

"No, listen. This is not like back in the day where you can just buckle down and balls up to push through the next fight. This job is going to chew you up. Taking care of yourself is just as important as any top-secret folder." She moved her hand back and stood.

Michaela looked up, "Nice outfit. Going home?"

Anna did a little spin, the scandalous black plunge halter dress flaring at a slit up to her mid-thigh. "No, got a date. Hey, there must be some perks to being the Chief of Staff. Maybe I'll get me some," she smirked, waving off Michaela's shaking head, "Take my advice, take a break. Eat a cookie, watch a movie, do whatever your crazy self does for fun." She disappeared out the door, having turned sideways to let a newcomer in.

Michaela watched Bert Renfield take Anna's place in the room. A veteran of the Secret Service, he was Special Agent in Charge for her entire personal security detail. He looked like an old pit bull who had seen one too many backyard fights. "Evening, Bert."

"Madam President." He stood ramrod straight, but his eyes never stopped moving, taking in data. "I'm wrapping it up for the day. Do you need anything?"

"No, I am good. I'm going to get through a few more briefs."

"Yes, Madam President. You know, Ms. Williams is right."

Michaela smiled. She had liked Bert from day one; he never minced words and didn't seem to have a false bone in his body. "Right about what?"

"You'll burn out if you keep this pace up. I've seen it. You're the third president I've protected. They all push it too hard in the beginning. The best is to pace yourself. It's like a marathon. Set a good pace and keep going."

"I know, Bert," Kai sighed in response. "I will find some downtime."

"You like to hike, don't you, Ma'am."

"Yes."

"I thought I read that about you. You should take a trip up to Camp David. It's a bit cold and nasty this time of year, but still good trails."

"I haven't been in office very long. The last thing I want to do is let the media have a hey-day with me taking off for a vacation in the first month."

"To be frank Madam, the media can go to hell. No one really understands how taxing your job is. And don't worry," he smirked, making his old war dog face look worse, "Camp David is all decked out. You will have plenty of time for work there."

"Okay, I'll think about it."

He nodded and moved to leave. "Good night, Madam President.

"Good night, Bert."

She did her best to look back at the open report, but the words would not come into focus. The late-night news report blurred on, harder to zone out. She closed the folder with a sigh.

"Two weeks have passed and still the police have made little progress in the death of fourteen people, murdered in their home and the fire that burned the home down. The house and group of people in question were linked to a drug trafficking ring that was suspected of being behind eight minors overdosing on tainted drugs."

A picture frame at the corner of the large desk drew Michaela's attention away from the news anchor. A massive, clear glass mason jar three quarters full with assorted rocks stood next to the picture. Nearly a decade old, the photo showed her standing between her parents, a majestic, snow-capped mountain standing in the distance. They had just finished a half-day hike. Her father, an amateur geologist and avid rockhound, loved going for long hikes in the remotest areas he could find. It was some of Michaela's earliest memories, walking with her father, his steadfast voice pointing out different types of rocks, what made them up, and how they were formed. It was the slow patience of rocks that drew her father. It appealed to his meticulous nature, something he passed on to his daughter.

The photo not only brought a wave of happiness from times bygone, but a lingering pain deep in Michaela's gut. Her father had passed away three years earlier, during Michaela's first year in the House of Representatives. He had died of pancreatic cancer. It was already advanced when the doctors found it and shortly after metastasized into his bones and liver. It was not a long and drawn-out fight. He went quickly, but painfully.

Her hand reached and touched the side of the mason jar. The stones inside gleamed and sparkled in a multitude of hues and gemstone facets. It was the best of the best of her father's collection. He had boxes and boxes of rocks, but this jar held the rarest of finds. She could see rough gemstones, from ruby to sapphire. Several pieces of gold and silver dotted the jar, but it was dominated by lustrous shades of green. Jade, in all its forms. Her middle namesake. Her father felt a deep connection and draw to jade. More than just a piece of décor or even a piece of their family's Japanese history to him. Michaela had added several items to the jar over the years, her worldly travels helping greatly. The only rule her father had set to the jar was that all pieces had to be found, not bought.

She stared at the jar of rocks for some time. *Maybe, I will go. I am the president.* She had thought that her recent yearly tradition would have to be given up, but maybe not. Each year since her father had passed, she had made sure to take a rock hunting trip on the anniversary of his death.

She stood and left the office/living room, thoughts of her father and the countless trips they took together. She decided she would speak to Anna the next day about planning a trip to Camp David; then at least she might steal a few hours walking, searching for something new for the jar.

Chapter 6

The air felt cold and fresh from the recent rain. Mal peaked the hill he had been hiking the last few hours. A great expanse of open wilderness lay out in front of him. His long hair had been chopped down to a buzz cut and firmly incased in a thick stocking hat. His beard too had been cleared away, showing the rough-cut line of his jaw and the wisps of several pink shifting scars coming up from his left side. His face had a woodsman look, strong jaw, straight-lined face. A heritage of Greek ran through his appearance.

It's been too long since I have gotten out. Away from it all, he thought to himself. A deep shattering sorrow boiled inside of him. He shook his head and moved forward, doing his best to lose himself in the woods. *Just one more step. Just one more.* He repeated as he went on, *this is it. The last hope. The last fight. If this works then maybe, just maybe, I succeed. Oh, my Sarah, how I wish you were here with me; how I wish this fight was for you as well.* Wetness having nothing to do with the winter wind formed at the corner of his eye. He pushed it away with a lifetime of practice and moved on. A few hours later, he found himself where he wanted to go: the tallest point in the great expanse around him. A grand view. He set a quick camp for himself and dug out his maps, several handwritten notes already on it. Soon to be more.

The days passed in a blur of hiking, planning, and dirty, back-breaking work. He felt most at home in that isolated land away from man and machine. He moved through the woods without a trace. Not leaving a broken branch or any sign of trespass. He could have lived in the woods for the next year and never be seen. A winter gale moved in sharply on the fifth day leaving in its wake a cold snap that seemed to freeze the air solid.

At the end of nearly two weeks, Mal looking better than he had in over a year, packed his gear and headed out of the woods. Part of him longed to never leave. He wanted to walk deeper and deeper into the unknown. To lose himself in the deepness of nature and unknowing of time. But he could not, he would not. He had a mission to finish and blood to be spilled. He grimaced and continued his internal chant of one foot after another.

○ ○ ○

"It is the end of February, and you not only want to go out to Camp David for some lovely winter mud walking, but you want to take a trip up further north to some dodgy wilderness mountaineer area?" asked Anna, looking doubtful.

"It's called the Wolf Run Wilderness Area. And yes, that is where I want to go. Just a day hike," replied the President sitting behind her desk in the oval office. Bert stood off to one side of the room a folder in his hand and Michaela's head secretary, Chance Gates, standing next to him, a crisp business suit on the young man.

"Okay, if that's the break you need, then we will make it happen," replied Anna. She went on a little more concerned, "Do you expect me to join you?"

Michaela let out a laugh, "Hell no. Hiking with you once on a dry and flat area was enough for me." Anna smiled in return.

Michaela had decided to go out to Camp David a few weeks earlier and made a last minute request to take a trip up to the Wolf Run area. It was not an uncommonly remarkable area but had something Michaela was hoping to find, a new piece of jade to add to her father's jar. Earlier that week she visited a website that couldn't be found on Google and that she had not opened in years. It was started by her father and a few other like-minded rockhounds. It was a living repository of geological data from all over the United States. It was simple, people would join the group and post anything of interest they had found. Everything from deposits of marble to veins of gold. The members of the online society were not looking to get rich, in it only for the hunt. A community of rock-loving people. The dues were basic: post everything

you found and never hide anything. If any member hid
a discovery, they were barred from the site, no longer
able to access the troves of data. In the last decade, the
members on the site had been getting increasingly
sophisticated, a little over a hundred-thousand strong.
Some of them had installed remote water sampling
stations on small rivers throughout the States.

It was a small river in central Pennsylvania.
The Wolf Run River, more like a stream, in the Wolf
Run Wilderness Area which dumped into Pine Creek,
more like a river, had traces of jadeite. Jadeite being
one of two minerals necessary to form the multiped of
jade stones. It was beyond rare in the area, and in most
of the eastern United States the other form of jade
taking the lead, nephrite. The purest of jadeite was the
bright lustrous green that most people thought of as
imperial jade. The online reports only showed trace
amounts of jadeite, but it had been confirmed by three
separate members and the source had yet to be
discovered. Michaela had no illusions of finding the
deposits, but she felt a deep connection to the mineral
as did her father. It felt like the best way to honor him,
to continue his passion even if it meant in a limited
way.

Bert stepped forward after the small exchange
and opened his folder. "I have done a preliminary
study on the Wolf Run Area, and it should not be
much of an issue to secure for the day. I have already
had our office reach out to the park rangers to be
ready to assist and shut down the area for the day. Do

you intend to take the Golden Eagle Trail that loops the area?"

"Yes, but I was hoping to go off the beaten path," said Michaela as Chance moved up to give her a new stack of papers to sign. "Not for long, but there are some rock formations I want to see."

"Very good, Madam," replied Bert. "I have no doubt the team is looking forward to it." He smiled, having already dressed down two agents for grumbling about the cold hike ahead.

"Have I given you and your team enough time?"

"Yes, of course Madam President," Bert answered. He excused then, as Chance could no longer be completely ignored by the President, something about triple booking her schedule for the next two days.

Chapter 7

"Another cup, honey?"

"Never say no to more go juice," replied Frostt.

"Go juice," laughed the plump woman as she poured some freshly brewed coffee into Frostt's cup.

"You keeping warm out there?" she asked.

Frostt let a gentle smile touch his lips. "Yes, Ma'am. Got many layers. And the cold doesn't bother me much as long as I can get the photos I'm looking for." He patted the camera bag sitting on the table next to him. A half-eaten sandwich and a massive dill pickle sat in front of him. "I didn't see a soul out and about on my hike yesterday."

"Well, it is a few days off of March, honey," replied the woman moving behind the sandwich counter to clean.

"Yeah, well it's about to get a lot damn more soulless around here," spoke up a man sitting a few tables away. The wrinkles of his face telling time, only a cup of coffee in front of him.

"Hey, Jonas. No cussing inside," spoke up a second person, standing behind the sandwich counter. Bob Jenson, owner of the fine sandwich station/general store/gas station/guidepost/tackle shop in the great community of Slate Run.

"It ain't going to be that bad, Jonas," said Bob. His thick frame was made all the thicker by a heavy layer of extra weight.

"It's just more damn government interference," spat out Jonas.

"Jonas," snapped Clare, the large woman behind the bar, "I am going to slap you silly if you keep cussing. This is a family place."

Jonas only grumbled in response.

Frostt spoke up, "I think I'm missing something here."

"You better get you as...butt outta here. The SS dogs are coming," sneered Jonas.

"Don't mind that old crugger," spoke Clare, her voice overwhelming Jonas's next few words. "We are having some visitors coming in a few days. And shortly after that the president herself is coming. You imagine that?"

Frostt's face bored a surprised look, his golden shoulder-length hair pulled into a tight man-bun. "You don't say. The President of the United States."

"Yeah, she don't mean the king of England, son."

Clare glared at Jonas, but it was Bob who spoke up. "Yeah, that's right, our little dot of a community is getting blessed by big government. I don't mind much, but it is kinda a hard sell. Them shutting down the entire area for five days and all." He went on to answer the quizzical look Frostt gave him. "Yep, five days. No one allowed on the trails or rivers. She is going to be somewhere up in the Wolf Run area, but they have to shut down a whole lot more than that. Her Secret Service advance team comes in tomorrow to set up."

"See? That's what I mean, they don't care about us. The little people. Come in here and shut down all the trade. A man needs to make a living."

"A man making a living, uh," said Clare. "When was the last time you worked Jonas." She waved him off. "It's a burden, but they're paying to rent out the entire Hotel Manor and even put in an order of supplies from us. So, it will be good, and we intend to advertise it. After the fact, of course, they made that very clear." She added the last bit, looking at Frostt.

"Now that would be some good photos to get. President Kai hiking around. But I'm headed out today any which way. Not that Secret Service would let me stay if I tried."

"It ain't right ya know," piped up Jonas feeling left out. "It ain't right a woman president. I da... darn sure didn't vote for her."

"And what is wrong with a woman president, you old cranky fart?" asked Clare. "You don't think a woman can do the job of a man?" She had her left hand firmly planted on her large hip and a meat cleaver in the other, a half-cut roast in front of her. Frostt thought that if he were Jonas, he would be heading for the door like a bat-out-of-hell.

"Calm yourself. It's nothing like that. Women are great and all, but just that job is the big one. The Leader. He needs to be logical, have an iron will and a pair to match…," he petered out at the glare from Clare.

"Know what, surrey-bob."

"Hey Jonas, you want some ketchup for that foot in your mouth," laughed Bob.

"It just that women tend to get more bogged down in their emotions." He held his hands up at the now murderous-looking Clare. "It's just the truth. Y'all know it."

"I don't know nothin' of the sort."

"Bob, back me up here," whined Jonas.

"Jonas, I have been married to this fine woman for forty-two years. And I have made a habit of not shooting my damn mouth off," said Bob.

"Hey no cussing," snapped Jonas.

Clare decided it was time to bring in a neutral party, "Mr. Archer," Frostt looked over at her, his blonde goatee holding onto a few crumbs of sandwich. "What do you think."

"I think Ma, that it comes down to the person, not the gender. A person is judged by their actions. If this new president is up to the challenge then we will see that sooner than later."

"Uh," groaned Jonas. "What a hippy answer."

Bob's laugh filled the small general store. "Oh boy, that is good. See Jonas? I think you could learn something from Mr. Archer here. He can give an opinion without making himself look like an old fool."

"Bah. Ya'll just too soft. That's what's wrong with this new generation. Just a bunch of snowflakes." With that final statement, Jonas downed his coffee and left.

"Sorry for that," said Clare as she came up to take away Frostt's plate.

"No worries, Ma'am. Each is due his own opinion."

"Yeah, but he is an old crugger any which way you skin him."

Frostt only nodded in response. His mind drifted to what this cozy little community was about to experience. After he was done, five days of shut down would pale in comparison.

Chapter 8

Bert Renfield stood at the start of a walking path, his wristwatch reading a few minutes past 0600 hours. The last day of February stood at a brisk twenty-nine degrees. Bert was thankful the wind had died down during the night. Nothing was worse than a biting cold. He could deal with it if he had to, but he was worried about the members of his team. The cold slowed people. The new batches of Secret Service agents over the last decade were lacking something undefinable, but lacking all the same.

He fieldstripped the cigarette he had just finished. A nasty habit he knew, but that never stopped him from opening the next pack. He had picked up the habit back in the eighties, on his first tour with the Corps. Since then, his only quitting time had been going down to a pack a day. Even with that and a diet of fast-food Bert could still run circles and open a can of whoop-ass, his words, on most of these new recruits.

Agent Meyers walked up, her hand covered with thick gloves and her breath coming out in steaming drifts. "Agent Meyers," greeted Bert.

"Morning, sir," replied the young woman, relatively new to the presidential detail. She had earned a reputation of being a strict professional. "What's the sitrep?"

"You tell me, Meyers. Four of my agents puking their guts back in that inbred county hotel. Food poisoning." He said the last two words like a curse.

"Yeah, you should have seen the old lady running the place. She was nearly apoplectic this morning when I questioned her. I guess she didn't like being accused of poisoning a group of government agents."

"Yeah, well, the health department will be making a trip up here after we're gone. Bad salmon, just son-a-bitch."

"Timetable still good?"

"Do you have to ask?"

Meyers shrugged in return and went on, "I'm as outdoorsy as the next girl, but this one is going to suck. Freezing cold and miles of trees to look at."

"Yep, it's not always fun," replied Bert. He liked Meyers a lot. Her full name was Bethany Meyers, and he could see real potential in her. Maybe even taking over his place as number one on the detail in the next few years. Bert knew he only had a few years left. Being too old was not allowed for a job like his. He would either be pushed to a desk or have to hit the retirement books. He tried not to think about it.

"Have Rogers and Juan split the difference in their coverage area for the missing men. Pull McLone from the primary circle and have him cover the high ground. I will make the rounds and close the gaps as needed. You take McLone's spot on point for the primary circle." Meyers gave the barest motion of excitement at the new position. It was a step up for her. First time running point for the primary agents around the President. Though it wasn't like anything would be happening on a hike through the backwoods of Pennsylvania.

"Yes, sir. I will pass the word."

"Also, lose the gloves, Meyers." He pointed at her hands. "That will slow your draw. Have someone go over to that general store and pick up all the pocket warmers and first aid hot packs they have. Pass them out. The team can use them in their pockets to keep their fingers from going numb, but no gloves."

"Yes, sir," nodded Meyers and went away to make it happen.

He looked at his watch again: 0623 hours. Twenty-two minutes till the President arrived. He pulled out a new cigarette and lit up. His Zippo was stamped with the symbol of the Marine Corps, a globe with an anchor through it and a bald eagle standing on it all. He pulled a long drag and looked up into the hills where their path would take them. Something nagged at him. Something too deep to register, but nonetheless there. He continued to stare at the forest-covered hills and tried to drag the feeling into a more defined shape. It didn't work.

○ ○ ○

Michaela kneeled on the bank of a small stream, her heavy-soled hiking boots already caked with mud. The sun lingered an hour before noon, she and her team of agents had covered near six miles since setting off. Mostly on an off-the-beaten-trail. She could hear the two helicopters circling above. One would be carrying the ever-present tactical strike team when she traveled.

The cold water bit at her skin as she plunged the gold pan into the stream. She moved it with a practiced hand. She could lose herself here. Forget the pressure and non-stop tension that filled her life. She could almost convince herself that her father would come walking up to pan next to her at any moment.

Why is it so hard now, she pondered internally. *He's been gone for years. It's so raw lately. So near.* She let out a long sigh, her breath still fogging in the above-freezing temperature. *It's the job. The stress. No, it's… It's 'cause I want to know what he would think now. He was so proud of me when I got elected to the House and so worried at the same time. Even more worried than when I would disappear on missions for the CIA for months at a time, but this is completely different. Would he still be proud of me? I so wish I could just talk with him one more time.*

Her hands moved slow circles, more for the moment of the thing than the search. She stopped. A ray of sunshine caught the barest hint of green. She circled the pan a few more times and there it was. A sliver, but still there. A deep, water-worn green piece of jade, jadeite to be specific. She used tweezers to pick it up; it brought a massive smile to her face.

"Did you find something, Madam?" asked Agent Meyers.

Kai held up the small piece for Meyers to see, the agent did her best to look excited. "Let's head farther up this stream. You can tell Bert not much farther." She added on the last part at the semi-hidden look Meyers gave.

"Yes Madam."

The group moved out, heading north. Michaela had a tough time not telling off a few of the Secret Service agents. They had no care for their progress. Making a mess of their path. She held her tongue. The last thing she wanted to do was to tell off someone who spent their time making sure she was safe. Another hour and half passed, and two more slivers of jade were found. The ground opened to a level field, sparsely wooded to the west, and a collection of small ponds dotted the clearing directly north. The east side of the clearing headed to higher ground, several small creeks visible in the densely wooded slope.

The three agents formed a rough circle around the President giving her space to explore the pond nearest the eastern slope, a rushing creek flowing into it. The rest of the team fanned out to set a perimeter around the clearing, Bert making the rounds.

"All posts report in," Bert spoke into his walkie mounted on his chest.

"Alpha clear, Bravo clear." The reports all came in clear and loud.

"What's wrong, sir," whispered Agent Meyers as she walked up, "that's your fifth check in nearly as many minutes."

Bert shook his head, "I don't know. Something feels off."

"Could be all those truck-stop tacos you've been downing lately."

"Yeah, or it could be a threat." His eyes moved around the soggy meadow without stopping. "Tighten up the primary circle around the President and have the outer perimeter close in half the distance."

Before Meyers could respond a voice cracked over the radio, the assault team leader in one of the helicopters. "We have multiple bogies airborne heading to Hawk's location! Small signals; possibly drones!"

"All teams close on Hawk! Double perimeter! Prepare to engage!" Bert was already moving, his Sig Sauger pistol out, towards the President, Meyers only a half-second behind him. Then several things happened at once, all a Secret Service agent's worst nightmare. Chaos.

A mind-splitting noise erupted from all the walkie-talkies on the agents' chests, a roiling of nails on blackboard static. Dozens of colorful detonations exploded from the ground turning the westside of the meadow into a frantic kaleidoscope of color and noise. To the north-side a cacophony of gun shots and muzzle flashes added to the chaos, several agents dropping to the ground for cover. Three other agents had already surrounded the President by the time Bert and Meyers joined them, the three rotating fire into the north tree line.

"Move!" bellowed Bert. "Up the high ground; cover fire!"

The five agents and Michaela sprinted up the slope, two agents laying down cover fire as three kept a tight body cover over Michaela. Bert had a flitting thought it was good to have a combat-tested President. She had been moving before he even needed to make the order.

"Bird Two…Bird Two," Bert yelled into his walkie, still screaming like a gang of angry cats.

Agent Juan led the party up the hill. It flattened out after a brief sprint. A new round of detonations ripped open behind them. Gunshots echoed closer, Bert and Meyers pivoted and lay down a clip each of cover fire to their rear. A fresh, close, scream turned them back forward. Juan was falling to the ground flaying his arms wildly. The group of agents had a challenging time understanding what they were seeing, Juan was dragged away and abruptly turned a ninety-degree angle up and hung ten feet in the air by one foot.

"What the hell," barked Meyers.

Before Bert could give any order, a loud thud and grunt sounded to the side of him. His blood went cold as another agent fell to the ground, eyes rolled back in his head. A round, black ball on the ground by his feet. Roughly fifteen yards past the agent was a newcomer, what looked like a small leather sling hanging from his right hand, homemade camouflage covering his body. Bert didn't need to give the order, the last three agents took aim and fired. The man darted to the left with blinding speed pulling up the sling to spin above his head, before twisting behind a tree he let his sling loose. A black blur rushed from the man and in a blink of an eye the agent next to Meyers let out a grunt as the projectile hit her in the stomach. She dropped her gun and fell to the ground bent double.

Michaela darted forward to help the fallen woman. Bert lunged and yanked her back, but not before she snagged the fallen pistol. "Move," he screamed and pushed Michaela in front of him and Meyers. The three darted forward less than ten paces before a new round of colored explosions went off a few dozen yards in front of them. A mad, rushing noise and breaking of wood followed the light show that could be felt in their chests. A massive log fell twenty feet to the right of them and ten feet forward. Another unknown sound echoed around them. Bert turned to lay down another round of cover fire. He could not understand what he saw. He had less than half a second. The camouflaged man was flying at them. Literally flying. A rope in one hand pulling him forward like some crazed video game. He slammed into Bert, tossing him to the ground. The man hit the ground in a fluid motion and in the space of a heartbeat, Meyers was laid on her back, her gun gone. Michaela only managed a single wild gunshot in the unexpected entrance of the attacker.

Bert found his gun and his feet faster than Meyers, turning to take aim, the burning in his chest barely registered. Meyers was rolling to a stop, still trying to gain her feet and draw her back up gun. What happened next chilled Bert to the bone and a cold sweat sprang out on his skin.

The attacker held President Kai in a choke hold, both arms bound, and a matte-black knife pressed hard to her neck. A round cylinder was just visible on her left side, gripped in the attacker's hand. Meyers had gained her feet, and both had the man in their sights, half-hidden behind the President.

"Drop your guns," said the man, as if commenting on the weather.

"That's not fucking happening," spat out Bert. "Let the President go, or we will kill you."

"You do that, and we all go up in flames," the man wiggled the cylinder. "Deadman lever. Two kilos of plastic on my chest with a pound of ball bearings." His voice sounded like gravel falling down a mountainside.

Michaela spoke up, slowly. "You don't have to do this. You can live through this. Let me go and my agents will not kill you."

"Hm," murmured the man. "I think not." He moved the double-edged blade just enough to bring a small drop of blood to the surface of her neck. "Again, don't even think about moving. I know your history, a better killer than these two here. You breathe wrong and boom." He had been taking small steps back, keeping Michaela as a shield. He held her with her body leaning into him, her balance completely dependent on him. If she moved forward, the knife, and moving back was impossible with his strength and grip.

"We can talk this out," said Meyer. "What do you want?"

"I think we left words behind a long time ago." More steps back.

"What do you want?"

Silence and more steps back.

The group heard fast movement towards them. Agent call codes yelled out; Bert responded. The pair of agents joined the standoff, weapons drawn. At the same time, the radios ended their death rattles. Voices breaking over the channel in confusion.

More steps.

"This is Agent Renfield. We have a situation, Red Alpha. Deadman switch is hot. All teams converge on my signal." The chatter died at once.

More steps.

"Now, listen, asshole. This is not going down any which way you want. Let go of the President and I promised not to put a bullet in your head."

"But maybe in both knees," smiled the man. More steps back, the agents forming a half-circle around him and the President.

"You have nowhere to go," said Meyers, "Whatever your beef is, we can sort it out."

"Maybe you all can give me a ride."

"Fuck you."

The man chuckled. He said to Meyers, "Agent Meyers, you should really get a better leash on your boss." He winked at Bert. More steps. "And you Madam President should expect more from your agents." More steps.

Michaela had been abnormally quiet, but not fear bound. She knew the key to any situation like this was patience. Waiting for her moment. It was not the first time having a knife to her throat. Something did unnerve her though. The raw power of the man was too intense and too calmly used. And where was his support? It would've taken a small army to pull this off. She counted her breaths and let her body slip into a relaxed tension, waiting.

The steps stopped.

"Now again, please drop your weapons."

"The answer has not changed, asshole. That's not happening."

"Good, I would've lost respect for you if you had." A faint click came from the man's left foot as he placed it back. Chaos once again joined the party. A chest-thumping concussion blasted out of the ground, up and at an angle towards the agents. Only knocking them down and giving them a good dose of pepper spray.

Michaela felt herself falling back. The knife moved away and the deadman trigger was gone. His arms wrapped her in a steel bear hug, pinning her arms to her side. Then the stop came, but not hard. Fabric and plastic bellowed up around her, and she felt the man give a hard kick to something, her body still pressed tightly up against his. A loud clang from a gear moving came after the kick, and they were moving, the light of the day slipped away as something carried them underground. The man's vice grip around her body shifted, she tried to get an arm up to strike with, but even one-armed, the man was absurdly strong. A rag covered her mouth and nose, and the darkness of the underground turned into the blackness of unconsciousness.

○ ○ ○

Bert wiped his eyes the best he could, but mainly pushed through with brute force. He moved over to the hole in the ground. He caught the barest glimpse of two people sliding down into a tunnel in the dirt wall of the hole through his pepper-burning eyes. He wiped at them again, only making it worse by adding pepper to them from his clothes, and moved to jump in. A dull pop sounded, and dirt and dust blew into the hole as the walls started to cave in. A pair of hands grasped at him even as he meant to dive into the collapsing hole.

He rolled over to look up. Meyers, half kneeling, half laid on him, tears running down her dirt-covered face, small beads of blood dotting it. Bert rolled to the side and vomited as he spoke into his radio. "Code Black. I repeat. Code Black. The President has been taken; last seen at my location, destination unknown." He spat out a new mouthful of bile, Meyers next to him doing the same. "Seal off this motherfucking mountain."

Chapter 9

Michaela did not let her eyes open when a faint registering of sense started to return to her. She kept her body still like a stone, even her breaths did not change. Even though every part of her wanted to roll about in wakeful fits of drug ending sleep. She let her senses come back to her fully picking up every smell, sound, touch, and even faint flickers of light through her closed eyelids. She was prone and her arms were not bound. She laid on something flat and hard, but not stone. A piece of fabric was under her, thin and scratchy.

What the hell, she thought. Her senses coming fully back alive. *'He who is prudent and lies in wait for an enemy who is not, will be victorious.'* She quoted to herself from the wise Sun Tzu. A line that had served her well over the years and too many bad days to count.

A sound of intently hidden steps came to her, not near her, but close. The place smelled of damp rock, stagnant air, and wood rot. A gentle hum she could not place, overlaid the entire space. *Time for the first chest move. Let the game begin.* She opened her eyes.

A rough-cut rock ceiling came into view, a basaltic formation she knew at sight. Two thick, rot-pocked, wood beams ran parallel to each other along the ceiling. She moved only her eyes, gaining more of the ceiling and wooden beams meant to hold it up. She let the words of Sun Tzu roll over her again.

A voice interrupted her inspection, like gravel under a mill. "You can sit up if you like. Please don't stand, both for the aftereffects of the drug and because I have no desire to fight you."

She took the advice but said nothing. She took in the entire single room in front of her in one sweep. The place measured twenty by twenty, if off by a few feet due to the rough stone walls, the same basaltic forms as the ceiling. More thick rotting wood beams held up the walls. The floor was a mix of broken, finger-sized rock and coarse sand. A table stood opposite of her, a small folding card table. A camp lantern gave off an unstable light. Another lantern was hung from one of the beams in the center of the room, giving the place a shifting shadow effect. The two lights fought each other. An open MRE and canteen of water sat on the card table next to the burning lantern.

Kai took a deep breath and steadied herself with it. "So, what do I call you?" She studied the man with a military eye. At least 6'1" maybe a hair more. Long dirty blonde hair was pulled into a tight ponytail, though the dirty could be from their current environment. A goatee of the same hair and cheekbones that stood high. A rounded nose dominated the face, and piercing green eyes finished off the package. His body was thickly built but lean like a racehorse. He looked like a coiled spring, but calm. She also could not help but notice the Colt 1911 pistol in a hip holster at his side.

"So, your name?" prompted Kai again.

The man gestured, in thought, "How about Mr. Frostt."

"Mr. Frost. Like Mr. Freeze from Batman. Not sure you're a supervillain."

"A villain is rarely a villain in his own mind, and you can make it Frostt with two T's if you like." He smiled easy, "Makes it more villainy, don't you think?"

Shit. Either he is nuts or beyond narcissistic. She went on out loud, "Okay Frossssttt," she stretched out his name like a snake, "What are we doing here?"

"We are waiting."

"For what?"

"For nighttime and the next stage of our journey."

"'Our journey?' You do understand what you have done?"

"You mean assault and kidnap the President of the United States of America? Then yes, I understand what I have done."

"Did you do this all by yourself?"

"Yes."

She played to his pride. "That is impressive if a little insane."

"Oh, I left insanity behind me a long time ago."

She moved gingerly on her fabric-lined piece of plywood. She inconspicuously tested her leg muscles to make sure they held no lingering effect of whatever drug he had knocked her out with. All good.

"Okay then. The big one." She smiled, matching his ease with the gesture. "Why?"

"Why do all this?" he moved his hands again in thought. "I need your help." He went on before she could continue. "I need the help of the President. As long as it has not reached you yet?"

"What reached me?" *Yep, nuts, and narcissistic. Good combo,* she didn't say it out loud.

"We will get to that later. For now, we wait and move to a safer location."

"Yeah, you don't strike me as the villain who would have his lair in a cave." She cleared her throat. "Can I have some water while we wait?" She cleared her throat again. "Whatever crap you knocked me out with has left a bad aftertaste."

"Of course. We don't have to be at complete odds." He grabbed the canteen off the desk and pulled a small pack, which had been hidden out of sight, from under the table. He poured some water into a Styrofoam cup. He smirked at her as he stepped forward. "Sorry for the precautions, but with a reputation like yours I would be amiss to give you even a plastic spoon."

"And what have you heard about my reputation; and from whom, more importantly," she said with a laughing pitch to her tone. She leaned

forward pulling both legs under her in a gesture to
lean forward for the cup.

"From people here and there." He handed her
the cup and turned to leave.

Kai sprang forward, her toned athletic legs
exploded her forward during the moment Frostt had
turned his head to walk away. She slammed her fist
hard into his kidney and swept a leg into his right one.
At the same time, she smoothly pulling the Colt from
his holster. Mal did the smart thing, fell with the kick,
and rolled away. He was lighting fast and back on his
feet by the table.

"Don't," she bit out. She racked the gun, a
bullet flying out, to make sure it truly was loaded.
Frostt had looked poised to lunge. "Don't," she said
with iron and drew a bead onto his forehead. "I can't
miss at this distance. Or five times further."

"There is no escape out of here. Even if you
kill me there is no way you will find your way out of
this old mineshaft. It is a twisted maze, miles and
miles long. You will starve to death."

"So, what then? Am I supposed to hand the
gun back to you?" she laughed. "We don't need to go
anywhere. People will come to us."

"I swept you for bugs and tracking devices.
All clean," he replied. "Even blasted you with a few
bursts of some super magnets just to make sure."

"This is the 21st-century asshole. We have
moved beyond tagging clothes." Her hand didn't

waver in the least, the muzzle trained between his eyes.

"Hey, at least we see where your head agent man gets his potty mouth from."

Kai moved her left hand to her right side and with two fingers pressed hard between her fifth and sixth ribs. She licked her lips; she was in fact very thirsty. "I have no clue how you pulled this off, it was good. Damn good. But you can spend the rest of your life in prison telling us all about it."

"Wow; that is cutting edge," he leaned against the table with an attitude of not having a care in the world. "Subdermal transponder. Who woulda thunk it?" He leaned over and picked up his pack.

"Don't. I will put a round in your knee if I have to. Maybe even one in the elbow for good measure," she snapped.

"That would suck," he replied. His hands sticking inside the pack. "And be super painful I have no doubt. Getting shot is no fun." He stood, pulling his hand up with a new gun.

Kai fired a single round into his leg. Or that is what she expected to happen when she pulled the trigger. She instantly racked the gun again, ejecting another bullet, and pulled the trigger. Only a sharp click answered her. She let her hand fall to her side and the gun to the floor. "Dummy rounds."

"Yep, made 'em myself to make sure you couldn't tell the gun was off weight." He raised his new gun, an odd-looking one with unusual parts.

"This place is still going to be swarming with federal agents and military soon," she said in one last desperate attempt to hold onto hope.

"Doubt it," he replied, and reach back to angle one of the lights so it shone steadily on the rock wall. A dull-colored wire mesh covered the entire surface, disappearing under the layer of sand ceiling. "Are you familiar with the workings of a faraday cage?"

"Well enough," she sighed.

"Good. Then you know that our little hiding place will remain secret." A dull rush of air echoed in the room and a sharp pain lanced into Kai's thigh. She looked down at a large cylindrical dart now lodged into her leg, red feathery ends coming off its back.

"Don't touch it. Unless you want another." Frostt had already loaded a fresh tranquilizer dart.

"Who in the hell are you?" she asked. Her voice sounding distant and muffled to her. She slid down the wall back to the plywood bed. *Supervillain indeed*, was her final thought before once again, blackness took her.

○ ○ ○

Mal looked at President Kai sitting half-slumped over on the other side of the room. He took a few steps closer and crouched down to watch her. Her chest moved up and down in slow rhythmic breathing. Her black hair, still held in her tight ponytail, laid over the left side of her face.

So, Michaela. Are you what you say you are? True and good? We will see, he thought to himself. He licked his lips, tasting the dust of the cave. *I will put it to the test. Live or die, I will know what you are.* He stood still, not able to look away from her. The news broadcasts did not do her justice. Her beauty felt like a sharp stab the longer Mal looked at her. Her face bore a regal quality that lent an air of something beyond skin deep. Something ethereal and coldly stunning. The type of beauty that people either worshiped or hated. Her whole effect was only intensified by her magnetic personality and wit. In their brief exchange, Mal had a painful urge to keep on talking to her.

He moved to his pack and pulled out several items: a pack of alcohol wipes, a sterile scalpel and tweezers, butterfly bandages, and a pack of gauze with surgical tape. He moved over to Michaela, pulling on a pair of new latex gloves. He pulled her shirt up to expose her right side, doing his best to preserve her modesty. He couldn't help but notice several scars on her side nor her toned stomach. An unmistakable bullet wound below the eighth rib, and several possible knife wounds, barely visible, on her stomach. He ignored them and focused on his task. It took less than three minutes to pull out the transponder from her side. He cleaned the cut, closed it with the butterfly strips, placed the gauze, and tape over it. He moved back to his camp table and washed off the dime-sized flat disc with some water. He put it into a small black cylinder, then into a lead box the size of his palm.

"Okay then, Madam President," he spoke looking back at Michaela, "Shall we move onto the next part of our long journey?"

Chapter 10

Agent Bert Renfield pulled another long drag on his cigarette, his third in a row. The bank of Pine Creek was only a few paces away and the only hotel of Slate Run was behind him, full of busy, mostly meaningless action. He stared to the south-east and the hills that rose into the dark night, broken by countless search lights and portable flood lamps.

He rubbed the side of his head, a mind-cracking headache bouncing from one temple to the other. He had just been dismissed from the worst meeting of his life. A little over fourteen hours had passed since President Kai had been taken. Not a trace had been found of her and her sub-dermal transponder could not be located. He cussed and dropped his cigarette into the dirt, digging it in with his heel.

The debrief had taken over five hours. Justin Figg, the director of the Secret Service, had flown in a few hours after the assault. The FBI, Homeland, State and local police, and a dozen other three-lettered agencies had shown up even earlier to fill the small community to bursting. Vice President Cever, now Acting President Cever, teleconferenced into the meeting. Also in attendance were a handful of other people. Within five minutes of the meeting starting, Bert had the clear impression that behind the official debrief and collection of information was a thread of political threat. A goat would be needed soon to be sacrificed on the doorstep of the nation, and Bert had a strong feeling he might get the honor.

Those cheap bastards are more worried about covering their asses than finding the President, Bert thought for the hundredth time. A new voice chimed in his head, *Yeah, but they wouldn't have to if you had not failed.* The thought burned him. He could not escape it. Escape the undeniable fact that he deserved to be the scapegoat. He failed to protect and serve. And for the first time in American history, a president had been captured by an enemy.

It had taken hours to find a way into the subterranean tunnels the man had taken the President into. An endless series of mineshafts and natural caves. It would take a week for the whole maze to be searched.

How in the hell did one man pull this off? He reached for another cigarette but stopped knowing he would have no time to get another pack anytime soon. He needed to stretch the half-pack a while. *He was so damn fast.* Bert shook his head. *He took us apart like paper dolls and moved us like chess pieces to where he wanted us.*

He turned as footsteps moved towards him. Meyers walked up and stood next to him in the gloom of the night. She handed him a fresh cup of coffee, black and hot. He nodded his thanks. The two stood for a few minutes before Meyers spoke up. "Do you think she's still alive?"

"Yes."

"Why?"

"Because a man would not go to that much trouble to take her away from us alive to just kill her elsewhere. He has a purpose. It's our job to sort that out before the asshole has a chance to use her for whatever he needs."

"Not sure if Director Figg is going to be too keen on letting us keep a job of any sort," she said with a bitter smile.

Bert shrugged in response and changed the topic. "Break it down for me again, Meyers. From the bottom."

Meyers cleared her throat and went into her analyst role, her first position with the Secret Service. "The first report came at 1234 hours from the overwatch team in Helicopter One. They had visible contact with what later were counted to be ten tangos. The assumption was made that the tangos were small drones. They lost visual contact with the tangos several minutes later. Three of the so-called drones were found afterwards. They were in fact black, thick-walled helium balloons. Each balloon had a rubber-band-driven propeller to give it forward motion. It is assumed they were released from tree tops as a way to redirect the attention of the overwatch teams. At 1235 all radio and cellular communication was jammed for nearly a quarter-mile surrounding the clearing the

President was in. The search team found several CB radios with amplifiers, a shortwave transmitter, and a homemade cellular blocker located at the base of a tree at the edge of the meadow. Five hundred and twelve separate copper wires had been run up the side of the tree, perfectly hidden in the bark, to turn the tree into a massive broadcast antenna."

Meyers paused to take a breath and wet her lips with the black bitter coffee. Bert still gazed at the Wolf Run area off in the distance. Meyers went on, "Eight car batteries were set up in series to power the makeshift jammer. The whole thing had been buried deep enough to not be picked up on the IR scan we did from the air before the President came; it had been covered with layers of aluminum foil as to not to be detected by any of our electronic device sweeps. All of the devices were common and a first pass by the techs hadn't found anything, but they are still reviewing it. All the tech is barebones and straight off the shelf. Even the homemade cell blocker they say is nothing but household items.

"This is where the timeline gets harder to track. Most agree within a half-minute of the radio jamming, multiple IEDs exploded in stages. After a review of the detonation pattern, they look to have been placed to herd the President up the hill. The IEDs were homemade, and once again off-the-shelf items, including firework powder. The bomb boys at the FBI said they were all-show IEDs, only meant for shock and awe. Hence all the pyrotechnics with them. Once at the top of the hill, things get beyond weird."

"Weird; is that in your official report?" said Bert, not able to put the humor in it like he wanted.

"I think not. Once on the hill, Agent Juan was in the lead and walked into a booby trap. A simple slipknot trap hooked into a counterweight that dragged him away." At a look from Bert she added, "He's doing good. I called the hospital before finding you and he's fine. Jenny and Mitch are good too. Jenny has three broken ribs from the hit in the stomach and Mitch has a severe concussion, but looks to have no long-term damage." She licked her lips and went back to her play-by-play. "As I just said, Jenny and Mitch both were brought down by the assailant with a sling and lead-shot-filled bean bags. After that, you, President Kai, and myself retreated while laying down cover fire." The next words she could not keep her voice monotone, it rose in anxiety. "The assailant caught up to us by pulling himself along with a rope pulley and counter weights. The team found multiple wood, hand-carved pulleys set up to keep the assailant on a straight and level path. The FBI has even flown in an applied physics professor from Harvard to help understand how the thing was possible with nothing more than a few hundred feet of natural fiber rope and pulleys that look to have been carved out of local trees."

A shiver ran through her body. It was not lost on Bert. "You okay?" he asked.

"Yes, sir." She held her coffee cup with both hands close to her face. "It's just... when he came at us. It was like nothing I have ever see. He went through us like we weren't even there. His speed and strength were mind blowing."

"I know," murmured Bert. He went on more clearly. "It even unnerved me. He was like a robot, so calm and cold."

"After that... after that, the assailant held President Kai in a chokehold. A knife to her throat and a self-proclaimed dead-man's trigger in his left hand, supposably tied to an explosive vest he wore. It was never clearly seen. It is clear now that all his talking was only in effect to get into position so he could make the fall down the hidden pit. The team is still digging that out, but found spent IEDs, the cause of the pit falling in on itself."

Meyers took another sip of her coffee and went on, her voice falling out of the monotone of facts, "I did see all the on-ground agents' reports and debrief notes."

"And how did you do that? No one can see those but the top brass right now," said Bert, not sure if he really wanted to know-how.

"I walked into the FBI room and asked to see the hard copies of all the files."

"And they just handed them over?" asked Bert, "You are cute, Meyers, but you're not that cute."

"Yeah, they handed them over," she said dry humor tinting her tone. "I told the newbie on duty that

I would kick him in the balls hard enough for him to taste them if he didn't get out of my way."

Bert only shook his head in reply.

"A good note is everyone's written report is nearly identical, minus the few details that would be expected in a combat situation like this. The assailant's description is pretty clear from the reports and they even match the townsfolk's accounts. A little over 6' tall, shoulder-length blonde hair pulled back tight, thin, blonde goatee, green eyes, and very physically fit. We know that he was in the area for at least four days before the advance team came in and is going by the name Michael Archer, an amateur photographer, a fake persona of course. A forensic team went over his room with a toothpick but found very little. Only two partial prints. They are not sure they will be of any use; looks like he wiped down the room before leaving."

"And the bad note?" asked Bert. He pulled out another cigarette unable to hold back the urge any longer.

"The debrief notes were," she chewed her lip for a second, "Not flattering to say the least." She finished with a note of apology.

"As it should be," he took a long drag and spoke through the smoke, still staring like a statue at the hills in the distance. "It was my fault."

"Sir, that is not fair…"

Kyle T. Davis

"Don't. It has nothing to do with it being fair. I am head of the presidential detail and the buck stops with me. I let her, I let all of us, walk into a trap."

Meyers did not respond at first, and before she could think of anything to say, new footsteps intruded on the pair.

Bert turned to see Director Figg, his leather loafers ill-fitted for the river bank terrain.

"Agent Renfield. Agent Meyers," he nodded to both in turn. "A word please, Agent Renfield."

Meyers could take a hint when slapped with one, she looked to Bert who gave a small nod, and then she left.

Figg looked after Meyers for a moment, the silence stretching too long. Bert had no intention of breaking it first. He didn't have to. "You have a very loyal team, Agent Renfield." Bert didn't respond; he only gave a small nod of the head and turned to look back at the hills.

"Not one of them would say a bad word *directly* about you."

"No matter how much you pushed them?" replied Bert.

Figg ignored the comment and went on. "This is bad business. Not a trace of DNA is left. The media is already having a fit. President Cever will be doing a press conference in six hours and we need to give him some good news. The hotlines are ringing off the hook since we released Michael Archer's photo to the public."

"We shouldn't use that name," stated Bert. "It will only create confusion."

Figg ignored him and went onto his next topic. "President Cever has insisted, against *my* recommendation, that you head the task force in the hunt of President Kai and Michael Archer."

Bert turned to fully face the director, "Why does Cever want me?"

"*President* Cever," Figg correct, "Thinks you are best for the job because you have had the most interaction with Archer and have the needed skillset."

"And maybe the fact that I am already a good scapegoat, so getting me a little plumper won't matter…sir."

"Listen, Agent Renfield. I strongly opposed this decision and you can be damn sure that you will be so far under my microscope you won't be able to itch your ass without it going into a report."

"Yes, sir," answered Bert. "I've no doubt."

Figg sneered and went on looking like he just drank down a pint of ipecac syrup. "The FBI will be running point on digging into Michael Archer and trying to sort out his real identity. Homeland is watching the border, and the US Marshal and National Guard have set up checkpoints at every state line, airport, and transit hub for all states east of the Mississippi." Figg adjusted his tie and went on. "The NSA will be sending over a team to make sure we have up-to-date intel in real-time. You will be headed back to DC; a helicopter is already inbound to collect you and your team." He paused for a minute. Bert held the stare and said nothing. "You will send me reports every three hours. And let's pray she is still alive."

"She is," stated Bert.

"And what makes you think that?"

"The assailant would not go to this trouble to only kill her privately. There is a motive here we don't understand."

"Unless he is just a sicko wanting to make it last with her."

"No, he is not. Too dedicated and methodical for that. He has a mission, and will drive to that if it costs him his life."

"Are you a profiler now?"

"No, sir. Just good at understanding people, especially assholes."

"Well for your sake, and President Kai's, I hope your asshole telepathy is working on overdrive." Figg turned without another word and started his awkward walk back up the rocky river bank.

Bert stared at his back as he walked away. "No worries. It's on full bore with you around.... sir," he said to the air around him. He pulled out another cigarette and lit up as he moved away from the river to find Meyers and collect his team. He had a job ahead of him and the same bad feeling in his gut as he did before the attack. This time, not from an unknown outside threat, but from a real, internal attacker.

Chapter 11

The early March morning felt abnormally warm in Washington D.C., the weathermen were talking about a new, record-high for March and at least a week left of sunshine. The burst of warmth didn't have any effect on the cold mood of the city. Forty-four hours had passed since President Kai had been kidnapped and it was the only thing on people's lips. From both the right- and left-wing media outfits came fear mongering and enough blame to pass around. Capitol Hill was a mess of special committees already looking for blood and political maneuvering to capitalize on the power vacuum and chaos.

Malcolm Frostt paid it all little attention, minus the report from the federal three-letter agencies and the Secret Service. The latter's director came across as more of a politician than a federal agent. Agent Renfield could be seen in the newscasts standing behind the Secret Service director looking tired but resolute at the same time. That steadfast look worried Mal more than any of the pompous reassurance the other federal agencies were puking out. He didn't let it deter him in the least from his mission. He would never waver.

The smell of dollar store candles and dirty sweat dominated the cheap wood paneled room where Mal sat. A single large bed, thrift store sofa, and battered pieces of cheap wood furniture dotted the seedy motel room. Lulu Candy sat on the couch smoking a cigarette and staring at Mal, who sat on the bed dressed in dingy blue jeans, a flannel button-down shirt, and a dusty leather jacket.

Lulu was of course not her real name, but a working girl didn't really need a name anyway. "Did you finish the job?" asked Mal.

Lulu didn't respond right away, she continued to smoke her cigarette, and switched legs being crossed, though that did little to hide anything under her panty-line skirt. Her top did even less to cover her ample chest. Her hair was straight as a board, and bright pink. Her voice was smooth with youth, but tinted with smoke, "Always down to business for you." She leaned forward making sure to give Mal a good view. "You know most men that meet for a third time want to do very little talking; well, most men on their first time," she smiled.

"Did you finish the job," Mal asked again. His eye never left hers, steady and unwavering.

She leaned back, a brief look of hurt on her face. "Yes, I finished. You do like to take on big marks, don't you."

"He didn't suspect you?" asked Mal. He ignored her question about his mark.

"He was out cold when I swapped out the ring. Well, out from too much vigorous activity. You know he's kind of a freak."

Mal held up his hand. "I don't want the details and I don't care any which way. As long as you switched out his school ring without him knowing it."

"Yes," she said waspishly. "I think I know my way around manipulating a man." She dropped her cigarette on the stained carpet and stamped it out with her high heel. "Now if you aren't going to take advantage of me and that bed, let's see the money and I'm out."

Mal pulled a roll of cash out of his pocket and tossed it over to her. She quickly counted through it, unabashed to count the money in front of him. After finishing her practiced count, she stood and went to the door. She turned back one last time, her hips pushed out in a suggestive angle. "You sure you don't want to have a little fun before I go? It's rare I get a man who's actually good looking. And I think your pay would cover a quick romp."

"No," replied Mal, still only looking at her eyes. "That is good money you got there. Buy a bus ticket and get out of town. Go to school, learn a trade, just don't burn your life out on the pleasure of others."

She shook her head. "It's not that simple, and I'm guessing you are one who understands the hold life can have on you."

"Yes. Yes, I understand that"

Lulu nodded to him. "Have fun with your senator." And she left.

As long as the bug you planted works, I am sure that Senator Otts and I will be having plenty of fun, Mal thought. *Just one step at a time. Plans within plans.*

Mal took his leave of the hourly motel. The section of D.C. he walked into did not look much better than the motel behind him. He moved down the street. His face had been restored back to its normal look with the itchy blonde wig stored for future use. People paid him little attention as he walked down the sidewalks and boarded a bus. He stepped off onto the north side of the National Mall, the warm March weather bringing out the tourists in hoards. Mal headed east along Constitution Avenue. The tall pillars of the National Gallery of Art flowed past him, though he had no eye for the sights. Only one place interested him.

The Upper Senate Park stood out in stark contrast to the warm winter day, barren trees creating a lined carpet of shadows from the full and warming sun. Mal never watched from the same place twice; he moved about the park for several minutes, always coming to the east side of the park by a different route. He leaned against a tree, pulled a digital camera from his jacket pocket, and attached an adjustable lens to the front of it. He made a show of capturing pictures of the mid-morning sun filtering through the endless branches of trees. In fact, his only focus was that of the Russell Senate Office Building. The Beaux-Arts architectural building first opened a hundred years earlier. Its purpose was to create new office space for the overcrowded Capital Building. Over the last century, it had been home to countless Senators, joined by two other Senate buildings rising from the ground to support the engorging government as the years passed. Mal's focus spanned the entire Delaware Avenue side of the building, but only two points held his attention. The first was a third-floor office window in the upper northern quarter of the building. Senator Andrew Ott's office sat behind that drape-covered window. The other point was the staff-only Delaware Ave facing door.

The day slowly inched its way to noon, and more and more people joined Mal in the park. The Russell building gained energy as the day moved on. A group of jabbering tourists moved past Mal; he paid them little attention focused on his non-tree art.

The voice of a child spoke out. "Pardon, sorry, sir," as the kid bumped into Mal as he tried to dart around the meandering group of oblivious tourists.

Mal's right hand snapped out in a flash and gripped the back of the boy's hoodie and shirt. He spoke without taking his eyes off the Russell building. "I doubt you are, but you will be sorry if you don't give me my wallet back."

"Yo, let me the hell go," spat out the kid. Mal's hand did not flinch as the boy tried to turn to face him. "Let go or I'll scream you're trying to molest me, asshole."

Mal let the camera fall away from his eye, and rest by its neck strap, he turned to face the kid and laid a look of ice on him. "Watch your tongue, boy."

The kid's prepped scream died in his throat at the look from Mal. He quickly recovered. "Yeah, whatever. Take it." He tossed the wallet back to Mal. "Now, let me the hell go."

Mal let him go, and caught the wallet. "Again, clean your mouth. Shouldn't you be in school or something?"

"I don't need that school. Bunch of tight-asses trying to brainwash me."

Mal shrugged. "Fair enough, but the street ain't no better." He could tell the kid was on the verge of bolting. "Even if you are good. I barely felt it, except your follow-through. Sloppy." Mal shook his head.

"Yeah, what would you know about it." The kid pulled down his hoodie to push his long dirty blonde hair out of his face. Mal could not tell for sure, but the kid couldn't be more than thirteen. Weedy-looking, puberty had not been kind to him; acne marked with deep hollow eyes and a nose that had been broken at least once in the last few years. His clothes were nearly worn through and dirty all over. His sleeves were rolled up and it was the circle burn scars that rounded out the street rat look, some new and some older. Mal couldn't help involuntarily move to touch the same scars on his own arm. They had faded with time, but only from the skin, not from the mind.

"What's your name, kid?" asked Mal. The boy caught the look at his arms and dropped his sleeves.

"None of your damn business," spat out the kid, "fake ass photo man."

"Boy, I should clean your mouth with soap. Some schooling would be good for you. Get some new words in ya." Mal made sure not to move forward at all, like stalking a scared rabbit. "And what do you mean fake photo man?"

"What do I mean, bah," smiled the kid. "You all standing here acting like the trees are the best thing on earth, but all you care about is that Russell Building behind me and the folk coming and going. And the third-floor windows, too."

Mal's eyebrows raised at the comment. *The little piss made me*, Mal thought. Doing his best to not show his concern, he scanned the crowd to make sure no one else made him.

"Don't worry," waved the boy, as if reading Mal's thoughts. "Doubt anyone else noticed. Most people are too busy with themselves to see anyone else."

"Yeah, that's a good bit of wisdom," replied Mal. "How'd you make me?"

"It's your stance, you're too serious. Like you got a stick up your ass." Mal gave him another hard look, "Okay, okay. Fine." The boy raised his hands, "Stick up your butt. That better?"

"What's your name?" asked Mal again.

"Milo."

"Well, Milo, you're just an odd kid."

"I ain't no kid," sneered Milo.

"Not in your head, I give you that." Mal rubbed the side of his face, where two days of stubble ringed his jaw and cheeks. "You want a job?"

"I don't do none of the punk-ass pervy stuff."

"I am going to slap you silly if you curse again," said Mal. Milo looked only slightly abashed.

"Yeah, well I don't need none of y'all charity. I can make my own way."

"I have no doubt of that, though it will end with you locked up or dead at some point. No, charity. One job. Good money, cash."

"Is it legit?" questioned Milo.

Uh, this kid has a good head on his shoulders. Shame it looks like someone has been using it as a punching bag. Mal kept those words to himself, and went on out loud. "Nope, not a bit."

Milo chewed on his lips for a second. "Okay."

Mal smiled. "Real simple then. Tomorrow, about eight to nine in the morning all hell is going to break out across the street in that building."

"Hey, you cursed," pointed out Milo.

"I'm big. You're not. Don't interrupt me. Now, do you know who Senator Otts is?"

Milo shrugged, "An as....bum. I've heard his name, but that's it."

Mal took a minute and showed a picture of the Senator to Milo on his smartphone. "Now, if you see the Senator, I want you to take photos of him and anyone he's talking to. There will be plenty of people snapping pictures of the building, so you will fit right in. Also, there are going to be some cars that show up, government looking."

"There are always government cars showing up," said Milo. He added, after a glare from Mal, "Go on."

"Yes, there will be hundreds of government vehicles showing up, but these won't be government, but will have the air of them. The men won't be feds either, but will...will have my look."

"You mean killers," Milo said matter-of-factly.

Mal could not hide the shock on his face this time. "Yes, that would be their look."

Milo nodded his head. "My dad served in the Iraq war; gets that look to him after a few drinks. Works nights, so days I'm out of the house. Now, how much are you paying?"

Mal handed over the camera to Milo. "You use this camera. And you will get five-hundred cash, two-hundred now, and three after we settle up." Before Milo could let the thought cross his mind, Mal went on. "And don't think about ditching with the money and camera. You might be able to pawn that thing for fifty, sixty bucks. You can keep it, minus the SD card, after the job, and the other three-hundred cash.

"We definitely can't meet here. Where do you live?"

"Nah, we not that much of buddies," said Milo. He thought for a minute, Mal waited. "We can meet at the Ferebee-Hope Park, down in Washington Heights. You know the area?"

Mal nodded. "Well enough to find it."

"Good, meet you on the south-side by the playground."

"Okay, tomorrow afternoon. Can't give you a hard time."

Milo waved the comment off. "Don't matter. Just be there before dark."

"Sounds good," Mal pulled two-hundred dollars and passed the camera and money over to Milo. Hiding the deal in a handshake. "Now remember, don't get too close to the chaos, I'm looking for anything on Senator Otts and non-fed looking feds."

"Got it, mister," said Milo. "See you tomorrow." He walked away, saying over his shoulder, "Don't forget the rest of my money." Mal watched Milo walk away, and easily disappear into the crowd, memories of a young boy full of fear, anger, and pain swinging in his mind. He pushed the memories away, mentally ignoring the scars deep inside, more than he could do with the dozens that littered his body from childhood.

o o o

Mal lingered in the park for several more hours, moving about so not to stay in one spot too long. A little after four in the afternoon, he headed towards the north-side of the park. He quickly ducked into a trio of trees, creating a pseudo blind spot. The jeans he wore came apart on pre-weakened seams, revealing a dark pair of slacks underneath. The same with the button-down flannel shirt, a purposely wrinkled white dress shirt under that. The leather jacket turned inside out created a sports jacket and a midnight black tie in his pocket. He stepped out from the tree, looking like a new person. A typical Washington suit, he tossed the discarded pieces of clothing in a trash can as he crossed Delaware Avenue on the northeastern most point of the Russell Building. He walked down C Street, putting on a pair of fake glasses from his pocket. He took a left at First Street NE. and made the walk north.

He never lost sight of his quarry, the reason for his flight from the park, just one of the myriad of reasons he had spent the day watching the Russell Building. The man, a block ahead of Mal, turned into a large parking lot and moved through the cars to a small, pale, tan building. Mal followed a minute later, though not straight to the building. He moved about the parking lot until he found a pair of trucks parked next to each other. He pulled from his pocket a fake, black goatee and used one of the truck's side mirrors to apply it to his face. After a quick look over his appearance, he deemed it good and moved forward.

The words of an old teacher, Gamba Eze, who was not one of any normal school, rang in his head. *Anyone can put on a fake face and new clothes. Those are only props for the disguise, only tools for any real master of deceit. The true disguise lies in the mind of the Other. The one watching. It must be carefully crafted and projected. It is the minor details that create the impression. Overdone, they create more suspicions than if not there, but underdone, they create no lingering effect to change the Other's lasting impression. This allows the Other's subconsciousness to come out with details that you would not want to be remembered. You must strike that fine balance between cunning but still human enough to catch the conscious awareness of your target that you will override any subconscious understanding that you are a fake.*

Mal licked his lips as he walked towards the building, not sure how to feel about the old lessons, all the old lessons. Pain too deep to even think about, but the only thing that allowed him to pursue his enemies and completely his mission.

A dozen steps from the building, Mal pushed all the thoughts of past times away and did what he had been trained to do: become someone new. From the bottom of his feet to the minor changes of his face, he forced his body into that fine balance of life and lie.

He rounded the side of the building, the pale tan walls replaced by a light lemon façade with forest green accents and an awning covered the front entrance, the same color as the trimmed windows and wall. Gold and white lettering stitched into the awning read: The Eyeglass Bar and Restaurant. Mal entered the space with a nod to the door man. A high end D.C. staple, the place saw no shortage of political players and power climbing sycophants. The Eyeglass was known for fine foods, weak beer, high end wine, and to Mal's pleasure, an excellent spirit collection including many top-shelf whiskeys. Even though a good drink was not the point of his outing, he thought of it as a pleasant bonus.

He sidled up to the bar. The suited bartender came over to him at once, "Blade and Bow Twenty Two, double. Neat."

"Yes, sir," replied the barman, then went about pulling the bottle down from the shelf.

A few patrons dotted the tables around the wood paneled restaurant, looking for an early dinner or late lunch. Only one other person sat at the bar, two seats down from Mal. The man sat, with a nearly gone gin and tonic in front of him, shoulders slumped forward. His short hair held the faintest traces of its original dark blonde, having been overrun by dirty gray. Years of lines dominated his face and a poor diet could be seen in his bulging gut.

The barkeep poured out Mal's drink and handed it over. Mal took a sip, enjoying the aged whiskey. *I hate to do this to a good man,* thought Mal to himself and he looked into his glass. *I have no choice. It needs to be done and that is all there is to it. He'll be okay.* Mal took a calming breath and let his new persona wash over him.

"Jonas, another please," spoke up the man next to Mal. The bartender nodded and deftly mixed up another gin and tonic.

"Double strong as always, Simon," smiled Jonas as he handed the finished cocktail over to the man.

Mal took the opportunity. "Rough day?" He motioned with his glass to Simon's, who had just downed a quarter of the drink in one go.

"Aren't they all," replied Simon, not looking over to Mal.

"Yeah, well that's why God invented liquor," Mal finished the quip by finishing off his bourbon. He motioned for another.

Simon gave a deep-throated chuckle in return. "True enough."

The two lapsed into silence. A few more patrons came into the restaurant. The TV at the bar turned to one of the endless news stations. More talking heads spitting out the latest theory about the President. A running timer of how long President Kai had been missing on the bottom of the screen: 51:08 hours. The talking heads were once again pointing fingers at anyone who would hold still for half a second. It had gone so far that the Republicans were blaming the whole thing on Democrats making America weak, thus encouraging an attack and the Democrats blaming the Republicans for organizing the whole thing because President Kai was a female.

"Hey, can you turn that crap off?" asked Mal, pointing at the TV.

Simon joined instantly. "Yeah, Jonas. Let's have something different."

"That's for sure," added Mal. "I mean it's sad and all, but talking it to death is not going to do anything for it." He pulled his glass up to his lips and muttered, "And it's not like she's still alive anyway."

Simon nodded his head, working on his third drink. "I agree. I don't want to be callous or anything, but the chances of her being alive are not good. We need to find the bastards who did this and go bomb them to hell."

Mal raised his glass at that. "Even my boss is acting like it's the only thing in the world and that it is our duty to support the *Cause* at all times." He let the perfect amount of bitterness linger on his words.

"You part of the investigation?"

Mal shook his head and gave a tired chuckle. "Nope, not at all. I'm a CPA. I work downtown for a financial management firm." Mal took a long drink from his glass. "My boss is up all our asses thinking we can have any effect on the investigation by supporting our Hill clients. 'It is our duty to make sure they have nothing to worry about so they can focus on their jobs,'" Mal said in a sardonic tone. "Like any of those pompous dimwits gives a damn about the President, only their next political move."

"I can second that," said Simon. "I work over at the Russell Building and it's chaos."

"And I thought I had it bad. I can't imagine what it's like in the thick of it."

"Yeah, well, my boss is nearly the same as yours and you are not far off the mark for all the senators. A bunch of manipulating two-faced phonies."

"I feel for you," Mal shook his head. "That has to be a tough gig. What you do there?"

"I am a Senior Building Inspector for the A.O.C., I work in the three Senate office buildings. It's nothing glamorous, but it pays the bills. Well, most of the bills."

Mal let a small pause lapse into the conversation; he didn't want to seem too eager about Simon's job. He motioned once again with his drink. "Is that a Florida State ring?"

Simon, no worse for wear working on his fourth drink, looked down at his right hand. "Yeah. Good eye."

"My uncle's got the same one. He played football there back in the day."

"Oh, really? What's his name?"

"Patrick Junt. I think he graduated in '84. If I remember right."

"I was '85, but he doesn't sound familiar. I wasn't into sports much back then."

"Yeah, he got a full ride for it, but never went pro or nothing. He got his degree, then his MBA, and went off to open a few car dealerships in Boston."

"Hey, yeah, I think I do remember him. Patrick Junt, huh? I was in the MBA program myself. I think I had a few classes with him."

Mal smiled inwardly, hook, line, and sinker. He pushed on, pulling the conversation back to work. "So how did you end up in D.C. working for the A.O.C. with an MBA?" He moved a seat closer with the question.

"Well, two failed marriages later and three kids on child support, work is work."

"Ain't that the truth. Me and my soon-to-be ex are signing papers next week," Mal spat the words out. "You know she's getting the house, the boat, and my dog. She claims psychological trauma."

Simon gave Mal a consoling pat on the back, "Don't worry buddy; it gets better."

"Really?"

"No, but as you said, that's why we have booze."

Mal and Simon toasted glasses. "So, what is one good thing about your job? There is always something, I mean my boss is a dick and all, but I get paid a ridiculous amount of money. Mainly so I keep my trap shut about how the people making the tax laws are cutting them."

"Best thing…" Simon polished off his drink and waved Jonas for a last one. "Well my pay is crap, but I get full access to some of the most powerful people in the country's highest offices. Man, some of the vices these people have."

"Like what?"

Simon shook his head. "Not worth my job to say."

Mal shrugged and held up his glass to the bartender as he passed, asking for another and brushing the top of his hand over Simon's cup. Simon didn't notice the extra bubbles in his drink. "No worries. I get it. The powerful must be protected at all costs, right?" He added a dose of sarcasm to his tone.

"Messed up city it is." Simon downed half his drink. "The hypocrisy of this city just kills me."

"You can damn well say that again," affirmed Mal.

"Okay, no names, but there is a small group of senators from both sides of the aisle and both genders who from time to time like to have some private entertainment come up from the street."

"No way, in the Russell Building?"

"Oh, yeah. Full-on orgies. And I have heard it even happens in the Capital Building as well."

"Well, that is tax dollars well spent," Mal laughed.

"I have even had to help sneak the girls in a few times. We have to use old abandoned service tunnels. All under the radar."

"No shit. Old tunnels, sneaking them in."

"Swear it."

Mal gave Simon a double pat on the back, "Now that tops my stories any day."

Simon finished off his drink. "It's been good, friend, but I got a good book at home and a microwave dinner calling my name."

"Take it easy and don't get lost in those tunnels." *And thank you for confirming that they are still open,* he thought the last part.

Simon laughed and took his leave. Unknown to him, he had given Mal everything he needed: confirmation that the abandoned tunnels Mal had discovered on some old prints of D.C. he had bought from a collector were still open. More important, was the ID card Mal had slipped off the man. The chemical cocktail he had added to Simon's drink would keep him sick for a few days. Lastly, Mal snagged the drink glass, still smelling of gin and tonic. Making sure to only touch the inside of the glass, not to mess up any prints on the outside.

Mal closed his tab and tipped well. He left the Eyeglass Bar and Restaurant, feeling a sense of hope. Hope that he might be able to pull this off. The first part of many. He did not dwell on the hope long. He didn't want anything clouding his judgment.

Chapter 12

Michaela woke with a mind splitting headache and a nearly uncontrollable urge to pee. Her entire body felt stiff and sore. A stabbing pain on her right side and in her left hand screamed at her. It felt like she had been chewing on sandpaper and a half dozen muscles in her back started spasming all at once. She looked to her side as she tried to move her hands, her left hand spiking in pain. She saw an IV needle stuck in the top of it, the line headed up to a clear bag of fluid. She cleared her mind and pushed all the pain away. A skill she had used too many times before.

"You can pull that out if you want," a voice spoke, familiar and gritty. "Just be gentle when you move, your side is still healing."

What the hell is going on, Michaela thought. Fear washed over her. That deep primal fear of the unknown. Visions of torture, both real memories and imagined ones, raged in the back of her mind. Eight months in an Iranian prison had left a lasting mark on her, both physically and mentally. This time was worse. The unknown tore at her. In Iran, she knew the game, the stakes, the players. But now she was lost.

She laid her head back and took several calming breaths, letting her body relax, as she cleared her mind. She let her surroundings flow into her. An unsteady motion instantly alerted her to the fact that she was on a boat or ship. The IV came out slowly, a trickle of blood coming with the needle. The pain in her side protested loudly. Pulling her shirt up just enough, she saw a gauze pad taped down to her side, right where her subdermal transponder should be. With eyes closed and head laid back down, she thought, *What the hell! He cut the transponder out. Shit and a half, who the hell is he?* "Did you enjoy the view when you pulled my shirt up, pervert?" The man did not respond to the jab.

Ever so slowly, Michaela sat up; she was on a small cot against a wooden wall. A single, multipurpose room lay out in front of her, just like when she woke up last time, but vastly different. Windows let in no direct light, but the inky dark sky was broken by a few stars. A kitchen table sat to the right of her, a work bench with dozens of items next to the table, a door to her immediate left. A small table covered in wigs and what looked to be makeup boxes stood next to the door. Across from her, a computer desk with what she could tell to be state of the art tech. Next to that, was a kaleidoscope of pictures, drawings, newspaper articles, and white and red string plastered on the wall. The most disturbing of the lot, multiple pictures of her. A large map of the Wolf Run Area with pins marking off different sections did not help the wall look better.

"The head is the door to your left. Guessing you have to pee like a race horse. I've been keeping you hydrated, but didn't want to cross any lines by using a catheter." The man, Mr. Frostt Michaela remembered, had not turned away from standing at the helm on the far side of the room. After another minute of quiet and no response from Michaela, he turned to look at her. He looked completely different. Same muscled build and snake coil tension in his stance, but a new face and something evening deeper. His hair was black as coal and his face looked like a Greek statue, Mediterranean complexation made him stunningly attractive.

"Go. I put a small, ditty bag in the bathroom for you. And I have some hot soup and bread here for you. It's been a while since you ate."

"You're going to let me go in the bathroom and shut the door? What if I try to escape?"

"There is only a single window in the head and you might be thin, but you ain't that thin. And I made sure nothing in the ditty bag is too dangerous." Frostt moved over to the table and micro kitchenette. He pulled out a bowl and a can of chicken noodle soup.

Michaela stood on weak legs and used baby steps to make it over to the door. The bathroom was anything but large or fancy. *And true to this Mr. Frostt's word, what a stupid name,* she thought to herself. A clear plastic ditty bag sat on the vanity. A cheap, flimsy toothbrush, a travel tube of toothpaste, two thin wash clothes, a single use deodorant stick, and a folding, child size hair brush. She quickly went about her business, and after a search of the room found nothing. Frostt hadn't been joking about the window, she could not have even gotten her head out of it. The view from it showed nothing new but a few lights off in the distance.

She came out of the bathroom feeling much better and cleaner, after giving herself a quick wet rag scrub down. The cut on her side looked clean and well bandaged. *Who in the hell is this guy? Fighter, tactician, con-artist, medic...* A steaming bowl of chicken noodle soup and some almost stale sourdough bread greeted her at the table. He had given her no utensils. She smiled thinking at least he took her threat to him seriously. He stood back at the helm, the boat moving at a steady pace. She had a fleeting thought the food might be drugged but dismissed the thought. He could just hit her with another dart if he wanted.

He didn't say a word as she slurped up her soup and dug into her bread. She used the time to exam the space and Frostt in more detail. The disguise he had worn had been perfect. It would have the Secret Service looking for the completely wrong person. He wore the same Colt 1911, no doubt truly loaded this time, on his right hip. Michaela felt the weapon to be a bit antiquated with all the modern pistols available. She turned her attention to the wall of chaos across the room from her. She could see several books, on a makeshift bookcase, all of them looking well worn. A quick look over the titles gave her little hope, over half the book's titles read about government conspiracy theories. The rest were technical manuals including an army issued manual on explosive ordinances and practical usage. The wall above the bookshelf was something straight out of a movie. Chaotic and impossible to understand Frostt's mad attempt at piecing his delusions together. She centered her mind and readied herself. It would be a game of wits. Pawns to be moved and a king to topple.

"How did you know where I was going to be? I didn't even know I would follow that stream up the mountain."

Mal turned away from the controls, throttling down the boat. "Easy. I've been releasing jadeite into that stream, which feeds the lower ones, for about a month now." At a wide-eyed look from Michaela, he went on, casually leaning against the wall next to the helm. "I created a water-driven device that released powdered jadeite into the stream. A day before you came, I started releasing pebble-sized jade."

"That was slick," Michaela muttered, pulling her shocked look under control. "You did your research well. My middle name, the anniversary of my father's passing, and making sure that your jadeite would be picked up by one of the water testing stations on my father's online network."

Mal shrugged his shoulders at the statement. "The strongest of all warriors are these two — Time and Patience."

"Agreed," nodded Michaela. "But Tolstoy was a chauvinistic pig who liked his women way to young."

"That was also a nice touch with the faraday cage, not to even mention the ploy with your pistol. I was completely duped." *Let's play to his narcissism a bit*, she thought, *create a connection. Put him at ease. Then crush his wind pipe.* She went on again out loud, "So that brings us to why? Why all this?" She pointed over at his paper- covered wall. "I am not going to insult your intelligence by telling you how much trouble you're in, but a *why* would be good."

"No, of course not, only don't insult me by trying to butter me up with false flattery," replied Mal. "I know the magnitude of what I pulled off and the cunning it took. Please don't try to humanize yourself to me. You have no need."

This time Michaela was able to hide the wide-eyed look that threatened to be exposed on her face again. "Well, aren't you a frosty bastard."

Frostt let out a sharp laugh. "Good one, nice pun."

"Yeah, by the way, I am not calling you Mr. Frostt or any sort of Mr. I will just stick with bastard for now."

"Whatever works for you, Michaela."

She glared at him. She knew she was at a huge disadvantage, him knowing more about her than she did about him.

Mal stepped over to the computer workstation, moving like a relaxed tiger, and picked up three file folders. He placed them on the table in a stack and pulled the only other chair to the side of the table to sit kitty-corner to her.

"Eighteen months and seven days ago my wife was murdered and my daughter kidnapped." Mal paused for a moment and unbuttoned the top of his shirt to reveal white and pink burn scars and a roughly healed bullet wound in the center of his left peck muscle. "The men who came for us were good. Some of the best I've ever seen. They surprised us, I got two of them before they were able to get to my daughter and use her against me, otherwise, I would have gotten all six of them." He said the last part in no way boasting but in solid fact. He went on, letting go of his shirt, the fabric covering the bullet hole once again, but still showing the ragged burn scars that licked the way up the left side of his neck, a few wisps touching his jawline.

"They shot me twice in the chest. Their mistake; should have done it properly. They did that to my wife. Two in the chest and one in the head. Two feet from me. I had to wipe her blood out of my eyes. They took my daughter and left an already dead little girl next to us. Their leader whispered to me as he left, 'We'll take good care of her. She's more special than you will ever know. Enjoy the fire.' They soaked the first floor of my house in gas and left as flames took over the place. I don't really remember getting out. I woke up about a day and a half later in the backyard. Luckily a hard rain had come sometime earlier and put out the house to only smoldering. We lived too far out for anyone to notice the fire. They even killed my dog."

Michaela sat in complete silence the entire time, soaking up all she could. She knew if she was going to find any way to this man it would be through the avenues only he opened. Frostt opened each folder in front of him and slid them over to Michaela. She took them and started skimming as Frostt went on. "I went to the police to start. Had detectives and officers all over my place, whole nine yards. Nothing. They would not believe me about my daughter, said her body was in the burnt-out house. No matter how many times I told them the new girl was a plant. Her body was burnt to a crisp, too gone for DNA, but her dental records matched my daughter's. So, they never looked for her. The case is still open, but murder not kidnapping."

"Not a lead nor even a peep from the police. I took the liberty of looking into the dental records myself. They had been digitally altered, pro job. I paid a local geek to scrub through the file. The hard copies had been changed out as well and no one with access to the clinic had anything financial that would have flagged them to taking a payment to switch them out. The strike group could have easily broken in without a trace and changed the hard copies. I did."

Michaela spoke up, flipping pages in the first of the folders. "Your daughter had congenital heart disease," she pointed to a page in the folder.

"Yes, she *has* coarctation of the aorta. She had to have a stent put in place to widen the aorta to get her blood flow up to normal. She was twenty months old when she had the surgery."

"In the autopsy report, which somehow you got, there is confirmation on the aortic stent. Badly damaged, but still intact enough to get a serial number that matched your daughter's."

Mal waved the comment away. "Same as the dental. Someone messed with the records."

Michaela let out a soft sigh and went onto the third folder. *Oh, shit. Way worse than I thought. A delusional conspiracy nut with trauma to create a massive psychological break, but with the skills to cause havoc,* she thought, making sure to not let any of the thoughts show on her face.

"I have confirmation of the tampering." Michaela raised an eyebrow at the comment. Mal answered her questioning look, "Of course I interviewed the doctor that installed her stent. He had been the one to register it with the FDA and had the hard copy records. He admitted to giving the model and serial number to an anonymous buyer."

"He did?" asked Michaela, hoping not to provoke Frostt by doubting him. "Was he under any *stress* when you asked him?"

"I made sure he was properly encouraged to answer truthfully," Mal didn't flinch making the statement. "I traced the payment he took back to a shell company in the Caymans. It's all there." He pointed to the folder she had in front of her. She looked; it was there. Payment of a hundred thousand dollars to the doctor from a company in the Cayman Islands, from there, the money disappeared into red tape.

"I also followed up on the ballistics from the crime scene at my house. The police said nothing came back positive from the bullets taken out of my wife, but I had reason to doubt them already. I used the three bullets I dug out of myself. All three bullets fired from the same gun, by the leader who talked to me, which has been used in three different murders over the last seven years all over the United States."

Michaela looked over the enclosed ballistics report and three other murders, no leads on any of them. She looked up at Frostt. "Were you able to confirm this as well?"

"Of course. The lead detective on the case was very forth coming with info. Same anonymous type of contact and payment, but from a different shell company. This time out of Switzerland."

"Did you kill him? The cop?" asked Michaela. Her body tensed.

"Yes."

"Why are you telling me all this? Why me?"

"Because I need help and because this is only the tip. Here is where the rabbit hole goes deep."

"And how in the hell, and why in the hell, would I help you? You have kidnapped me and are by now the most wanted person in the country," she shook her head, then stared into his intense eyes, the color of fire-blackened steel.

"Because you have a cancer eating at your government. And I'm not even sure if you are part of it."

"Part of what?," Exasperation edging her voice.

"I am not sure, but it is large, multifaceted, and goes higher than the U.S. Senate," he returned her stare with a soul gazing look. "You are my last hope. Either you are part of it and I have failed or you are not and we must cut out the cancer in the government. Either way, I will see this to the end, even if that means my life. I will find my daughter, with your willing help or with your forced help."

"I can help you," Michaela answered, doing her best to keep a smooth voice. "But you have to let me go and turn yourself in. I will personally look into the investigation of your daughter and we can get you some help."

Mal's only response was to shake his head. He ignored her suggestion. "Go to the last dozen pages in that folder." He pointed to the third and thickest one.

Michaela did as she was told and started flipping through the pages as Mal went on. "I was not able to get straight looks at either the Swiss or Cayman accounts, but I did get some sideways looks at them. A few transaction codes and pieces of account numbers. That with my research into the other murders tied to the gun that killed my wife and shot me I was led to several different companies and the initials AO tied to several key legal documents for each separate company."

It was all in front of Michaela. Lists of accounts, company tax forms, and ledgers. The initials AO and several documents from separate companies seemed to have no ties, minus the two letters. Then she turned the last page and a picture of a man she instantly recognized stared back at her. Andrew Otts, the senator from New York state and one of her most outspoken opponents before and after her election.

Mal tapped a finger on the picture in the center of the page. "It is all here, yes, some might be a little thin, but still more than enough. Senator Otts is a key linchpin in what is going on. He served on two of the city councils where three of the companies are based. After that, he moved into the federal realm and worked in the office of customs and the IRS, in which he used that power to help all these companies dozens of times. His run for Senator was funded from many different sources, but I have been able to track at least forty percent of the money coming out of these same companies. There even was a local newspaper that did a story about voter fraud in his district that helped him get office. The story was never picked up by a major station and the reporter whow wrote the story went missing a month after it was released."

"That doesn't mean he's in on some sinister plot to kidnap your daughter and murder people. At most, he used dirty money to get elected and sold favors. Sad to say, that is not uncommon." Mal shook his head, but Michaela went on. "As I said, turn yourself in and we will look into your daughter and this should be enough info to start an investigation into Otts. I will be the first to admit that he's an asshole. A pompous, stuck up pig, but we have processes to deal with corruption like this."

"You either don't get it or you are in on it," replied Mal, and stood up from the table.

"Okay then. What now? Do you keep trying to convince me, which will get real boring fast, or drug me again?"

"No," Mal manned the helm again. "I have better plans."

When he offered no more information Michaela spoke up, "Do you want to share that plan with me?"

"Nope."

"Didn't think so. Do you have more food?"

"Yes, in the fridge. Help yourself," he didn't look back at her. "Also, if you open anything but the fridge or pull anything out but food, I will shoot you in the knee cap."

"Well, you got to earn the bastard title somehow." She went to the fridge and found a collection of leftovers, beer, and deli foods. She grabbed an assortment, focusing on protein and carbs. She wanted staying energy. She went back to the bed to eat her food and give herself a better view of the entire cabin. She noticed a small nightstand next to the bed; a single picture frame stood on it. A picture of a beautiful, auburn-haired woman and a young girl with the same hair color in pigtails. Both were laughing with delight.

This is beyond bad, Michaela thought. *Not only is he skilled and has had a huge mental breakdown, but he has found just enough good info to create a full-blown delusion. If he truly thinks his daughter is still alive, there is nothing he won't do to get her...even kill me if he has to; or anyone else who gets in his way.*

Chapter 13

Mal steered his trawler into the marina on D.C.'s South Waterfront. The coming dawn was a glowing hint over the eastern horizon. The boat was no gem to behold. The whitewashed vessel gently moved into one of the many boat slips.

Mal turned away from the helm. Kai had not moved or spoken in the last hour. Only looking around the room, trying her best to dive into the mind of the crazy man that held her. *More likely she's waiting for her chance to break my neck or find something to cut my eyes out,* thought Mal. The few stories he had gotten about her from her time in the CIA spoke well of the iron in the woman's blood. He tossed a small bundle over to Kai, "Put that on. Make sure to tie your hair up so it's completely under the hat."

"Well, at least you're letting me keep my clothes on," replied Kai as she unwrapped the bundle to find an oversized zip-up hoodie, a baseball cap, and a pair of large aviator sunglasses.

"If you want to take them off, I won't object," smiled back Mal.

Kai tossed him a glare that would have cracked ice. "Boy, you have had all the look you are ever going to get under my shirt." She snapped her fingers and went on. "That's it. Bastard Boy. That is your new nickname."

Mal just shook his head and pulled something out of a compartment above the helm.

Maybe I shouldn't piss him off, but better to get him on edge and keep him dancing, thought Kai. She went on aloud, "So where are we going? Into D.C. by the look of the skyline. You are one far out crazy dude, you know, that right? Bringing the President of the United States who *you kidnapped* back to D.C.. Unless you have a death wish and, in that case, why wait? I can help with that anytime."

Mal looked up from what he had pulled out of the helm cabinet. "Don't worry, you just might get your chance."

"Don't get my hopes up."

"As to where we're going, you will find out soon enough. I'll just say I need your help to acquire a few special items."

"Robbery? So, you're a thief as well now."

Mal ignored the question and jab. He held up a small device, three inches long, an inch thick, and an inch and half wide. It was black, with several wires and two small antennas sticking out from it. He tossed it to her. "Do you know what that is?"

She barely even glimpsed at the device. "It's a signal receiver. Homemade. Looks to be shortwave and I'm guessing cellular. Meant for remote bomb detonation." A cold sense of dread washed over her.

"You know your bomb tech. That's good. Not surprising with your history and record." He pulled out a disposable cellphone. "But that is just an example." He looked her dead in the eyes. "There are six bombs spread throughout D.C.. Nothing too large. Three pounds of my own plastic explosive mix up, and three pounds of ball bearings with each. Good locations though." Kai could feel the blood in her veins turn cold and her heart start pounding , urging her to kill this nut job. He went on, "Two schools, one park, one busy intersection, and two prime tourist locations. All very well hidden. Each is on a timer." He looked at his watch, "As of now each has eight hours and forty-two minutes till they go off. This phone," he shook the phone in his hand, "Is the only way to deactivate them. One phone call with a twenty-two-digit code. It cannot detonate them, only disarm. If you do what I say and don't cause any fuss, I will give you that code once we're done with our task. If you betray me though, even manage to get me captured, there is no way you could beat the code out of me in time."

Kai thought to herself that it was unlikely any amount of torture could break this man. She spoke, "You're not even worth the air you breathe. Rat vomit has more value than you."

"Wow," Mal nodded his head. "That was creative, I will give you that." He tossed the phone over to her. She caught and stared at it. "You can hold onto that. I will give you the code once we're done."

His voice dropped several levels, becoming like shifting tectonic plates. "Do not test my resolve in this. I will do whatever it takes to get my daughter back. If that means blood on my hands, I will happily break this entire nation to get her back." And with that, he turned and opened a floor hatch that led down to the small cargo hold and disappeared under the cabin.

Kai stood for a moment, looking at the phone in her hands. The desperation of her situation continued to shock her. She shook the feeling away and put the new layers of clothes on. She could hear Frostt moving around under the floorboards. She darted noiselessly forward and in less than twenty seconds found a steak knife and wine corkscrew. She stowed both weapons in the folds of her clothes, both ready for a fast draw.

Mal had changed his clothes and moved back up the ladder. Jeans and flannel shirt had been replaced for a black pair of tactical cargo pants, a black t-shirt, a long, charcoal jacket, and a black, canvas backpack. A black baseball cap and reflective aviator sunglasses finished off the look. Kai could just make out the Colt 1911 on his hip under the coat and she saw the telltale bulge of a second gun on the waist line of his back. Kai had been trained by the best to read people, to read a tactical situation in a matter of seconds, and know all the possible threats. A weapon changed the way a person held themselves. Even people who had been trained to be the best of fighters.

She had worked with Delta operators who still had the minute signs of carrying a gun. Not Frostt though. She had been watching him for a few hours and the man showed not the slightest sign. It was like the gun was the least important weapon on him.

"Let's go; we have a little less than two miles to cover."

The two walked out into the new day, the sun just coming over the horizon fully. Mal tied the trawler off in the slip, and the pair walked off the marina and to the waking streets. The morning was brisk but warming quickly despite being a March day. They walked in silence for some time before Kai spoke again, "So, where did you learn it all? Military, Delta I'm guessing?"

"Nope, never served," was Mal's terse response.

"Then how did you become supervillain of the year? Foreign training?"

"Nope, American made, all the way."

"Then where?"

"That is a good question."

"Are you going to answer it?"

"No."

The two once again lapsed into silence. Kai tracking their progress through the now awake city. The streets clogged with cars, and people filling the sidewalks. No one gave them a second look, her face and figure hidden well under the clothes. They headed north, towards Capitol Hill. With each step, Kai's feeling of impending doom grew. Why in the world would he bring her back here, the most secure city in the world?

o o o

Bert Renfield sat at his desk, a fresh cup of thick, black coffee in front of him. It did little for him now, sixty-eight hours since the President was taken and he had barely slept a handful of hours. He knew without a doubt that his career was over. It was over the moment he let even a nail break on the President, much less not find her in three days. It still made no sense to him why Acting President Cever had overruled everyone and appointed him head of the investigation. His new office sat on the third floor of the Eisenhower Executive Building, across the street from the White House. The entire third floor had been converted to a command center. Each federal agency had been given space to work, with all reporting back to Renfield, most of them bitter about it.

Bert forced his mind back to the report in front of him; he knew worrying about his career was pointless and selfish compared to what the President must be going through. He once again started at the top of the report, for the third time, and headed down. Top Secret in bold bright letters plastered on each page of the report.

The report detailed the full research into Michael Archer. A complete and useless dead end. They knew the name must be fake, but they didn't think the prints in Archer's hotel room could have been faked, much less the single strand of hair they had found. Even worse Michael Archer himself was not fake, just dead already. Michael J. Archer of Kentucky died eight months prior. A bad heart, a bad liver, a heavy smoker, and an even heavier drinker. Neither the NSA nor the FBI geek squad had any idea how the suspect had gotten both a good fingerprint and usable hair sample from a dead guy. Bert was convinced that even the man's looks must have been faked. The whole operation had been planned to perfection and executed to a T.

Nearly to the last page of the report again, his office door burst open and Agent Meyers rushed in, followed by the head FBI agent, Casic. Before Bert could even ask, Meyers blurted, her words falling in a barely understandable rush. "NSA just got a hit off President Kai's transponder." Bert exploded to his feet, his chair falling over. "The transponder is live and broadcasting a current signal. It is on E Basin Drive Southwest headed towards the Thomas Jefferson Memorial, roughly three hundred yards out. Moving at a walking pace."

"Who knows about this?" asked Bert, he could feel his heart turning to ice. If the President was in D.C., much less at a famous attraction, that could mean her body was about to be dumped or she would be held hostage there. Most likely to be killed once all the news stations showed up for the lunatic holding her.

Agent Casic spoke, a towering, thick set man, "Us three and the NSA team that sent the report in. I have local HRT already prepping; they will be in the air in four minutes. I haven't told them why yet."

Well that is something then. He at least didn't blab to his bosses about it. But he sure is itching for the FBI to get the glory on this, thought Bert. He went on with his orders, sharp and direct. "Good thinking. HRT will take point on the assault. We are going in quick and hard, but we must secure the scene. I want local PD onsite ASAP, shutting down bridges to or from that island. Have the HRT come up from the south and land directly behind the Jefferson Memorial. Meyers, get us a chopper to the scene." The three moved out of the office in a collective rush and let the news break to the room of agents and support staff. They would have that area, including the waterways, completely shutdown within seven minutes. The NSA already summoning a surveillance drone to take up station over the President's beacon.

Three-and-a-half minutes after Meyers barged into Renfield's office, the three agents were rising off the ground in a Bell 412EP helicopter, supplied by the FBI's Critical Incident Response Group. The twin-engine Huey surged forward, the rotors beating a thrumming rhythm in the cabin. Bert already had his headset on and issued more orders over the radio waves. Next to him, Meyers and Casic did the same. He had a nearly irresistible urge for a smoke but knew that might come across poorly especially considering

he could barely breathe for the speed of his beating
heart and his rapid-fire orders.

Chapter 14

Mal and Michaela stood at the intersection of Constitution Avenue Northwest and Delaware Avenue Northeast. The sounds of car horns and the chattering crowded lingering all around them. The tourists were out in full force, the sun drawing them out like ants to sugar water.

"Can you finally tell me where we are going?" asked Michaela.

Mal raised a hand and pointed to the building kitty-corner to them. A large building by most city standards, but not in D.C.. The front entrance was filled with small crowds of people moving in and out of the building, most of them tourists.

"The Russell Building? What in the hell can you steal there?" Kai shook her head. She hated the baseball cap she had been forced to wear. It made her head itch. "That building is nearly as secure as the White House, you know that right?"

"Every place has its weakness," he turned to face her. She could see her baggy reflection in his large sunglasses. "Remember those bombs. No one needs to get hurt. We are going to walk in there nice and quiet. We are going to head to the basement and borrow- "

"Borrow?" Kai interrupted with a huff.

"Okay, we are going to steal some documents from the subbasement from the secure Senate records room. And *you* are going to talk our way in."

"Sure," retorted Kai. "The second I show my face they're going to go ape shit and most likely shoot you."

"Well then I guess you'd better be creative and make sure that doesn't happen. If I go down, so do the codes."

Kai only scowled in response.

He gently touched her arm as the crosswalk sign turned white for them, she snapped her arm away from the gesture. The pair walked up the marble steps joining the throng of people streaming in, some people looking in awe and some looking in disgust for double talk the building spit out daily. Both Mal and Michaela had thoughts along the lines, *Here we go. Let the game begin.*

Once in the vast rotunda, Mal motioned Kai over to the side, away from the metal detectors. He whispered in her ear, "You're up. Get us through without any noise." He pointed to a single guard standing off to the side, stationed at a standing desk filling out paperwork.

Kai looked the guard up and down. The man looked to be in his late twenties with already thinning hair and a body shape that did not hold his extra weight well. A line of sweat beaded up on his forehead. Kai could see the man wearing not only the lapel American flag, but both of his cufflinks were

American flags and she caught a glimpse of red, white, and blue socks. *Smooth and steady girl,* Kai thought calming herself, *he is just another mark. Like the old days. Control his attention and create self-importance for him.* The thoughts of the six bombs lingered in her mind.

She spoke two paces from the guard. "Excuse me, sir. Can you help us? We need to get into the building."

The man did not look up from his paperwork. "The main line is over by the front door."

Kai finished the last two steps and stood next to his raised desk, placing a hand on the wood top. "I know, but we can't use the main entrance."

The man finally looked up at her. Before he could retort again, Kai pulled her sunglasses off and tipped her hat up so he could see her face full on. She dropped her voice low and smooth, "We need your help, sir." She could see the near-instant recognition cross his face. His hand moved for the walkie-talkie sitting on his desk. Kai reached out and placed her hand over his before he could touch the call button. "Please, don't."

The man finally found his voice, "Madam President, is… is that you? What- "

"Yes, it's me," Kai interrupted urgently, "Please, you can't tell a soul I'm here. It is too dangerous."

"But you're dead!" He exclaimed.

"No, just kidnapped; and that only faked."

The man shook his head like a horse ridding a fly, the folds on his neck trembling. He started to stammer again, but Kai cut him off quietly.

"I wasn't kidnapped. It was all staged. There is a threat, a catastrophic threat to this nation and I need *your* help. This nation needs *your* help."

Kai did it, easy as that. Hook, line, and sinker. His posture straightened and he looked around, not doing a great job of looking normal. "What can I do to help, Madam President? I am here to serve."

"Good. What's your name, sir?"

"Jack Jenson."

"That's good. I'm guessing your friends call you JJ." It was clear on his face that no one called him JJ, but his eyes lit up with the familiar address from the President.

"Yes, Ma'am. What are your orders, Ma'am," he almost threw a salute, but held himself in check. "You know Ma'am, I applied for the Secret Service. I want to work in the White House. I am sharp as a tack in spotting bad guys. I always know who the bad guys are right away in any movie I watch."

"Is that so," replied Kai, her voice still low and smooth. "That's great. We need more people who come into the service already trained. I will make sure to look up your application once I, once we, have dealt with this threat."

"What is it, Ma'am? The Chinese? Muslims?"

Kai kept her face neutral at his last comments and went on. "I can't read you in here, JJ. Me and my associate," she nodded to Mal. "Need to get to the subbasement without causing any fuss. All I can tell you is that the threat has internal ties. We need to access the secure records room."

"Of course, of course," said Jack, like he already knew where they had to go. He called out to another guard standing a dozen paces away by the metal detector. "Frank, I gotta hit the head; be back soon."

Mal heard Frank mutter, not too quietly. "Yeah, soon. Takin' an hour to shit."

Jack motioned them to follow discreetly, Michaela putting her glasses back on and pulling her hat low. The trio moved around the desk and strolled across the rotunda, eighteen Corinthian columns encircled the massive space. Early morning day light flooded in through the glazed oculus at the pinnacle of the coffered dome above them.

They stepped past a statue of the building's namesake. Two dozen paces later brought them to a door, Jack used his ID card and fingerprint to open it and the three entered a stairwell. The white marble walls echoed with their steps as they went down the flights of stairs. They came out another locked door. Jack spoke up, bravado coloring his words. "This is a shortcut. We'll go around the backside of the kitchen. I could walk this building in my sleep. I probably know more about the building than anyone else."

It crossed Mal's mind to shoot the guy, Kai probably would have let him. Jack led them through another door, not locked this time, and into the backside of a massive commercial kitchen. The front of the kitchen was filled with busy cooks. Upright freezers and fridges bordered the walls around them, a pair of walk-in cooler and freezer doors sat to their left. Racks of dry goods and stainless-steel tables also filled the space, creating a maze to navigate.

Jack pointed to a door on the other side of the maze of tables. "Through there, a short hall, and down another set of stairs, and we're there. Again, I know this place great. They're always asking me to train the new guys."

Kai only half listened; she scanned the space. Not a single table was empty, a bank of cooling racks filled with pastries stood eight feet in front of them. Kai double stepped to come to a stop ahead of Jack. Mal also scanning the space looking for threats. When his head turned away she acted. Grimacing, knowing the next few seconds were going to hurt like hell. Both from her current injuries, her side stitches were going to rip for sure, but also from the new ones Mal was sure to deal. She hip checked one of the cooling racks; it jumped to the side and into Jack, tripping him. He went down hard, taking the rack with him, screaming and flaying his arms. Before a single pastry hit the floor, Kai pivoted around pulling the steak knife hidden in the folds of her clothes and pitched it at Mal. Not a balanced throwing knife by any means, but a flying knife of any kind could still wound.

Mal reacted with lightning speed, as Kai expected, and batted the knife with his left hand and drew his Colt with the other at the same time. Kai had also been multi-tasking, she horse kicked the table separating them. It slid, slamming into Mal's legs. She moved with the table, rolling onto the top of it, scattering the clutter and bringing down a side kick to Mal. The kick and table forced him back into a defensive position. Kai wasted no time and pressed the attack. Fast as the wind, she came in hard and low.

But not fast enough. Mal moved with precognitive speed. He parried the perfectly placed strikes and lunged back, landing a ringing closed fist to the side of Michaela's head. She used the strike to her advantage and stepped into his guard, having to take another strike for it, this time to the ribs. She now stood too close for him to use his pistol. As she had observed earlier, he did the opposite of what most men would, he let his pistol hand go soft. The pistol flew from his hand with a simple disarm, but she knew the real weapon was still against her.

The next five seconds were filled with screams from Jack, the kitchen staff joining him, and nonstop strikes and blocks by Mal and Michaela, neither landing a blow, but Michaela was losing ground each second. A new table stopped her from taking another step back; Mal pressed the attack. Again, sacrificing her defense and taking the hits, she lunged into his guard and sprang up, her leg muscles straining with the effort. She broke his guard and landed a pair of elbow strikes to the side of his face, the skin of his cheek splitting open. She used the opening to land a horse kick to his chest knocking him back and opening up room for her to breathe. A quarter second scan, and she saw what she needed; a roll and slide, and she was up on one knee his Colt 1911 in hand. He did the only thing sensible when someone points a hand cannon at you.

He ran.

The trigger pulled once, then again, and finally for a third time. The first shot missed by a hair's breadth, the second grazed his side, and the third blasted pieces of concrete from the door frame as it impacted, Mal barely rolling out of the door in time. Kai let out a curse and moved to Jack, keeping the door covered.

He had his hands covering his head and had rolled into a fetal position, the best his large stomach would let him. "Call it in," spat out Kai, "get this building locked down and a tactical team here double time." Jack did not respond, only moved one arm to peak up at her. She barked out, "Get your dumbass up and call it in. Now!" He scrambled to his feet, stuttering into his radio. The chaos of the kitchen staff did not help and the screams of the people in the cafeteria on the other side of the far wall added to the chaos.

"We are going to the secure records room. Have armed guards join us there ASAP," ordered Kai.

○ ○ ○

Bert stalked towards the front of the Jefferson Memorial, looking as pit bullish as ever. The area had been completely secured and swept in a matter of minutes, but chaos still reigned. Protesting cries were coming from several clusters of people, phones out and recording. Bert had no doubt that within the half-hour, YouTube would be flooded with hundreds of videos of the debacle in front of him. Meyers walked a pace behind Bert, talking nonstop into her radio. Agent Casic walked a dozen feet abreast of Bert, both men heading for a group of men in full tactical gear. A couple laid flat on the ground, hands zip tied behind their back and not happy about it. The cursing coming from the woman impressed even Bert, who had picked up his bad mouth in the Marine Corps.

The man on the ground next to the woman, dressed in an expensive sports coat, was spouting off threats, "I am going to own you by the time this is all over. I will sue you all into the ground."

The HRT team lead ignored the man and held up a digital camera when Bert and Casic came to stop. Half of the camera housing had been ripped open, knife marks all over the opened edge. The man on the ground went even louder, "Get your hands off my camera. Do you know how much that cost? That is a Hasselbald X1D II. How dare you break it open! I will press charges for destruction of property. I will see you behind bars." The bleach blonde woman added a colorful stream of words describing the men's mothers and their penis sizes.

Bert shot a glare at the man. "Shut the hell up before I have them gag you. And just maybe we won't charge you with terrorism and ship you off to Gitmo."

"You can't," whimpered the man his face going pale. The woman still acted like a rabid dog.

Renfield knelt and held his hand out to the HRT team lead for the camera. He spoke with ice on his lips, "Now if you do not shut up, I am going to have these very large men say you were resisting arrest. Then I am going to stomp on your face." The man's eyes went wide hearing the earnest truth in Renfield's words. He went quiet. "Now tell your trophy bimbo to shut up or I'll still smash in your face." It took nearly a minute for the man to calm his wife.

Renfield went on holding the camera close to the man's face. "Now, I only want yes or no answers. Is this your camera?"

"Yes."

"Have you had it longer than a week?"

"Yes, about six mon…" The man cut his words short with a glare from Renfield.

"Has anyone had access to your camera in the last three days?"

"No," the man paused for a moment and then rushed on. "Yes."

A few seconds lapsed. "You are a dumbass." Renfield shook his head. "Explain."

"Oh, yes. Yes," stuttered the man. "I had it cleaned at a local shop yesterday."

"What shop?"

"Camera Depo on Grand."

"Yes, now was that hard?" Bert stood. "Take them to lock up and debrief every scrap of info out of them."

The pair on the ground started shouting again, but Bert had walked away. Casic and the team lead joining him. "Have a team over to Camera Depo on the double. I want every employee gone through. Tear that place apart." He looked down at the camera still in his hands and into the guts of it. There, glued to the inner casing was the President's subdermal transponder. "He wants us here." Bert looked around the area; it was chaos. Agents everywhere, the crowd in confused groups, the protesters already gaining steam. "Why?"

Casic and the team lead were busy talking into their radios, getting the next round of bedlam going. From across the front plaza of the memorial, Bert could see Meyers running towards him. His stomach dropped. Before he could make a comment on how he hated the look on her face, she blurted out, "Shots fired at the Russell Building. Reports coming in that the President is the shooter."

The chaos of the scene around them paled to the next few moments. Bert shouted orders, all agents dropped their posts, and all rushed to converge on the chaos across town. The screaming woman and now sobbing man were left tied on the ground.

Chapter 15

Piss and a half, she is good. She moves like a dancer, but hits like a steel cobra on crack, thought Mal as he sprinted away from the kitchen, not up the stairs they came down, but down a new hall. He could feel the stinging welts on his face from where her strikes landed, and his side burned with white-hot pain. "I damn sure wouldn't want to go toe to toe when she was at her peak."

He stopped at a door labeled Maintenance. His snap gun opened the tumbler lock and he stepped in closing the door behind him. He flipped on the light switch; a spastic, florescent light stuttered to life. The space was twelve-feet wide with a small worktable to his right. The rest of the space, minus a wall hatch, was covered in light-duty shelving. He pulled his pack off and stripped his coat to reveal a tactical vest, the pockets full of needed tools. He pulled up the shirt on his right side and found that Kai's shot had only grazed him. The wound was half clotted already, blood running down his side. He dropped his shirt, ignoring the wound for the time being. He had a critical timetable to hold to. From the pack came his silenced H&K, placed in his hip holster, eight smoke grenades, half dozen flash grenades, and two non-lethal black stinger grenades. The last piece he pulled

out of the pack was a black tactical face mask.
Modern and sinister looking, he placed the full-face
mask on and stepped over to the wall hatch. It
measured three-feet by three-feet, and had been
painted countless times over the decades. He used a
razor blade from the pack to cut the paint lines and,
with a hard pull, the hatch squealed open. The space
beyond was dark and musty. Several pipes ran down
blocking the opening, the largest being a three-inch
copper pipe that ended in a large bell catch. Several
smaller pipes dripped into the bell catch, a building P-
trap. It took Mal less than fifteen seconds to spray the
bell catch and copper union with WD-40 and spin it
free with a crescent wrench. With the pipe moved, he
had just enough space to wiggle into the cavity.

He had attached his pack to his leg with a
short piece of paracord, and after some whispered
curses, he stood up in the cavity. He knew from the
original prints he had bought off a D.C. historian that
this cavity ran from the basement to the attic plenum,
an old air chase. *Forty-two feet up. Sixty-five-second
climb,* Mal chanted his timetable in his head. A dull
alarm sounded. "Right on time," he whispered. He
popped an orange glowstick hanging on his tactical
vest and in the pale orange light started his way up.
The old mason walls gave great hand and foot holds,
alarm sounded a non-stop staccato rhythm.

Halfway up the shaft, Mal came to a hole in
the mason wall, an HVAC vent. He dropped the pin
from the smoke grenade down the shaft and tossed the

grenade into the vent. A little less than ten feet from his goal, another vent cut the wall open. He did the same with another smoke grenade. He stopped at another wall hatch in front of him. The thin copper lines between him and the hatch bent out of the way and with a hard push and sharp crack, the hatch popped open. With his arms only, he pulled himself above the hatch and swung his legs into the light filled square. He came out into a hall, sliding on his back and, fast as a cat, up to standing with a pistol in hand to sweep the hallway.

A well-dressed grey-haired man and a young lady in a long skirt and blouse stood frozen like field mice out in the open, roughly twenty-feet away. Mal could hear the clamor of the main rotunda behind him and one level down, his hall ran twenty feet then opened up into the second-floor balcony that overlooked the main floor. A half-second later, the clamor turned to fearful shouts as some started yelling about smoke and fire.

"Down," barked Mal at the pair. The man had moved behind the woman. Both dropped to the floor, hard enough to bruise their knees. He added to the chaos in the front of the building. The stinger grenade soared down the hallway and detonated just over the lip of the balcony, the panicking crowed dissolving into screams as the non-lethal, but extremely painful, plastic BBs found soft flesh. Mal moved past the shaking woman and whimpering man, and headed away from the rotunda, ordering them to stay down, eyes closed, or take a bullet to the head.

○ ○ ○

"You and you, cover that hall," ordered Michaela. "Dammit, not like that. You're going to shoot each other; stagger your positions. Just, shit; where is a Delta team when you need one? More like five teams." Michaela stood at the end of a hallway, a single door behind her. The hallway went twenty feet and then split into a four-way intersection. Five armed men had joined her, three building security and two local cops. She did not count JJ as part of the team. He currently sat slumped against the wall, behind the makeshift barricade they had placed in the hall of two steel tables on their sides back to back. The chirp of the radio on Michaela's side was a constant stream of voices. She knew that the entire building was in chaos now, smoke coming out of the vents, apparently on the first floor. She also knew that the Secret Service Counter Assault team or CAT was three minutes out and the FBI HRT team one minute behind them, both coming in for a fast rope down from choppers. Local police SWAT teams were also inbound, with what seemed like half of D.C.

Michaela had set up her rag tag team as best she could to create a crossfire if Frostt made an attack. The single door behind her led to the secure documents vault. The cellphone in her pocket felt like burning coal. She had given the order at least ten times that Frostt must be taken alive at all costs. She did not say why; that type of info over an open radio channel could cause citywide panic.

There is more going on here than I know, she thought. *I can feel it. He does not play straight. He moves like shadows and plays games in games. Oh, I hope I get to shoot him again.* She smiled at the last part, her split lip protesting.

○ ○ ○

The pair of guards didn't even have time to draw their weapons before Mal knocked them both to the ground and out cold. He had crossed a quarter of the building, stopping twice to toss smoke grenades into HVAC wall vents. He came to a sliding stop in front of his target door, two minutes and twelve seconds since he had left the kitchen. One second ahead of schedule.

He heard over his earpiece, the radio built into his tactical mask, that the CAT team would drop in one minute and forty seconds. The CAT team didn't worry him; they would only be worried about getting to Kai and then back out. It was the HRT and local SWAT teams that would want to give him new air holes.

The door's electronic lock flashed green with the stolen ID badge and faked fingerprint Mal had taken off his drinking buddy, Simon, the day before.

He stepped into a deserted office foyer with fake plants and tacky décor filling the space. He made his way over to the far office, overlooking Delaware Avenue, his pistol out and covering all the corners. The red oak door had brass letters emblazoned across it: Senator Andrew Otts. It was not locked.

The office was a complete reflection of its occupant. Gold trimmed art, boastful awards, and articles about Otts covered the walls, deep money all over the place. Mal holstered his pistol and scanned the space. He smiled, "Got ya." He stepped over to a large portrait of Otts, the artist taking many liberties in granting the man in the painting an air of power. Mal tried not to gag. He pulled his gloves off and started to run his fingers over the gold leafed frame. The bottom right corner of the frame was the ticket. He pulled from one of his many pockets what looked to be a pale gray ball of clay. He molded it around the edge of the frame, going an inch beyond the lock point. A small pull fuse finished it all off. He pulled the fuse tab and stepped back looking away from the flash of light.

A dull thud filled the room and the picture frame swung open with a noise of rending metal and cracking wood. Mal wasted no time and moved up to the now exposed wall safe. An AMSEC WS1214 wall safe looked back at him. One of the best on the market, with a three-quarter-inch steel door, exposed hardened hinges, and three one-inch steel locking bolts.

Thirty seconds till CAT team landed. Another forty-five seconds after that the FBI HRT would come into the building looking for blood. Mal took a deep breath and deftly went to work on the safe. He had no time for a delicate opening. Instead, he opted for the power of chemistry and brute force. He quickly pulled out a linear shaped charge and attached it over the left side of the safe, over the locking bolts. He then added two cylinders with double sided tape on top of each exposed hinge, wires coming out of all three devices. The two cylinders were prefilled with a homemade mix of thermite. When ignited, the thermite, a mix of iron-oxide and powdered aluminum, created a highly exothermic reaction reaching temperatures pushing five thousand degrees Fahrenheit. He tied all three wires together and into a micro transmitter.

The CAT team had entered the building. ETA to President Kai's location: forty seconds.

Mal stepped away and adverted his eyes, the charges going off a split second after he pressed the transmitter. The linear charge sent a molten, hot thin piece of copper through the locking bolts. The thermite hissed and popped as the hinges gave way, the powder coating on the metal blistering. The moment the thermite flash could be looked at, Mal jumped forward, slamming a flat, twelve-inch crowbar into the rent the shaped charge had made. He grunted with the effort, but after what felt like an eternity, the safe door started to move. It crashed down, denting the hardwood floor. Mal took no time to look through the contents of the safe, patting out the smoldering edges of paper and swiping everything into his pack.

His earpiece crackled with more news. The CAT team had the President. The HRT team and the Secret Service details had just arrived, including Bert Renfield. Mal pulled his pistol from his holster and headed for the door whispering to himself, "Now the real fun starts."

Chapter 16

"This way, Madam President," said a member of the CAT team.

Michaela tore her arm out of the man's hand. "Like hell."

"Ma'am, we must go now," he and another CAT member moved to pick her up by the arms. Much to their surprise, they both ended up on the floor, one holding his stomach and shoulder, the other sporting a bloody nose and out cold on the floor.

The other three members of the CAT team looked at her, not sure what to do. The glare she leveled on the three hardened men made them all take a step back. Her voice like jagged ice, "I understand your first duty is to get me to safety, but my first is to this country and its people. Now the man behind all of this wants into this room." She pointed at the room behind her. "We will secure this hallway until proper reinforcements show." She looked at the several building guards still looking nervously down the hallways. The three remaining men, and the one on the ground still awake, gave a nod, "Aye, Madam President."

Kai motioned the team lead over and in military-style relayed the info she could not on the open radio: the bombs around D.C., the needed deactivation code, and to secure Senator Otts as soon as possible. The info was relayed to all needed teams.

The next minute and a half crept by, Kai had a growing feeling in her stomach that something was not right. It had been too long and Frostt had yet to make a go at the secure records room. She was about to order one of the building guards to open the door to make sure Frostt had not found another secret way into the secure room when eight local police officers and five Secret Service agents rounded the corner, calling the all safe as to not get shot by a twitchy guard.

The CAT team lead stepped over to Kai as the Secret Service agents moved to surround her, "Madam President, it's time for you to go."

Kai had the nearly irresistible urge to break the man's jaw and stand her ground, but she knew better. She was not an operator anymore. She was the President of the United States and needed to respect her new role and the people protecting her. She nodded her head to the man. "Okay, your team stays here until another full tactical team can take over." She turned to look at the lead agent. "You and your men take me to the local command center." She tucked Frostt's Colt 1911 into her waistband at the small of her back.

"Madam," replied the lead agent. "This way." The five agents created a tight circle around her. They wasted no time in moving out, taking the north hallway away from the records room. The pair had barely made the next turn when a newcomer joined the team.

"Madam President," said Bert as he took up the rear guard position. The lead agent nodded to him. Bert outranked him, but the agent had the lead and knew the most updated info so Bert deferred to him.

All the agents heard the report over their earpieces, the lead man relayed it to the President. "Shots fired. Main entrance." And sure enough, they could all hear a distant thud and pop of automatic fire.

Kai snapped the order again. "He must be taken alive at all costs."

None of the agents responded to her. They took several more turns at full sprint, the two front agents clearing each turn and knocking down several building employees as they dashed deep into the building. More downward steps and turns.

Bert spoke up from the back of the group to the lead agent, "Johnson, where are you taking us?"

"Maintenance bypass to the underground foot tunnel. We will come out near the far side of the Hart Building's pedestrian tunnel."

"Good thinking," gasped back Bert, never breaking the pace.

Another turn brought them into a hall that ended in a gray metal door. The two forward agents doubled their speed and broke the lock off the door and held it open just in time for the group to dart in. The room was broken into two sections., The upper section's walls were covered in electrical and control panels with the door just opened, and another door on the opposite wall. A lower section accessed by a short iron ladder bolted to the wall sat off to the right, a guard rail blocking the six-foot drop. Huge air handler equipment hummed in the lower section. The smell of oil and damp stone dominated the space. Michaela knew something was wrong before she heard the dull thud and gasp of pain from behind her. She spun, pulling the colt out with the movement, a sharp whole-body stinging pain surging through her before she could pull the weapon to the ready. She felt the barbs of the taser through her shirt and bit firmly into the flesh of her stomach. She landed hard on the ground and could see Bert's face down on the floor a few feet away.

The Secret Service agent, Johnson, looked down at Kai taser in hand, "Madam President, I have some questions for you." He pulled the trigger on the taser again before any questions came.

○ ○ ○

Mal lunged forward, kicking the MP-5 pointed at him away, the wall next to him burst open in a cloud of sheetrock dust. He spun, moving his head to the side as the pistol brought to bear by the next HRT member went off inches from his head, he broke the man's arm. At the same time, he brought his left leg up and knocked the MP-5 man down with a spinning kick to the side of the head. The pistol man fell with an elbow to the face, cracking his helmet. The man already down went dark with a boot to the face.

The H&K pistol sounded off, the silencer ditched minutes before, and two new attackers fell. One with three bullets to his bulletproof vest and one with a bullet to the leg and shoulder. Mal turned and sprinted letting more bullets crack off. Bullets tearing the walls all around him as he darted across the second level of the rotunda. The last stinger grenade and his second to last flashbang went down to the main floor as he slid into the next hallway, disarming the two men that came around the corner. They both lay with broken bones as he moved on.

His pistol moved in sweeping arcs as he ran, he dropped two smoke grenades as he moved. Several people still lingered, cowering in corners as he moved past. He moved into a second-floor foyer, a bank of windows on the far side, a receptionist desk in front of them overlooking the internal courtyard. A four-man tactical team converged on him, two from either side. Three of them fell, bullets to their vests and legs, the fourth man took cover. Another group of federal agents joined the mayhem. With the odds stacking even higher against him, Mal lunged, emptying his gun into a window as he vaulted the desk. The glass exploded out as he went through it and he felt the sickening feeling of freefall. Not for long.

The impact came with a resounding crack, a whiplash to Mal, and a sharp pain through half of his body. The wood pergola cracked under the impact.

Mal rolled off the pergola and landed hard on the manicured grass. Dirt and grass started exploding around him as he surged forward, changing out his clip and ducked behind a large leafless maple tree. He tossed his final flashbang and his last two smoke grenades back into the courtyard and started scanning the area.

Two seconds and more bullets passed. *Crap and a half; if those plans are wrong, I am dead.* His heart rate held a steady pace, just as he had been trained. A second more passed and he saw it, he could physically feel the relief wash over his body. He guessed he had about thirty seconds before they truly rushed him; they would set a perimeter around him and then charge in for the kill. He took the two steps needed forward, making sure to keep the tree between him and the majority of the courtyard. He swept away the dead leaves and half-inch of dirt that caked the small metal grate locked with a rusty 1980s padlock. Mal pulled three of the cylinders of thermite out and soon the two hinges and padlock turned to molten metal. He tossed the grate aside and jumped down without a thought, a bullet grazing the top of his left shoulder, drawing a thin line of blood. He landed in a dark and damp hole, years of detritus from nature and man created a soft, uneven floor. He dropped a lit cylinder of thermite into the debris and moved forward on all fours into the pitch black, leaving the rubbish pile sparking to life with the exothermal reaction.

○ ○ ○

Whap sounded the boot as it connected with Michaela's ribs. She let out a grunt and then a gargled cry as Johnson let on the taser again. Three of the five agents had their guns drawn and Michaela was lined up in their sights. Johnson held the taser, an evil smile playing on his lips, and the boot kicker was lining up for another rib denting thrust.

"One more time and then it gets worse for you," said Johnson, swapping out the battery pack on his taser, "Who is the man that kidnapped you, and what has he told you."

"Kiss my ass," spat out Michaela. She did not mention the agent's oath to protect again; she would have gotten a boot stomped on her face for that and a round of laughs.

Johnson squatted down, four feet away. "Oh, there is a lot of things I would do to that ass don't worry. Only if we had time," he licked his lips. "I don't think any of us here has had a president before." The group laughed. Bert made a moan on the floor and got a kick to the side for it.

Johnson looked at the bootman. "Cut off her left ear." He said it like ordering an appetizer at a restaurant. He gave another jolt of power to the taser when Michaela started to crawl away. The boot man and another agent, holstering his gun, came up to pin her down. The first man pulling out a large tiger striped pocket knife. Michaela eyed the knife counting her breaths; she would only have one chance to get that knife. She readied her body, though it screamed in pain at her.

The two agents were only a foot away from her when the door to the mechanical room burst open. Frostt slid through the door, his gun deafening in the concrete-walled space. Bootman and the agent at the far end of the room both took a single shot to the head. Johnson did the smart thing and dropped the taser, rolling back and twisting around to face Frostt.

A wave of near giddy euphoria washed over Kai. She couldn't pin the feeling down and would not, by force of will reflect on it later. It was a feeling of unhindered security, safety, and bone deep reassurance. It burnt deep and hard like melted steel.

Her combat instincts overrode her flux of emotions a quarter second later. She twisted, kicking the agent who was about to grab her in the side of his knee. He screamed, as his knee blew out of place. He fell to the ground as Michaela took out his other leg, the same time pulling the taser barbs out of her stomach. The now loop of wire fell over the man's neck and became a makeshift garrote. Her knee in his back, both laid on the floor, the man pawing at the wire as blood started to well up from his neck. Mal's pistol having been knocked away, he stepped into Johnson's and the last agent's guard. Both men went down, the last agent with a broken neck and Johnson with a knife driven into his right eye.

The man in Michaela's grip stopped twitching finally a moment later. She pushed him off, blood covering her hands and forearms.

"You look like shit," said Frostt. He stepped over, taking off his sinister face mask, and put his hand out.

"At least I'm not taking fashion advice from a thirteen-year-old boy. Nice helmet," retorted Michaela.

A burst of gun fire interrupted the banter. The pair moved at the same time. Frostt fell back, twisting, and came up to one knee with his pistol back in hand. Michaela rolled over and spun around, the 1911 once again hers. Two shots each, and the two men dressed in tactical gear, firing bursts from their MP-5s, fell to the ground. Frostt wasted no time, slamming the door shut as three more men in full tact gear came around the corner firing. The metal door rang with the bullet impacts.

"Move," barked Mal, as he reached down and grabbed the collar of the still unconscious Bert's suit and dress shirt, dragging him to the far door. Michaela needed no order, already on the move for the second door. The first rattled with a hail of bullets, several holes already blasted through as the bullets chewed the metal away.

The three moved into a new hallway in complete contrast to the manicured basement behind them. Bare concrete walls showed water stains and pipes of all sizes lined the walls and ceiling. Frostt pulled his last thermite cylinder out and placed it on the largest pipe, hot steam warning signs stenciled on it. The pipe ruptured after a dozen sprinted paces away, Bert now tossed onto Frostt's shoulder like a rag doll. A scalding hot wall of steam screened their escape down the hallway.

The bullets coming out of the wall of steam leaving small swirling eddies in their path gave them no time to stop. They turned one corner after another and soon were utterly lost into the bowels of the underground space. Frostt came to a sudden stop. The moldy hall before them stretched on but for an alcove in the north wall. They ducked into the space, roughly ten-feet deep and eight-feet wide. The floor bore old marks of equipment anchors, the space now empty and forgotten.

Frostt sat Bert down none too softly against the south wall and turned to see his own Colt 1911 pointed at his face, a foot away.

"This time I know I have real bullets in here. So, what the hell is going on? Who the hell are you really? And why did members of the Secret Service and what looked to be FBI HRT try to kill me?" hissed Michaela. Her eyes at a new level of icy blue, cold, and steely in the hallway's dim lights. She lined up the pistol for his right eye and spoke with dripping venom. "And what is the code to the bombs?" She pulled the cellphone out of her pants' pocket.

"Should I just pick which one to answer first at random or would you like to ruminate on it for a while," replied Frostt striking a full tooth smile.

"Don't fuck with me."

"Never crossed my mind," he stared into her eyes in his unsettling way. She moved the gun an inch closer and before she could blink, it was gone. The muzzle of the gun was now in her face. She took a step back, the speed unnerving and frightening her. She was good, was one of the best…but him. *He is still toying with me. Games in games.*

"There is no code," he started, "Never was. Because there were never any bombs."

"Liar."

"No, I am not. Phone is fake anyway."

Michaela looked at the phone in her hand, gripping it hard and splitting it in half. The inside of the phone was empty, minus a few pieces of lead for weight.

He spun the Colt pistol handle towards Michaela. "I am not your enemy. Shoot me if you want; stay, or come it makes no difference in the end. I will find the truth and nothing but death will stop me. Now, the choice is simple: You stay here and see if any more people who swore to protect you instead try to murder you, or you follow me down the rabbit hole. I promise there will be answers. Unpleasant and disturbing answers I am guessing, but answers none-the-less." His entire face burned with a hidden heat, the hard lines of his jaw stone cut. He spoke his words with the resolute and undaunting force of a slow-moving mountain range.

Michaela's body reacted, taking the pistol back without thinking. And with that, Frostt stepped around her and into the alcove. In the far corner, he uncovered a manhole covered in decades of grime. He used his flat bar to pry up the edge and with one last look at Michaela, he disappeared deeper into the ground.

Michaela looked over to Bert, who was starting to come to. His head listing side to side. "Oh, shit and a half." She turned and let herself down the rabbit hole.

Chapter 17

Kai cursed at herself. Her legs burned, her ribs screamed in protest, and each breath felt like a knife. A half dozen years earlier, this mad dash through dark tunnels, abandon maintenance lines, and even the Washington subway system would have been difficult but well within her abilities. Being a full-time politician for the last four years and the president for the last three months had cut into her physical training routines. Though at one point that routine was full-time training to be the best operator she could be. She always had to work twice as hard as her male Special Operations Group counterparts. She needed to be faster, more agile, and above all, quicker of mind. What concerned her was that the man she tailed made her look like a JV track runner in high school, even at her best.

What felt like an eternity in truth was only forty minutes, both Frostt and Michaela came to a locked fence gate, bright sunlight poured in through the gate and the noise of cars filled the exit alcove. Mal quickly picked the lock and both stepped out; he locked the gate again, making sure not to leave any trace of their passage. A bridge towered over them, the area cast in permanent shadow. She could see several homeless people milling around on the other side of the dirt field.

"What in the hell am I doing," Michaela panted out loud, more to herself than Frostt. "I am the President of the United States. Not only am I aiding and abetting the man who kidnapped me, I killed a Secret Service agent." She bent over, her hands on her knees, her side where the agent's boots had tenderized her throbbed in pain. Her hair was matted with sweat, blood, and dirt.

A scraping noise drew her attention to Frostt. He had taken a few running steps up and used the wall as a step to reach the backside of a support beam. He came back down the strap of a backpack coming with him, the pack pulling free from its hiding space behind the rusted metal support. He went to a knee and opened the pack. He stood back up with two dirty and frayed jackets in his hands. He tossed one to Kai and then swung his own on, after taking off his tactical backpack which he shoved into the battered backpack. Before she even had time to register what was going on, he tossed a ragged ballcap at her feet.

Michaela looked at the jacket in her hands; it had seen far better days, better days back in the 90s. Not even the trashiest thrift store would sell something this bad. It smelled like sour cabbage. She stood holding it in her hands not moving.

She felt hands grip her firmly on her shoulders and she looked up into the intense, burnt coal eyes of Frostt. "Michaela," he said her name like longtime friends. "We have little time and even less chance of success. Yes, you are the President, and yes, you just committed major crimes. But the people meant to protect you just tried to kill you. I can't guarantee any of this will go well, but I guarantee we will find answers." He let only a half-second pass. "Now get your ass in gear. We are in evade and escape mode in an urban setting with some of the world's best forces on our tail."

A shift in posture passed through her at the last words. She knew that the shock of it all would do nothing more than kill her. With ease that comes from long field time and even longer training, she pushed the thoughts away and pulled herself into the moment. She again looked over the coat in her hands and no longer saw a rotten ball of fabric but a tool. She broke away from Frostt, pulled on the jacket, put her already knotted and messy hair into a tight ponytail, and donned the ball cap low and forward. Frostt didn't acknowledge her new attitude and only went back to work.

A pay to park car lot laid to the south. Frostt led the way the dirt lot under the bridge, covered from the DC weather, crunched bone dry under their feet. The fence surrounding the car lot barely deserved the name fence, more holes than not. The pair moved through the field of cars, cheap white slips of paper on the dashboards showing the time left until the tow truck would come calling. A single-person hut stood sentinel at the front entrance to the right of them. The sole occupant did not bother to look up from his book.

Michaela peered into each car and truck as they walked on. Halfway through the parking lot, her luck struck; she pulled a white plastic trash bag out of the back of an old pickup truck, edges of beer cans bulging the thin plastic. She slung it over her shoulder adding to her street life appearance. Mal gave a stoic nod of approval.

The pair moved through another hole in the fence and emerged out from under the bridge and onto a small grassy knoll. The traffic of the freeway rushed on behind and above them. The grassy knoll lent to a commercial parking lot and then to side streets, cutting through a mix of commercial and light industrial buildings. Cars and delivery trucks moved along the road, a small spattering of people walked the sidewalks, enjoying the rare winter sun. Michaela, even in her intense tactical focus, could not help but wonder at the people moving about their day. Completely unaware of her and unaware of anything beyond their daily life. The next work meeting, the kids to pick up, dinner to make, bills to worry about. Part of it all allured her, a simpler life, but in the end, she knew that she could be nothing else. The thrill of the fast pace and challenge, one of the reasons she went into politics, another warzone to join.

The side streets soon disappeared to a main road and the path they had walked earlier in the day away from Frostt's boat, now she walked willingly towards it. The sounds of distant sirens could be heard over the busy street. A police car, lights flashing, sped past as the pair turned into the marina. The cop riding shotgun scanned the crowds as they drove by, his eyes passing over the grimy homeless couple without a thought.

They soon stepped onto Frostt's trawler. He didn't even bother to untie the two ropes holding the boat to the dock. Two quick hits from a hatchet released them. The engines up and running, the boat turned toe and headed out of the slip and south into the center of the Washington Channel.

o o o

"What?" scowled Kai.

"You heard me," said Mal. "Take it off," he repeated.

"Pervert," Kai also repeated.

Kai sat in one of the two chairs around the small table in the main cabin of Mal's boat. He had just finished docking and securing it. The short trip had only taken a little more than an hour. The slip they bobbed in sat a little less than seven miles south of D.C., the busy city of Alexandria sat across the river basking in the noon sun. Mal had just turned off the radio from a local news station, blaring about the President being kidnapped again and reports of multiple federal agents dead at the Russel building. D.C. had been placed in lockdown; all major roads, ports, and airports were locked down, though it was noted it would be impossible to secure all the side streets and paths that led north and south. Several members of Congress had already started blasting the Secret Service and FBI for incompetence if not intentional miss-action.

Mal had noticed the grimace of pain on Kai's face as she twisted in the chair, reaching for a bottle of water. The pair had not said a word the entire trip. She had ditched the homeless attire, but her clothes didn't look any better. The same ones she had been wearing in the Wolf Run area days before.

"You got your ribs kicked in," said Mal softly. "We have to make sure nothing is out of place." He stared at her in his unnerving way. "Now ditch the shirt and let's see."

"Kiss my ass. I'm fine," spit Kai. "And you have already seen all the skin you are ever going to from me." Mal continued to stare at her, leaning against the side of the helm. "Don't, "she pointed at him. "Don't give me none of that super stare down shit." He didn't flinch. "I want answers and I want them now." He again did not answer, only waited, his face unreadable and his eyes like x-rays.

A few moments passed. "Dammit," bit out Kai. She quickly pulled off her shirt, the pain of it making her gasp and flinch. She tossed it to the ground glaring at him, her black bra grimy and sweat-stained from days of wear. "You stare, or your hands go anywhere I don't like, I swear I will throat punch you." She leveled an equally intense glare back at Mal. "Now you better be talking and spitting answers while you work."

Mal stepped up, taking a knee next to Kai. He rested one hand on her hip to twist her to see her left side better. "Where would you like me to start?" he asked. His small smile gave Kai the urge to break his jaw.

"Well, what is your name to start. I am not going to keep calling you Mr. Frostt, with *two* t's. Bastard Boy,"

Mal chuckled as he inspected her side, gently touching each rib. The bruising had already turned to a deep black and blue, tinted with pale green on the edges. It started an inch below her twelfth rib and disappeared up under the side of her bra. Kai kept her face in check as his finger ran across each rib, her skin protesting in pain. "Don't punch me, please," he said as his hand went up to inspect the rib under the side of her bra. He went on "My name is Malcolm Frostt, with two t's. Most call me Mal."

She looked at him skeptically.

"You're shitting me."

"Nope," smiled Mal.

"You used your real name with me," she raised an eyebrow.

"Not like you believed it." He pulled his hands away. "Nothing is broken, which is a miracle. Well, this time." He could see the evidence of several broken ribs, bullet wounds, and several thin, white knife wounds across her exposed skin. "You can take a beating, that is for sure."

Kai fought down a flush at his admiring tone, irritated with herself. The intimate contact of his medical examination hadn't fazed her at all, but his admiration of her resilience put her off balance somehow.

"Your twelfth rib though is out of place. I am going to have to push it back." He gently placed two fingers and his thumb wide open on the rib. "You ready?"

Kai did not answer out loud, only nodded her assent.

Mal pushed forward with just the right amount of pressure, satisfied to feel the pop under her skin as the rib moved back into place. She let out a gasp of pain and gripped Mal's shoulder.

"All good then," he stood, turning away from her. He pulled down a battered metal box from the top kitchenette cabinet. "There are new clothes for you in the footlocker by the bathroom. Go get cleaned up, and I will get some grub on. Then we will have all the answers together."

"You first, hot stuff," replied Kai. She gingerly put her grimy shirt back on. Only then did Mal turn around.

He tossed her two red prescription bottles. "Two of each and lots of water." He eyed her, his face unreadable.

Frostt & Kai

"Don't ignore me, Bastard Boy," continued Kai, opening the two bottles. "I know I clipped you at least once. So off with it," she gestured at his chest with a smirk, "Quid pro quo."

Mal grinned. Without hesitation he dropped his jacket and pulled the shirt over his head. Kai gleaned nothing from his devilish grin. It was a well-worn mask over his true thoughts and intentions, one that was flawless. She had never been so lost in reading anyone.

He tossed his ripped shirt onto the kitchen table. Kai struggled to keep her eyes from the chiseled lines of his body, like a Greek statue, focusing on the task at hand. She stepped closer, taking a knee next to his side as he had done with her. A bloody rent started at his tenth right rib. About four inches long, her grazing shot had taken a good chunk out of his side. The wound appeared to have clotted and opened back up three or four times, the trail of blood staining the top of his pants and drying on his belt.

"It's not bad; just a flesh wound. Needs cleaning and some butterfly bandages at least." She stood up and looked through the first aid box, pulling out a few sterile cleaning rags, rubbing alcohol,, and lastly a handful of butterfly badges, skipping over the less caustic antiseptics. She kneeled back down, soaked a few rags, and roughly started cleaning out the gash. "You can take care of *that* yourself she said, gesturing to the blood on his belt and pants.

Mal made a show of flinching dramatically as she worked. "If you're this gentle all the time, I will be more than happy to clean it all myself." Kai pushed harder and splashed on more clear alcohol, smirking with satisfaction. She passed a trained eye over his stomach and chest, a story told on his skin. A collection of pink burns littered his left side, moving up into his neckline. Recent by the rest of his scars, minus the fresher bullet holes in the center of his chest. She could see at least two other bullet wounds, one had to be rifle caliber. He also had dozens of thin white lines that only sharp blades could have made, round cigarette size burns on his arms and back, and what even looked like a set of lash marks on his back. Add all of that to the fresh blood and the black and blue of fresh bruises, he looked like a walking ad for a bandage commercial.

"Keep on talking; answers should be pouring out," said Kai. "You never did go to the secure records room. Did you plan that?"

"Yes, I never meant to go there, but I had a feeling you might. Which meant most of the reinforcements would go there."

"And you went to..." she let the question hang.

"Andrew Ott's office. I recovered some material from his safe."

"You stole them." Mal shrugged in response as Kai finished with the butterfly strips. He placed his shirt back on. "How did you know where I was? And come to think of it, how do you know for sure you can even trust me? Wasn't that one of the main points of all of this? To test me?"

Mal nodded. "Good; you're catching on. I like to get several things done at once. Stealing from Otts and vetting you at the same time, among other things, worked out well." He moved back over to the helm. "And as for knowing where you were, there is a locator in the Colt in your waistband as well as listening bug."

Kai's face turned into a glare. She shook her head as she spoke, "So you meant for me to take your gun and to get away." Mal shrugged again in response; she hated that response. "Again, who the hell are you?"

"As I said, most call me Mal."

"Is anything you've told me true? Or is all this just one head game and manipulation after another?"

"Yes, and yes. My wife was murdered and my daughter was kidnapped. And I will find her…at *any* cost."

Chapter 18

Michaela sat at the kitchen table working her damp hair into a French braid. A hot shower and clean clothes made her feel human again. The simple khaki pants, cami undershirt and form-fitting t-shirt Frostt had provided surprised her. She looked at him across the kitchen table where he sat fully immersed in the papers and items spread out there. He had cleaned up also, changing into charcoal cargo pants and a black t-shirt.

He knew he'd need new clothes for me, and even chose clothing perfectly to my taste. He has played me from the beginning. Games within games.

Seeming to sense her thoughts, Mal spoke up, not looking away from the papers. "Like the new clothes? And I made sure to get proper shampoo as well."

"Yeah, they're fine," shrugged Michaela. She had a much clearer mind than twenty minutes before, a bag of jerky, sliced cheese, and whole wheat rolls on the table for sharing. "So, answers. And no more games or plays. Straight answers."

Mal finally looked up at her, his face unreadable as usual. "Answers, sure. Some. Questions... more."

"Going monosyllabic on me? I know it must be hard stringing full sentences together, but I have faith in you," she popped a slice of cheese in her mouth followed by the tangy and smoky jerky.

"Cute," nodded Mal. "Careful with them big words, don't want to be messing with that well practiced double talk you got down pat."

Before she could shoot a quip back, Mal slid several pieces of paper over to her. "Otts's laundering money through half a dozen companies, including his whole reelection campaign."

"Wow, a dirty politician. That is shocking." Michaela took the paper offered to her and started looking over the numbers. It was clear as day that Otts had huge money off the books and was channeling it through half a dozen places. "This only means Otts is getting payoffs for political favors," she shrugged. "Honestly not that uncommon, unfortunately."

"Look at the account codes for at least half of those payoffs." He pulled out another sheet of paper and slid it over to her; and then another, this one from the folders she had seen earlier. "The payoffs come from the same shell company that paid off the doctor that sold my daughter's stint info." Michaela started looking at both pieces of paper as Mal continued talking. "Also, see the transactions on that other sheet from his safe? He is not only getting payments but helping channel money for someone else." He handed over several other pieces of paper and a small black book, clearly a ledger, with all the names written in short hand code.

Michaela took it and started adding up the numbers in the ledger, then the transfers and payments on the pieces of paper. She looked up sharply, only half way through the ledger. "There's over ten billion here and half the book left."

"Hell of a payoff."

"No way it's all his, not this much," she shook her head. "The personal transfers don't match up either. The money is coming in and then going back out."

"Yeah, did you know that Otts worked for the IRS before becoming a senator and is currently on several oversights and tax audit congressional committees?"

"No, I did not. How does that fit into all of this?"

"I am only guessing here, but of what I know of Otts's career, and I know a lot of it, he has been involved with the IRS for a long time. He has voted more than once on bills focused on complicating the tax system and even a few times against bills that would create more transparency. And can you think of a better place to launder money, than through the IRS?"

Michaela shook her head. "Not possible. No way. Too many checks and reviews in the system. Sure, some John Doe might scam the system on his taxes, but you are talking about billions of dollars.

And not cheating on taxes, but dirty money in and clean out."

"Why not? We have one of the most complicated tax systems in the world. All it would take is the right people in the right places and a person or company claiming extra money, then it gets taxed, washed, and returned in federal rebates or tax credits."

Michaela stopped shaking her head, but still could not agree. "No way. Too many weak points in that type of plan. Also," she waved her hand at the papers, "all of this is circumstantial at best. You have nothing concrete or truly linking Otts to your daughter, minus some payments out of a shell company you can't track."

"I would say it's more than enough, but for the unbelievers, we can always dig deeper." He held up a flash drive. "You don't lock up a flash drive unless it has sensitive material on it."

"Like classified congressional documents."

Mal shrugged in response. He stood up and moved over to his computer desk. A half-minute later, the computer was scanning the flash drive. Lines of high-level encryption rolled across the screen.

"That is impressive stuff," Mal noted on the encryption as a username and password prompt popped up on the screen. "Is an ASE 128-bit encryption on a Kanguru drive standard practice for senators?"

"Depends on what info they need to be stored, but that is not an official drive. It doesn't have any of the digital seals."

"Well, there is no way I am going to crack this thing. It would take a team of hackers with a super computer and a billion years to go through all the key logs."

"Move over," Michaela pushed him hard. "Move Bastard Boy," she snapped when he didn't get up fast enough.

"Yes, Ma'am."

Michaela took the worn leather seat. She opened a web browser and in a matter of minutes was plugging data into a command prompt window on the browser, the IP addresses nothing like Mal had seen before.

"Got yourself some dark web stuff there," he sniffed. "I didn't know you were into the nasty stuff."

"Bite me," she retorted. "This makes the dark web look like a child's playground. It's a CIA black site, deep... deep web."

"And it does?" prompted Mal when no more answers were forthcoming.

"It's a field tool. Set up for operators to use when they come across digital devices they need to access on the fly."

"Well, that's cool. So, some super computer is hidden somewhere for CIA lackeys to use."

Michaela ignored the jab, "Not exactly. It's not a brute force or key log attack. It...well it's a back door hub basically. The CIA has *many* hidden doors into systems."

"Ah, the CIA accessing info it should not. Shocking. Really, so shocking."

Michaela only let out a sigh and went to work. Fifteen minutes later, she moved away from the computer, numbers moving about on the web browser. "Okay, it's running and narrowing down the back-door access. We should have access in less than two hours."

"Well, good. I need to go see a boy about a horse." Mal moved his H&K pistol to the small of his back and slipped on a long black wind breaker. "You can come or stay, your call."

Michaela looked at him quizzically. "Like hell I am staying. I'm not letting you out of my sight."

"Ain't that sweet."

"And it smells like wet socks in here."

Mal shrugged.

o o o

"You can't smoke here," said the tenuous voice of the AV tech, monitors splayed out in front of him.

"Do I look like I give a shit," snapped Bert.

"Oh, okay. Okay," replied the tech and went back to punching keys.

"Run it again, the whole thing. I want to see the full narrative of events again."

"Yes, yes, sir."

A cloud of smoke lingered around Bert in the cramped, badly ventilated security office. He held a cigarette in one hand and the other held an instant ice pack to the back of his head. The last three hours had been a blur of manic chaos. Bert had woken up in the dark basement tunnels and barely crawled around a corner when several men came through. His first instinct was to call out, to report the President was gone, but something stopped him. Either the bump on his head or the fact that he could have sworn that the man who kidnapped the president just saved his life. Saved it from his own agents at that.

The pause saved his life, the men's radio cracked, no call sign he recognized. The words chilling and the response worse. The president was gone, but that was not what the radio voice cared about, it was more worried that they had failed to kill the president. The men moved on and Bert slowly made his way out half an hour later.

He had emerged into a scene of chaos. Federal agents and local cops running about doing their best to secure the scene and the panicked crowd. Most of them were still searching for the president who was long gone. Through a mind-splitting headache, he gained control of the agents and local PD. Soon the crowd was contained and the minor injuries treated, the worst being a broken ankle only due to a mad dash to the door when the stinger grenade went off.

Most importantly, Bert had gotten the message off that the President had left the building. He did not include that it seemed to be by her own volition. The call went out to lock down D.C.. Every road, airport, riverport, and dirt path locked down completely. He knew it would never happen. DC was too big and had too many egos to manage for something like that to happen with any needed speed.

As soon as Bert could, he left a senior agent in charge and got away from the main level chaos. His first stop, helped little, the basement mechanical room he and the president had been ambushed in. The details were too fuzzy, like looking at a painting through fogged glass that lay at the bottom of a pond. He knew from the hit on the back of his head to when Archer, or whatever his name was, had been several minutes. Archer was not the one who hit him. He had come to in the last of the fray, the president blood on her hands from a dead agent. The room though had been swarmed by dozens of agents since then, too many big, three-letter egos going for the glory.

He then made his way to the second story, deftly avoiding Director Figg who was out looking for blood. The two building security and three Secret Service agents in the Security Operation Center, SOC for short, paled under his glare and orders to get out. Minus the one shaking AV tech.

A minute later and half a cigarette, the AV tech had brought up the first video feed of the President. She had been in disguise, but after backtracking to follow her, they picked her out entering the building. No luck identifying the man with her as he never looked at a camera. Not once. Though he did disappear for more time than not. He had spent a little less than three minutes in Senator Andrew Otts's office, which of course was also a swarm of agents. The Senator in question had already been secured and was currently being debriefed by the FBI as to why the most wanted man in America had been in his office.

Again, the video showed the President moving through the crowd, talking to the security officer, *yeah his ass is hamburger*, Bert mused, then off to the kitchens, where all hell broke out. Bert could not remember a president under his sight with balls as big as President Kai. Starting a gun fight in the kitchen of a government building and busting the asses of multiple agents. He smiled at the thought of it and then it faded as he saw Agent Johnson enter the picture, the lead agent of five going for the President.

"Pause it," said Bert. The AV tech did. The screen showed the hallway down from the secure records room, the President, and the Secret Service agents, including himself. "Get out," he stated.

The AV tech swiveled around in his chair. "Um, sir…sir that is against the SOP. Sir. There must always be two people in the SOC at all time."

Bert glared down at the still-shaking man. He let the last drag of the cigarette bellow out of his nostrils and flicked the still glowing cigarette butt at the AV tech. The man flinched away, nearly falling over in his chair, as the butt bounced off his chest, the glowing cherry sparking away. Bert whispered low and deep, "Get out before I break your face in."

The door closed behind the tech, nearly tripping him in his haste out of the room.

Bert didn't give the man a second glance. He plopped down in the man's chair with a sigh and worked the controls awkwardly until he came to the group of people on the screen walking off camera one of the few dark places in the building. He saw the kidnapper come down the hall shortly after. A few minutes later the FBI HRT team came down the hall, a four-man team. The two in front opened fire down the hall into the mechanical room. The mechanical room where the President was. Not just against the HRT protocol, but no one would send rounds where the President might be hit by an errant bullet. Unless they meant to.

"I need a drink," Bert said to himself. He pulled out another cigarette and let out a string of curses hoping to ease his headache. It did not help. He watched the same clip several more times, until a noise in the hall pulled him away. He dropped the video back to the beginning of the day and turned just in time to see Director Figg storm through the door.

Figg laid right in. "What the hell are you doing? I have been looking for you for the last hour! What in the hell is going on here!? You lost the

President again," he bellowed the last, his face a splotchy red.

"Well, currently I am abusing AV guys and smoking a cigarette," replied Bert coolly.

"What…what," stuttered Figg, taken off balance by the comment.

"What is going on here is a complete shit show and what I am doing is my job."

"Your job, your job!" Figg screamed apoplectic, bits of phlegm flying from the corners of his mouth.

Bert stood in a rush, causing Figg to take a defensive step back; Bert smile inwardly at that. "Yes, my job. In fact, that is what I have always been doing. And that is what I am going to keep doing until you and Mr. Vice President decide to toss me to the wolves as the scapegoat."

Figg was shaking his head, unable to form a sentence both from rage and from astonishment.

Bert stepped closer to Figg, forcing him back another step. "That has been the plan the whole time. You need a scapegoat. Either way, it would not matter; I find her or I don't. When this firestorm is over, someone needs to fall and fall hard." He stepped even closer, Figg out of space to step back. "So, either drop me now and pile on the blame, or wait and get the hell out of my way. Because I am going to find her and I will not let some snot nose paper pusher get in my way."

"Paper pusher," squeaked out Figg, flushing with embarrassment as his voice failed him.

"Make sure the city gets locked down. Flex some of the paper muscle and make it happen." And with that, Bert left the room. Steaming hotter than Figg, he wanted to go back and take his rage out on the man's face. He decided that would not be a good idea, even though he could not do much worse. He knew he was done. Beyond done, maybe looking at criminal trouble. He was right; when all was said and done, someone was going to pay.

He stormed through the building and emerged into the noon sun. Meyers ran up the steps towards him. He raised his hand, stopping her words. "Get a car. I need you go to the White House and look into something for me." Meyers turned toe without a word and barked down for a car.

Can I even trust her? Bert thought to himself. He banished the thought. He had to trust someone. If he was surrounded by enemies, then it was best to keep the most dangerous close by.

Chapter 19

"What are we doing here," asked Kai. She and Mal stepped out of a nondescript black early-2000s Camry. The cold, winter light reflected on the weathered, black paint. They had no issue getting back into the city since there were too many side streets to close down.

Mal did not respond to her. He scanned the area. Kai did the same. He moved away from the car and across a sidewalk into a large playground area. The smell of fresh bark dust lingered in the air, a few kids were climbing on the structures, and more were off in the open field near by burning off their endless energy as parents watched.

"Hey Bastard Boy, are we meeting someone?" snapped Kai. Mal walked down the cracked asphalt path bordering the playground. He continued to look around, not responding. Trees lined the path and a large rec building stood twenty feet off the path, half-dead grass separating the path and building. Mal frowned, still looking around. Kai was about to speak up again, planning to add a kick to his backside for effect when a voice called out.

"Who's the chick?"

Mal and Kai spun towards the voice, both falling into relaxed, defensive stances.

"You are a quiet little shit," said Mal.

"Hey, cursing," Milo pointed at him. "and yeah. Thought I should step up my game. You know, super spy kid and all."

Mal stared at Milo, a look of confused amusement on his face. "How did you sneak up on us?"

"I put one foot in front of the other."

"Smart ass."

"Who is this kid?" interrupt Kai.

"Oh, me and KM go way back, don't we," smirked Milo.

"KM?"

"*Killer* Man," answered Milo.

"Your face looks like piss. Somebody's been tap dancing on it," stated Mal, all the amusement in his tone gone.

"It ain't shi...crap," changed Milo midstream at a glare from Mal. In fact, it was quite bad. Milo's lip was split open and swollen, his left eye was solid black and half-closed, a bruised gash on his left cheek finished off his face, and he favored his left side, most likely bruised or cracked ribs.

"So who's the chick?"

"Chick?" Kai turned to Mal. "Don't tell me this is one of your contacts."

Mal ignored them both. "Where's my camera, Milo?"

"You mean my camera. All you want is the memory card."

"Fair enough boy," smiled Mal, "Let's have it."

"Let's see the money."

"Unbelievable," huffed Kai. "Hiring kids."

"Yeah, bet you never did anything like that running ops," replied Mal, still eyeballing Milo. Kai's expression sobered up.

Mal pulled a roll of bills. Milo did the same with the SD card. "Your old man found the other money?"

Mal could see the comment rocked Milo off the edge. Pain, anger, and a profound fear washed across his face. He tamped it down well, too well. "It's none of your damn business," snapped Milo. "And don't give me any shit for cursing. You want the info or not?"

"Yeah, of course." Mal tossed the rubber banded rollover. Milo matched the move. "Just make sure you hide it better this time."

Before Milo could snap back, a loud yell echoed from the other side of the playground. Milo's face went a pale white. "Milo, damn you."

A middle-aged man walked towards them, hairline pulled back, a beer belly hanging over his dirty jeans. As the man walked up, a splotchy redness dominated his nose and center of his face. Kai wrinkled her nose at the smell of the man, cheap spirits and lack of showering.

"What the hell you doing, kid? You were supposed to be back an hour ago with KFC. What did ya do with the twenty I gave you?"

"Nothing, just…just.."

"Spit it out, you little shit."

"Hey," spoke up Kai. The man ignored her.

Milo's father's eyes darted down and before Milo could hide it, he spotted the roll of cash in his hands. "Oh boy, yeah. I will assume you are not going to try to hide it like last time. I hope you learned your lesson."

"That money was not for you," said Mal matter of fact.

"Who the hell are you?" snapped the man, rubbing the scruff on the side of his face.

"I am KM," replied Mal.

"What? Oh, whatever," waved the man standing next to Milo, "If you are the man paying, I don't give a shit. The boy's finally doing something good for his family, not just a useless life suck." He put his hand out, "Let's have it, boy."

"I said the money is for him. Not you."

The man sneered at Mal. "Go screw yourself man or that hottie you got." He looked Kai up and down. "Don't butt in between a man and his boy."

"I see no man standing by Milo." Mal tilted his head and gave a mocking flick of his hand.

"I should kick your ass, but I don't want to ruin my boy's future chance of more work."

"So, just kick his ass then. And steal his money. Father of the year."

"Screw you, you rich yuppie. Maybe I will kick your ass anyway. Maybe my boy deserves more pay for whatever he's doing for you or to you." He let out a short wet laugh. "That is probably all he is good for." He slapped his hand onto the back of Milo's neck, grabbing hold, "being some pervert's play toy."

"Enough," snapped Kai, but before she could lunge forward. Mal already stood behind the man, his arm now off Milo and in a half chokehold and armbar.

The man tried to yell some obscene words, but failed when Mal tossed him to the side completely taking him airborne. He fell hard, another round of curses coming from him. Mal waited until the man made his feet, shaking, but that was it. He walked into the man, a wild swing coming up short, and dropped him in less than two seconds. The man's right arm broken backwards at the elbow, his nose broken, and several cracked ribs. Mal looked down at the man, a painted rage on his face that Kai had not seen before.

Mal bent down, his foot on the broken elbow joint, he spoke in a cold, halting voice. "The money is Milo's and only Milo's. I will be back. I will watch you. You will never see me, but I will see you. One cut, one bruise, one day with lack of food in his belly and then you will see me. The last thing you see. I will kill you in a way that can only be described as beyond depravedly graphic." He pushed down hard on the man's already destroyed arm. The man let out a whimpering scream. And then Mal let up and walked away.

He came back to stand next to Milo, his face back to his neutral, unreadable state. His voice was clean and slightly humorous as always. "To cover the loss. I promised five hundred to *you*." He handed Milo another roll of bills. Milo's expression was a mix of mortal fear and awe-inspired admiration. "Be good kid. See you around." And with that he walked away, Kai flabbergasted once again.

Neither said a word as they got into the car and it came to life with a faint knocking noise. Mal pulled away from the curb, the brakes whining as he came up to the first stop. The peace of the little neighborhood was surreal to Mal, kids playing and people going about their normal days. When the core of the city, the heart of the nation, lay in completely panicked chaos. The president still missing, death a stone throw from the White House, and more political agendas gaining steam.

Kai turned to Mal, doing her best to stay afloat in a sea of unknown waters. "Can you fill me in a little," she nodded her head back to the playground.

Mal did not respond for a minute; Kai was deciding whether to push harder or just let it lie, but he spoke up. "The kid was just a random pickpocket I found. I paid him to watch the Russell building this morning and take pictures of the entire scene and any vehicles or people that looked out of place. "

"Well that was smart," replied Kai.

"I also have a listening device currently on Senator Otts."

"What, how?" asked Kai.

"Paid one of his hookers to swap out his school ring for one I made."

"*One* of his hookers?" Kai raised an eyebrow.

"Yeah," Mal smirked. "The ring is a short burst transmitter that will only activate once the memory is full. It is a bone inductor, using Ott's own hands, skin, and bones to pick up sounds, so nearly undetectable. There is a receiver hidden in the park near the Russell building to pick up the signal and boost it out onto the cell network and into a half-dozen cloud drives for us to access."

"'Us?' Are we a team now then?" Kai raised an eyebrow, an honest question hidden in her mocking tone, but she went on without giving him a chance to answer, "That is top-line gear. Black ops tech. How did you get it?"

"Anything is purchasable if you know the right people."

Kai did not press the subject; she was no stranger to black ops contacts. It did put another note in her log of who this Malcolm Frostt was. The two lapsed into silence on the quick drive back to the marina, new roadblocks forcing several detours.

Chapter 20

"Do I need to paint a picture for you, agent," snipped Andrew Otts. He sat in a high back chair, his dusty, charcoal, three-piece Desmond Merrion suit laying with ease on his soft frame. A single lock of thick golden hair lay astray, the only sign of stress. He had spent over eight hours going from conference room to conference room in the Russell building and Hart Senate Office Building. From one federal agent to another, to emergency committee meetings, some with him on the committee and some with him in front of them.

Once again, he sat with the infamous Agent Renfield, the man responsible for losing the President in the first place. The audacity of the man to make Otts repeat himself for the hundredth time. "Once again, Agent Renfield, I do not know why my office suite was targeted." Even Otts was impressed with himself on the amount of disdain he was able to put into the words. "As I have told you earlier today and the other hundred people that have asked me, who knows what that psycho wanted? And I would add that you should be out looking for the President instead of interrogating me, but that might be beyond your skill, since you've already lost her *twice*."

Renfield ignored the comment and did not look up from the papers in front of him, much to Otts consternation, this agent seemed to not react to any jab. Renfield went on in his matter of fact tone, the smell of cigarettes heavy on him. "I know you have gone over it many times Senator Otts, but we will go over it again. And trust me, things would be much different if this was an interrogation." He looked up at Otts, his stare direct and unnerving. "To start, you would not be sitting in a comfortable chair while your bimbo assistant fetches a chai tea latte for you."

As if on cue, the assistant entered the room again, her tight skirt looking hard to walk in, her blouse skimming the levels of propriety in the Senate office building, low cut and clinging. "Here you go Senator," she placed the artisan latte in front of Otts and took her place a few steps behind him. The man didn't hide a lurid look at her backside as she turned away.

"This is beyond pointless," said Otts taking a sip from his latte.

"What was in the safe?" asked Renfield.

"Can you not listen the first time? No wonder you lost the President."

"The safe?"

Otts shook his head and replied without trying to hide the aggravation in his voice. "As I said. There were several things in the safe." Renfield continued to stare at Otts until he went on with another dramatic sigh and drink of his latte. "Several reports from the healthcare committees I'm on, several non-classified intelligence reports, and a few personal notebooks. The last does have some sensitive notes in it from meetings and also a few things that might be seen as uncouth."

"Such as," prompted Renfield when Otts did not elaborate.

"Uhh, such as a few personal notes on the other senators and the President. And a few crude sketches of the President. I have always dabbled in art."

"Crude sketches?" Renfield raised an eyebrow.

Otts shrugged. "I can't say I think much of her as a president, but any man has to admit she is not lacking in the way of stunning *assets*."

Renfield shook his head, but before he could respond or go onto his next question, the door to the conference room opened and Director Figg walked in. "That is enough Agent Renfield. Wrap it up," the deep hatred for Renfield barely held in check.

"I am not done. I will be shortly." Renfield did not as much as shift in his chair to look at his director.

"Yes, you are," stated Figg trying to sound tough, but failing.

Renfield turned to face his boss and saw Meyers walk around the corner of the hallway through the open door and wave to him, a file folder in her hand.

"Okay, you're da boss." Renfield stood collecting his notes and quickly left, not saying another word to Otts, who had a smirk plastered on his face.

"Thank you, Director Figg. These questions have been getting tiring, to say the least."

"Of course, Senator, I am sorry. You should have been out of here hours ago. We will be in contact if any new questions come up."

"Yes, I am more than happy to help. As long as it's productive." He stood, buttoning his suit jacket, leaving the coffee cup for his assistant to pick up on their way out of the room.

The pair made their way through the clamor of activity in the building. The acrid smell of the flash and smoke grenades still lingered in the air. Not to mention the much fainter, but much more pervasive smell of panic induced fear and sweat. The place made Otts want to go home and shower. He felt tainted by it all, tainted by his own fear.

The sun shone brightly still in the late afternoon sky, the top edges of the marble façade of the building burnished with a fiery glow. The steps and streets around the building fared no better than inside, just more air to thin out the smell. Otts walked down the steps with his assistant and into the throng of people, her high heels clicking on the marble steps. They had made him park in the general parking lot; he would be having someone's ass for that as well as other offenses. He was keeping a list.

"How about a ride, Mr. Senator," said a tall, blocky man stepping out in front of Otts.

"What," snapped Otts, his next words dying in his throat with another voice joining in.

"We insist, Andrew," said a new man. He leaned against a black SUV. Dressed in black, a well-tailored suit, black tie, and exposed undershirt under his open jacket. His face had a gaunt sallow look to it; a slim jaw and short-cropped salt and pepper hair framed his naturally tanned skin. No one could call his face weak, not for the features but from an unseen characteristic that flowed from the man.

The man opened the back door to the SUV, "Get in the SUV, Andrew." His smile did nothing to lighten his face, it only gave him a more predatory look. "And lose the titty bitch."

"Ye…yea..h," stammered Otts. "Go home Steph. I'll call you later."

"Are you sure, sir," replied his assistant in a high-pitched voice.

"Get," he snapped his head to the side and Steph followed the move and quickly walked away. Without another word, Otts climbed into the back seat of the SUV, the black leather cold and gleaming. The predator man followed, talking the seat next to him, and the one from the sidewalk took the driver's seat and started up the SUV.

"What are you doing here, David?" demanded Otts, doing his best to take the lead, adjusting his pearl cufflinks.

"What am I doing here?" replied David as the driver pulled the SUV into the street. David did not look at Otts; his attention was completely focused on a minuscule fleck of dirt under his finger nail on his ring finger. "I am here because it seems you can't manage your affairs properly."

"What the hell does that mean," snipped Otts, still fiddling with his cufflinks.

"What was in the safe, Andrew?" David held up his hand to inspect the ring finger for any other hints of dirt or flaws.

"How...what? How do you know about that?"

"Andrew. What was in the safe?" David turned to Andrew, his face smooth and placid. His skin smooth as polished granite.

Otts wanted to protest, but the look from David and the rumors he had heard about the man stopped him. "Nothing important," he lied, "As I told the FBI and the Secret Service. It was some memos, reports, and personal notebooks." David did not respond. His eyes never came off Otts. "What dammit?"

"Are you sure that was all there was in the safe?"

"Yes," snapped Otts, adding a couple of religious curses for good effect.

"So, there would be nothing in the safe that would tie you back to us?" The SUV moved at a snail's pace through the clogged streets. It looked like every cop and federal agent within three states had descended on the city. "Nothing to show the billions of dollars that you have moved around? Nor the payments to yourself? Or heaven forbid you would have kept a record of any communication, bribes, or IRS tax black booking."

Otts adjusted his tie without noticing, his cufflinks would not lay right on his wrists. It was driving him mad. "Of course! I only keep the most basic info needed to track the money and that in the shorthand you trained me to use." He went back to adjusting his cufflinks, wanting to rip them out of his sleeves. "It would look like nonsense to anyone who read it."

"That is good, Andrew. I am glad you took to heart the methods I showed you. Mr. Voste will be most happy to know we have nothing to worry about." David went back to looking at his fingernails. "Then the next question would be why did this attacker single out your office and your safe?"

"Beats me," answered Otts. "Just some nutcase. Probably upset about me not voting or supporting so and so. It is quite common for unbalanced people to focus on a political figure. Especially one as prominent as myself."

"We are quite aware of your fame. Not something I would say is a good thing in our business."

"That is separate. I have it under control as always."

"I am so glad to hear." The SUV pulled up to the sidewalk and the driver stepped out and opened Otts's door.

David did not look to have anything more to say, so Otts stepped out of the car. They had barely gone two miles away from the Russell building. David's voice drifted out of the open door as soon as Otts took his first step away. "Andrew, please keep yourself safe. We would hate anything bad to happen to you."

"Of course, of course," replied Otts. "Please let me know if there is anything more I can do."

"We will, we will," were David's parting words. The SUV door closed and pulled back into traffic.

Otts wanted to rip his cufflinks out and toss them to the ground. He let out a stuttering sigh and pulled out his cellphone to call for a limo.

Chapter 21

The last traces of sunlight faded in the distance, the dark waters of the river gently lapping at the side of the trawler. The interior lights of the cabin shone burnt orange in the small space, the smell of fried meat and mustard dominated the air. Mal stepped away from the small kitchenette, two plates in hand. He set one down in front of Kai and one on the other side of the table for himself. He stepped back and pulled a bottle of Buffalo Trace bourbon from a shelf. He motioned with the bottle at Kai.

She raised a hand, "No, gave it up years ago." She looked down at her sandwich of thin sliced fried spam stacked high, melted cheddar cheese, and mustard all on a toasted bagel. "But this sandwich might kill me faster than booze."

"Don't knock it till you try it," Frostt dug into his sandwich, chasing it with a pull of bourbon from his nearly-full cup.

"You eat like a slob," commented Kai, taking a bite of her sandwich… and enjoying it. She thought it would be a cold day in hell before she admitted that to Frostt.

"I make sure to keep my etiquette tailored to my company," he smiled, finishing off another drink with a deep throated burp. He turned his attention away from Kai's blue, gem-cut eyes. The sharp lines of her face had almost imperceptibly softened since Frostt had kidnapped her. As if the stress and combat of the last few days had chipped away at her normal rigidity. The change had only made it harder for Frostt to concentrate.

He let his eyes drift across the table at the mix of papers and photos. Printouts from the camera and even the transcript from the Ott's conversation with this mysterious David in the SUV. Without speaking, they had both come to the same agreement that beyond the man's diminutive stature and feeble frame lay a man of considerable violence.

They had learned the man's name was David and that Ott's was petrified of him. He worked for a Mr. Voste, and they had confirmed Otts was not only using his IRS connections to launder money, but had been a part of sending out bribes.

The computer still labored away at the hard drive from Otts's safe, the CIA deep web hacker site streaming numbers away. Kai had commented on how long it was taking, much longer than she thought it should. The pair finished their sandwiches at almost the same moment as the computer beeped. The screen turned from a scrolling line of numbers to an open file folder. They both jumped up and move to the computer, Kai barely faster getting the seat. Frostt glared at her.

"Wow, damn." Kai opened the flash drive folders and property bar. Tens of thousands of folders scrolled down the screen. "There is a little over a terabyte of info here."

Frostt leaned in, his hand on the back of the chair much to Kai's annoyance. "Start a search for Voste and then lets go to the last modified file."

"Good call, Sherlock."

"Bite me."

"Have to get my shots first."

The newest data was of little use, from what they could understand. Nothing but money values and nonsensical transition numbers. A search for Voste rolled on with no luck in the first ten thousand files. The next dozen recent files only showed staggering amounts of money. Even in both of their wildest guesses would they have thought this amount of money could be moved without being notice, over a hundred billon in the last three months alone.

The search popped up its first result, then quickly another few hundred. Kai opened the folder with the most search results in an archive of Otts old emails, hundreds of them.

"Looks like old Otty was keeping a record of his wrong doings," chuckled Kai. At the same time, Both of them said. "Blackmail."

"Just in case they turned on him."

They opened the first ten emails highlighted with Voste's name. The first being simple exchanges of needed bribes and new avenue of money, nothing of great use. Only acronyms and number strings used in relationship to the bribes or money. Then Frostt's attention was caught in an email that had never been sent, it looked more like a personal note to Otts himself. Voste's name and the letters IIC were repeated several times.

"Look at that," pointed Frostt, leaning closer to the screen. Kai batted his hand away.

"Yeah," she replied, already reading the same lines.

Frostt's mouth opened to keep going, but stopped suddenly. Kai's hands froze above the keyboard at the same time.

Then several things happened at once.

The portholes looking out into the black night and barely tinted with the lights of the nearby dock and marina buildings, suddenly burst to life with a white, blinding light. Frostt and Kai moved at the same time, as if of one mind, the first round of shots cut through the plywood hull with a sharp crack as they hit the deck. The sharp pop of a silencer was quickly covered by new shots. The hull of the trawler started shredding into splinters of wood, the computer ripping apart, dishes, books, and bottles exploding as hundreds of bullets from multiple directions tore into Frostt's home.

He spoke calmly but like cold iron, "Move." He pushed Kai's side, pointing her to port and towards the hatch down to the hold. A staccato of silenced shots ringed his words. He moved away from Kai, aft, debris exploding creating a cloud of wood, glass, sparks, and plastic. Kai got to the hatch, opened it, and slid down head first, looking back to see Frostt grab a photo off the nightstand and start a quick sliding crawl towards her.

A sharp sting tore into the side of Frostt's face as he went head first into the hatch, taking the small stairs in a tumble and kicking Kai in the back as she tried to move out of the way. The cramped hold already smelled of river water. The lights failed in a spasm of sparks, more bullets tearing into the craft. Frostt pushed Kai to the far aft of the trawler and with one armed pulled a storage cabinet over, ripping the mounting screws out. He roughly pushed Kai into a small cavity behind the storage locker; she didn't protest. He joined her, after grabbing a duffle bag out of the fallen storage locker, the space barely enough for one person, he wrapped his arms around her and pulled her tight. The thick duffle bag on Frostt's back making the space even more cramped.

"Close your eyes. Hold your breath," Frostt hollered over the growing noise. Kai did as she was told, her final breath filled with his scent. Unable to forget the lingering smell of bourbon, but more than that a subtle scent of old oak and fresh cut pine. She felt him press hard against her and reach for something behind her. A hard click followed.

A blinding light exploded a half-second later, throwing shadows in sharp relief even through her closed eyes, and the heat felt nearly unbearable on her face. Then it was gone, replaced with a cold that crawled and gnawed its way into her skin, like a dull knife slowly grating against her bones.

Chapter 22

The desk phone continued to ring. A trilling noise reverberating off the glass and teak paneled walls. The desk it sat on had been handcrafted from Brazilian mahogany and inlayed with Egyptian cypress and gold leaf. The center of the room was dominated by a ten-foot by ten-foot handwoven cashmere rug, deep rivers of blue and purple ran through it with true gold threads tracing the edges. The rest of the office suite bore the same look, fine woods, polished leather, and fine crystal decanters of even finer scotch.

The solid wood door opened without a sound, and David walked into the office, an easy confidence radiating in each of his steps. Behind the desk a panoramic view of the New York City skyline could be seen out the window. A magnanimous view if any, one of the best in all the city. The man sitting behind the desk wore a black suit no brand could claim. One of those outfits that was named only by the creator behind it. A Patek Phillippe rose gold watch with matching cuff links were the only jewelry the man wore. He reached for the phone with bare hint of apprehension in the movement, too minuscule for most to see. David saw it. The brought the phone up to his face, the barest hint of white stubble on his cheeks.

His pure white hair hand thinned to the point that not even the most skilled hair dresser could make it look full. His face showed the red marks of a life of heavy drinking and hard living, the skin tight, but only due to Botox.

His voice was raspy and cigar tinted when he spoke, "Yes." He waited for a moment; a line of sweat had sprouted on the stretched skin of his forehead. He swallowed deeply and wished he had poured himself a third drink before picking up the phone. "No, we have it handled…. No, Sir." A faint distain colored the last word.

The person on the other end of the phone spoke for some time before the man at the desk responded, "Of course. I have Mr. Levi here now; he just came in but he gave me his report over a secure com before coming. The boat was completely destroyed; it looks like it was some sort of fail safe. We're not sure if they triggered it or if it was triggered by a stray bullet. The rough onsite analysis makes it look like the man had his boat rigged with white phosphorous and magnesium charges meant to burn everything incriminating and sink the vessel. Couple that with the amount of ammo David and his men poured into the boat there is no way anyone could have survived the explosion, not to mention the cold river. That would have done the job in a few minutes as well."

Another pause and the man at the desk listened and then went on, doing his best to keep the defensiveness out of his tone. "No, sir. We did not find any bodies and neither has the local PD. We are tied in with them of course, so we will hear when or if they do, but it is doubtful anything will be found."

A short pause. "But sir-" the man at the desk was cut off abruptly and quickly recanted his statement. "Of course, we will consider them alive and a threat until we have confirmation of their bodies. Do you want me to update you through the normal channels?"

The man at the desk did not receive an answer; the line had gone dead. "He hung up on me that bastard."

"I am guessing he's unhappy, Mr. Voste," spoke David for the first time.

"That is a gross understatement," Voste sighed. "He made it clear that he and the people above *him* will not consider this closed until we have the bodies of President Kai and this mystery man cold and dead on a table." Voste stood abruptly from his desk, grabbed his empty crystal glass. And walked over to a table laden with fine spirits. He poured a double measure of Macallan single malt scotch and downed the entire dram in one go, worth more than most would make in a single month. He poured another and turned to look back at David; he did not offer the slim man any, he never drank. In fact, Voste didn't know of a single vice David had, unless he counted hurting people. David had worked for Voste for nearly a decade, steadfast as a mountain and he never failed.

Voste was in no way naïve of the fact that money and opportunity to do his gruesome work kept David loyal to him; he was one of the very few men that Voste feared.

David had spent several years bouncing around as a mercenary and in the clandestine world before coming to work for Voste full time. Before that, he spent the early part of his career working for Mossad out of Tel Aviv. He came out of the deep dark of the secretive Mossad, a black ops agent to his core and a man fighting for survival since his birth in the West Bank.

"Is the scene clean?" asked Voste, more out of habit than need.

"Yes," replied David. "The local police report will come back as mechanical failure which led to the fire and sinking of the vessel."

"And the bodies?"

David shook his head; he showed no sign of being agitated by his boss's pestering questions. "Not as of ten minutes ago when I checked in with my local asset. The police will send down divers at first light. I do have my doubts they will find anything." He held up his hand before Voste could interrupt him. "I don't mean that either of them survived, only that the currents are strong in that area and my review of the tidal charts beforehand would point to the bodies being pulled away quickly."

"How do you know they didn't make it out somehow?" Voste took a long drink of his scotch, his hand already reaching for the bottle unconsciously.

"The probability of them surviving is near zero, but beyond that, my men watched both sides of the river for a mile each way, and the assault team was outfitted with thermal imaging gear, though the boat fire interfered there slightly. Six drones are running a cross pattern survey of the river as extra insurance."

"You and your probabilities and analyses." Voste shook his head, he never understood how a man as brutal as David could be so precise in his operations. "It is near zero or zero?"

"Nothing is perfect zero, you know that, Mr. Voste," replied David in his cold toned. "All the facts point to neither of them being alive."

"Okay, I can live with that, but we need to find some hard proof. Their bodies or body parts, I don't care." He downed the rest of his drink. "Please follow up with the local PD to see what we can get and reach out to our friends in the Coast Guard; they might be able to send in resources to help if we can get a good cover story for it."

"Will do, sir." And at those last words, David turned and left the office, leaving Voste alone with his thoughts and scotch, although neither did any good for his mood. The voice from the other end of the line haunted him. He didn't even know who the man was, that's how it all worked. Separation and compartmentalization of assets and information. He swallowed hard at the thought of failing; it would mean more than criminal charges, which would likely carry the death sentence, but the death from the men he worked for, which would not be swift nor pleasant in any sense of the word.

o o o

The black coffee burned Mal's mouth, but he didn't care. He downed the cup, the fourth in a row. A bone chill still ached all through him, despite the seedy hotel room heater pumping out as much heat as it could. He stared at the computer screen in front of him, a picture on it of a man from a news report, white haired and beyond finely dressed. Duncan Voste, CEO and Chairman, largest stockholder, of IIC, Intulus International Corporation. A conglomerate of hundreds of subsidiaries and fully controlled departments mostly in the medical field. From big business health insurance, biomedical research, medical manufacturing, CDC contracts, and majority interests in half a dozen hospital and healthcare groups. IIC reported a little north of a hundred-and-fifty billion in revenue in the recent public stockholder's report.

Mal had little eyes though for Duncan Voste; he stared at a lone figure in the background of one of the photos, nearly out of sight, lingering in the shadows. David. David Levi, as a matter of fact. Once

Mal knew he too was connected, it was not hard to track down employment records of David, a full-time employee of Voste, with the title of Special Assets Director. Mal had neglected to mention to Michaela that he recognized David from the photos Milo had taken and he would never forget that face. The man that pulled the trigger at his wife's head; the man that told him they would take great care of his daughter before planting two rounds into his own chest.

The running water turned off in the bathroom. Mal could hear Michaela moving around through the paper-thin walls and even thinner door. A few minutes later, she came out of the bathroom dressed in the clothes they had *borrowed* from the small department store, same with the cheap laptop Mal worked on, new shoes, and a handful of general sundries. Michaela walked over to the single heater in the room and started brushing her raven hair in front of it, doing her best to suck up the heat. By the time the pair had made it out of the river, the first stages of hypothermia had set in. It would have meant death if not once again for Mal's forethought.

The go-bag had two full, thermal wetsuits, instant chemical hot pads, six mini air tanks, and a waterproof container filled with cash and a Glock-19 with four clips. They had used the intense heat and light of the sinking boat, still burning underwater, the miracle of burning metal. After lingering in that spot, they slowly made it over to the pier and crawled out sometime later, blue lipped and past the point of shaking. A mad dash, some breaking and entering, and a cash payment to a drug thin hotel clerk brought them into the dingy room.

Mal pointed to the computer screen. "The magic of the internet." He moved out of the chair to let Michaela sit. She read with rapt attention. Mal went over to the queen bed in the center of the small room. He started laying out their supplies: an extra pair of clothes each, one five-inch fixed blade knife, a little under twenty thousand dollars in cash, Mal's H&K pistol, and lastly the Glock-19 with barely two boxes of 9mm ammo between the pair.

Finishing reading the half dozen webpages Mal had left open, Michaela sat on the edge of the bed, braiding her hair into a tight French braid and looking over their meager supplies. "I've been thinking about how they tracked us down. It can't be from the CIA code breaker site," she hesitated only slightly. "They must have found something you left behind and tracked it back to the boat."

"Nope," Mal replied flatly as he started stripping down the two weapons.

"You have planned thousands of details and you can't control everything. A street cam could have caught a glimpsed of us or a street bum just happened to talk to the cops."

"Nope."

"Dammit" snapped Michaela, "Can you have a real conversation here? I don't need your dumbass monosyllabic responses."

He did not look up from his task, though he could have stripped, cleaned, and reassembled each pistol with his eyes closed. "Even if we had been seen and/or if I had messed up, which I did not, it would not have led back to the boat. It was too well insulated to be found so quickly. All things will fail given enough time and enough inspection, but I created the layers to point to each other and create contradictions within any evidence found. At my best estimate it would have taken someone at least ninety-six hours to trace down the false lines I created and find the boat. And that's only if they were given enough information to start with."

He looked up and handed the Glock to her, fully put back together. "It is not a question of competence on my part, but an issue with the amount of data that could be absorbed and sorted by any given government team. Time is our main evidence; thus, Occam's Razor gives us the only solution. It had to be your CIA site, cause that was the singular entity that had a direct tie to the boat."

Michaela took the Glock, staring at Mal. "I hate you. You know that right?" Mal nodded in response. Chambering a round into the pistol, she placed it in her waistband at the small of her back. "You have to be ex-intelligence or something even more sinister."

"Nope," answered Mal, back to his monosyllabism.

She shook her head in disbelief but went on. "You don't understand what that would mean. Not even the director of the CIA knows about those code breaker sites. They are set up by the Architects. A group of hackers and think-tank eggheads who aren't tied to any agency. They are kept completely isolated, not even their handlers know who they are, and they work on only pieces of each site or program so not a single person ever understands the whole thing."

She stood from the bed and started pacing the room. "I have no idea how someone could have traced us. They would have to be beyond connected and have access to info not part of any network. And it would have to be several people, tons of them, to pull something like that off."

"We already know for a fact the Secret Service and the FBI have been infiltrated."

She waved that off. "Those were grunts, soldiers. Extremely dangerous and worrisome, but just grunts none the less. We are talking about high ranking and powerful leaders deep within our own government." She went quiet, her thoughts racing a mile a minute. The implications went way beyond anything she could wrap her mind around.

Mal rubbed his hands and blew warm air into them. He hated the cold, since being forced to live out in the cold and wet for months on end as a kid. Michaela stopped noticing his hands. "Enough for now. We know who Voste is, and we can sort out the next steps shortly. Go take a shower; there should be some hot water left but piss poor water pressure. Warm up, then we can get a bite and figure out the next move."

Mal only nodded in response and went into the bathroom. Michaela sat down at the cheap desk and read through the webpages again. The clock read a-quarter-past one in the morning, and she felt an overwhelming foreboding that the storm surrounding them would be coming to a head sooner than later.

A few keystrokes later, a community college website lay open on the screen, one of those schools that only the people living within twenty miles knew about. After a few clicks on hidden buttons and a few hacks, she had a draft email typed up. She could hear the water from the bathroom, even so she had continued to listen for motion and look over her shoulder every minute. Then the mouse cursor lingered over the send button. *We need help. I need help. We can't do this…I can't do this without some more help,* she thought to herself and pressed the send button. *I hope she still remembers the old codes.* The message sent, a message buried into the junk mail, a spark of hope lingered in her chest. The water in the bathroom shutoff.

Chapter 23

Bert stood, a just finished cigarette between his lips, looking over the active scene before him. A few police cars and several Marine officials looked over the dock area. The report he'd been given by a green police officer made it seem like some boat had a mechanical fire and then sank. The police officer quickly retreated from Bert's unfriendly stare as he made it clear he thought the man was a dumbass. In fact, Bert already had a better report, from a homeless man who overlooked the marina from his box home. After several twenty-dollar bills and a whole pack of cigarettes, the homeless man recounted what sounded like some war scene in a bad movie.

His phone buzzed with a text message. He looked down at it, the screen reading 2:03am. The text was from Meyers: Break in reported at Fifth and Scott Avenue, retail store. Men's and women's clothes stolen, laptop, other small items. Alarm completely bypassed.

He ran the map of the area in his head, that location was about two miles away. He thought for a moment that he should head over there, but thought better of it. It would do him no good. He had come straight over to the marina after waking up a very agitated and aged man, a professor of history and an expert on D.C. historical architecture.

His phone trilled again, another text from Meyers. He scanned it and ignored it. He knew she was pissed for being left behind, mainly because she had told him and cursed at him for it, but he needed to do this alone and needed her back at the office running down info for him as needed.

He tossed the cigarette butt to the ground and turned away from the riverbank and walked back to his car, his breath coming out in foggy bursts. He started the car up, the heat already turned to full blast. He looked out into the clear night sky and sank deep in dozens of lines of thoughts and next actions. He picked one at last and put the car in gear. His fingers already twitched to pull out another cigarette, but he was low, after giving his spare pack away.

o o o

"What? Not fancy enough for your highbrow tastes?" said Mal.

Michaela glared up at him, pushing around her eggs and greasy home fries. The diner's lights hummed above. The clock above the dented diner bar struck three in the morning.

"Or maybe you would rather have some raw fish and rice."

"Racist asshole," whispered Kai. She downed her fourth cup of coffee. "I am just not that hungry."

Mal picked up the last bite of syrup-dripping pancake and washed it down with coffee. He had already finished off a meat-filled omelet, six pieces of bacon and sausage, two pieces of buttered toast, three biscuits, three cups of orange juice, and at least one pot of coffee. "I didn't think a little stress would affect you so bad. I thought you CIA COG types were made of stiffer stuff."

"Kiss my ass."

Mal shot her a smirking, raised eyebrow.

"It has nothing to do with the action. You just can't grasp what's going on here. The magnitude of it all. There looks to be a deep-seeded conspiracy going on at the highest level of the US government and the President of the United States is sitting in a nasty diner talking to the most wanted man in America."

"Yep. And don't forget about garroting the Secret Service guy to death," Mal stood and tossed money on the table, a good tip included. "Stop focusing on the implications of it all and focus on what the hell you are going to do about it. What is the President of the USA going to do about evil people doing evil things?" He took a step and stopped in line with her and looked down. "I'm leaving for Voste's house in thirty minutes. Come join me or not. Just remember, inaction is still a choice." And with those last words, he left. Kai looked down at her plate of food.

"You look like shit, MK," said a voice. Kai looked up to see Anna slide into the seat that Mal just left minutes before.

"And you look like a high priced hooker," replied Kai, a surge of hunger washing over her as the weight of stress on her chest lightened at the sight of her friend. *Finally, someone to help and to trust.* She started piling food into her mouth. "I didn't know you would get the message, much less this fast."

Anna let out a small laugh, her bright blonde hair pulled back in a tight ponytail, her low-cut blouse, and skirt that did little to cover her panty line made her stand out like a beacon in the place. She placed her black leather clutch on the table. "Of course, I've been looking. I've been scouring all the old boards, posts, and dead drops an hour after you were taken."

"You know you could have dressed less conspicuous," Kai eyed her.

"No, I couldn't. That would've drawn attention to me. If I read your message right: danger, being watched, don't be followed, trust no one. First thing to draw attention to me would be changing my habits and in this part of town," she scanned the diner while snagging a piece of toast off Kai's plate. "This outfit is just fine." She took small mouse bites out of her stolen piece of toast before going on, the questions lingering in the air. "What the hell is going on here MK? What is this place? Why are we here? Why are we back to the days of secret spy shit? And most importantly, why the hell is the President of the United States of America in hiding?!"

Kai looked around the diner, pulling her ball cap lower. "Keep it down." She cleared her throat. "Things have gone dark, Anna. I mean real deep dark." In less than three minutes and in terse chopped whispers, Kai laid it all out for her: from the best she had seen in Malcolm Frostt, to the Secret Service team trying to kill her, to Duncan Voste, and the tracing of an untraceable CIA hacker site.

Anna summed up the entire story with a single word, "Fuck."

"Yeah," nodded Kai and took a sip of her coffee, her plate cleared of food.

"Where is this Frostt right now?"

"He's back at the hotel across the street prepping to make an assault on Voste."

"Let's go then. I gotta meet the stud who is making the infamous Kai swoon."

"I am not swooning," glared Kai.

Anna laughed and stood up. "Sure MK. It sounds like you have a little idol worshiping going on."

Kai stood, shaking her head, the pair left the diner. "No, don't you get it, Anna? He's not just good. I'm good. He, he is a ghost. He's the boogeyman we told the new recruits about."

"He can't be that good; everyone makes mistakes."

"He single handedly kidnapped me from a team of Secret Service agents using not much more than woodcraft. He broke into a senate office building in broad daylight with me in tow. He seems to always be a dozen steps ahead and just getting further the more info he finds."

"Yep, swooning; like I said."

"Kiss my ass," bit back Kai. "You probably would have tried screwing him by now in my place."

Anna nodded her head. "For sure. If he held still long enough, I would have been all over that."

"Whore."

"I call it fun," Anna smiled back. The pair left the dinner and crossed the street to the back of the motel. "What room is he in?"

"We're room eleven."

"*We,*" Anna shot a knowing glance at her. Kai only shook her head in response. "You two armed?" The pair walked into a covered breezeway; half its lights burned out.

"Not much. A pistol each and not enough ammo for sure," answered Kai, "Why?"

The question came at the same time the sound of silenced gunfire echoed into the breezeway. Not at them, but close around the corner, farther into the courtyard. Kai's hand moved to the small of her back, but stopped as a sharp click came from behind her.

Anna's voice came still full of her normal flirtatious tones. "Don't go for it. I know how fast you are. You even twitch and I will put a pair in your back." Before Kai could say anything, Anna went on. "Turn around slow. Put your hands straight into the air, elbows locked."

Kai turned as instructed, her hands pushed straight into the air, shock and confusion directed at her friend. "What the hell are you doing, Anna?" The sound of more silenced shots and several yells reached them.

Anna stood in a shooter's stance, purposely a half dozen paces back, a chrome single stack pistol in a shooters grip. "I said elbows locked. If any part of your arms lower or you take even the smallest step towards me, I will put one in your knee to start. And you know how good of a shot I am."

Kai's brain felt like mush, but she forced herself to focus. This could not be happening, but it was. Her best friend and closest confidante had her at gun point, a fight raging on the other side of the motel. "Anna, *not* you," Kai let the words hang as a statement and lingering question in the air.

"Sorry MK; you know how it is," Anna smiled.

"No, *I* really don't. I haven't betrayed you."

Anna nodded. "Fair enough. But you're a stuck-up self-righteous bitch. *Girl*, I want the good life. And man, the money I am getting will set me up on a nice beach, good house, great wine, and better dick for the rest of my life."

Kai heard footsteps behind her. Her mind raced through the possibilities. "You don't have to do this, Anna. We can find another way."

"Ha, like working my ass off for the next thirty years. I want to enjoy life while I still got the body to be enjoyed." She firmed up her stance. "Now twitch and I will put a hole in you." She then spoke to someone behind Kai. "She has a pistol at the small of her back. She is ambidextrous and can kill you with her hands. So, don't fuck around and don't get in my line of fire."

Kai could hear the footfalls of two men as they came up to the side of her. The shadows they cast showed both armored and carrying silenced MP5s. One submachine gun trained on her head, the second man lowered his weapon and reached for her arms. *It's going to be close,* she thought. *And man this is going to hurt.* She twisted toward the man who reached for her arms and at the same time, craned her body into a half moon, losing her balance on purpose to get her profile slimmer. A loud crack echoed in the space and a searing pain lanced into her leg, but she did not stop. The MP5 next to her head exploded the bullets coming within centimeters of her head; she felt the skin on the side of her face burn as the muzzle gases struck. Bits of concrete debris stung on the other side of her face as the bullets hammered into the wall.

Then it was over. Over for her opponents. Her hands were down and she stepped behind the MP5 shooter, causing him to interrupt Anna's line of fire and take her bullets. The second man fell backwards, already dead, his nose shoved into his brain. Kai fell with the armored shooter, a bullet to his head from Anna, and fired twice from behind her human shield before hitting the ground. Anna screamed in pain.

Kai pushed her armored meat-blanket off and sprang to her feet. A dashed sprint, then she kicked Anna's pistol away and stared down at her. Blood welled from Anna's messed up hand, at least one finger was gone and her left leg was covered in blood leaking from a hole in her thigh. Kai had her pistol pointed at her head.

"You okay," asked Mal, as he stepped up next to Kai. She had not heard him walk up. He had an MP5 in his hand and blood spattered most of his body.

"Yes, flesh wounds only."

Mal looked down at Anna, who glared back. Her bloody wounds had done nothing to quiet her fire.

"You both are dead," she spat. "You bitch! You destroyed my hand." She spat a wad of spit onto Kai's shoes.

"I am thinking of doing the same to your face so shut the hell up."

"Do it quick," said Mal, looking over his shoulder. "More are coming. I would say two minutes, three at the max until we are surrounded again."

Kai looked down at her friend, steel in her eyes, her voice even harder. "You have thirty seconds then. Tell me who paid you, who else is involved, and I might not put a bullet in your head."

Anna's face broken into a huge smile. "Couldn't if I wanted to, MK. Doesn't work like that with these types of people. Plus, a bullet to the head would be better than anything they will do to me, or heaven forbid, prison. Can you imagine this hot bod in prison? I would be fighting the dikes off with a stick."

"I can't believe I ever called you my friend," Kai leaned forward and repeated. "Last chance; tell me who else is involved."

"You know even after this, I still wish I had your rack. Damn you need to start using that body," smirked Anna. She went to continue but stopped as Kai kicked her in the face.

"Let's go," she turned to Mal.

He raised his eyebrow, questioning her.

She shook her head in response. "Let her deal with the fall out."

"Like hell you will," wheezed Anna through her broken nose.

A loud crack filled the space, and Anna fell back with a hole in her forehead. The thin throwing knife she had pulled from under her skirt fell away, clicking on the cracked concrete. Smoke rose from the end of Kai's pistol, like the ending fragments of a bad dream. Kai stared down at her friends ruined body, a pool of blood spreading away from her. A visceral rage born of fear and shock surged in her. The fragments of the dream trying to coalesce and crush her. And the antithesis of the latter, a cold and detached analytical review of the lifeless corpse in front of her, fought the waking dreaming.

Mal waited a full three seconds, a miraculous show of restraint and sensitivity for him, before prompting Kai to move. The pair wordlessly moved out, disappearing into the night.

Chapter 24

Two stolen cars later, a half dozen backtracks, a handful of miles on foot, and a small stint on a late-night public bus, Mal brought their latest stolen car, a nasty beige colored sedan, to a stop against the sidewalk. The car's brakes protested with the hard stop. Michaela let out a grunt as her seatbelt locked up.

"What the hell?" she snapped looking around for a threat she had not seen.

Mal slammed the car into park hard enough to rattle the entire dash and turned to face her. A murky, orange light from a street pole did little to light the darkness inside the car and only made the shadows worse. Mal's eyes were pools of arctic ice.

"What," snapped Michaela, her ire building. Mal did not respond. "Don't try the cold eye stare on me you bastard. What did you expect? Of course, I reached out to…" she could not bring herself to finish the sentence and say her best friend's name.

"I have put my life in your hands," spoke Mal, his normally calm voice verging on the edge of rage. "I have put the life of *my daughter* in your hands." His voice shook. He turned away from her and gripped the steering wheel. The wheel protested under the pressure of his twisting hands. "Either you are with me to see this all the way through or get the fuck out of the car."

Michaela took a page from Mal's book and did not respond; she only stared at the man sitting next to her. Minutes passed. A police car drove past; a few minutes later an early morning garbage truck.

"You are a real asshole, you know that." Michaela finally broke the silence. "I am not going to apologize for doing what I thought was best. So put the damn car in gear and let's go. I am in this until the end whether I want to or not." She did not break her stare. "But get this straight. I have every desire to help you get your daughter, but in the end, I have a larger duty to this country. A cancer has gotten into the government, all the way into the White House," Michaela grimaced like a bad taste coated her mouth. "I am going to do everything in my power to cut it out. Right now, our goals are aligned."

"And if they get out of alignment?" asked Mal, his normal detached calmness returning to his voice, though a hint of lethal challenge brushed the edges of his tone.

"We will cross that bridge when we come to it. If we come to it."

Mal turned back to her and the pair locked eyes. A palpable heat resonated in the car. "Understand that I could give a flying rat's ass about the country. My mission is my daughter and nothing else." The arctic ice in his eyes lessened by a visible force of will. "But, as you said, for now we are on the same path, so…fair enough." He put the car into gear and pulled back onto the street. A few more cars joined them, the predawn workers coming out onto the dark streets to start the day.

"So where to now?" asked Michaela, still not completely sure where the pair stood.

"Now we go talk to Voste," replied Mal, "He lives east of New York City, large house in Huntington Bay."

"When you say 'go talk' do you mean beat the piss out of him until he tells us what we want?" asked Michaela. Mal shrugged in response. "Yeah, I thought so."

"We need fuel," said Mal after a few minutes of silence. He pulled into an all-night gas station. "Fill her up, I'll go pay." He stepped out of the car, Michaela right behind.

"Get some food while you're at it." Michaela opened up the gas tank. "and don't just get Twinkies and soda. Get some real food."

"Stuck up health snob."

"Juvenile dickhead."

"Sure, I'll see what health food a gas station has," smirked Mal as he walked away, flipping her off over his head.

"Bastard," Michaela glared a hole into his back. A few seconds later the pump turned on; she could see Mal talking to the sleepy clerk and then step away to the food aisle. The gas pump clicked to a stop a few minutes later. Mal emerged from the store, three plastic bags laden with supplies in one hand.

He got into the driver's seat; Michaela joining on the other side. He handed over the bags. An assortment of junk food, soda, energy drinks, a box of crackers, and some off-brand green tea. A local paper topped it off. "Nice food," sneered Michaela, opening the paper.

"Hey, I got you some crackers and green tea."

She shook her head in disgust and opened the paper. Mal reached for a Twinkie. A car alarm sounded off behind them; both turned to check the scene and whipped back their attention to the driver side as a sharp click sounded through Mal's open window.

"If that Twinkie moves an inch, I will put a hole in your head," said Bert. Mal stared at him through the open window, the business end of a Sig Sauger P229 looking back into his face.

"Evening, Agent Renfield. Fancy seeing you here," replied Mal his eyes not paying the pistol any mind, only looking at Bert.

"Bert," exclaimed Michaela.

"Don't move; either of you," snapped Bert. "I am going to ask a few questions and I want straight, simple answers."

"What the hell, Bert," cracked back Michaela. "How much did they pay you to turn."

Bert's left eyebrow rose at her comment, but he went on undeterred with steel in his voice. "I just watched you, Madam President, shoot your Chief of Staff in the head. And then steal several different cars, and willingly go along with whom I presume is Mr. Archer, your kidnapper. Does that about sum up the last few hours?"

"Well, you are forgetting the eight-man strike team I killed at the hotel. And the two other members that the President killed," said Mal.

"Only one of those guys. Anna shot one in the head for me," quipped Michaela.

Mal heard the trigger of Bert's gun creak as he applied a fraction more pressure to it. "Madam President," whispered Bert, a whip like tension in his voice. "As of right now, I know that agents on my team tried to hurt you or even kill you. And that an FBI HRT did its best to fill you and Mr. Archer here full of holes. So, what is going on?"

"The name is Malcolm Frostt," said Mal calm as always, "and you really should lubricate the trigger assembly of that pistol. I can hear it rubbing. It will slow down your trigger pull and even lead to a stutter."

"Dammit, answer the question," Bert's eye unconsciously looked down at his gun as he went on. "What the hell is going..." He never finished his sentence stunned as the gun was pulled from his hands and now firmly in Mal's grip. The speed stunned Bert, his mind racing trying to replay the man's movement, but it was just too damn fast.

In full two seconds it took Bert to get his mind under control he faced Michaela out of the car, pistol in hand a bead on his chest. "Get in the car," he did not move. "That's a direct order." He shift then, his body moving out of trained habit more than anything.

Bert got in the back seat and Michaela took her seat again. Before he could say a word, Mal turned around in his seat and spun the stolen pistol around, its butt pointing at Bert. He took it back, looking even more deeply confused. Michaela, her own pistol holstered again, turned into her seat as Mal pulled the car onto the street.

The story that was told made Bert go pale. "That is not possible," he stuttered, his collected demeanor completely shattered. "Do you know what you're saying, Madam President?"

"I completely understand what it means," replied Kai. "It means that not only is there corruption at some of the highest points in our government, but that they are connected enough and powerful enough to not have an issue with killing the President of the United States."

Bert only nodded in return.

Mal smirked. "Thinking pretty highly of yourself, ain't ya."

Kai beat Bert to snapping at him. "Kiss my ass Bastard Boy. I am talking about the office of the president, not just me."

Mal quirked his eyebrow in mock agreement.

"So, you two intend to keep this small war going, drive up to *just talk* to Duncan Voste, and then what? Kill more people?"

"Yep," replied Mal in his normal monosyllabic style.

Kai turned in her seat to look at Bert. "What would you do, Bert? Go back to the White House and try to sort it out? Go public?" She stared at him. "The Chief of Staff, my best friend, just tried to kill me." She shook her head, wetness staining the edges of her eyes. "We need to know more. We need to find the head and cut it off. Then...then we go home and chop the rest into pieces." Her voice dripped with malice. Her voice smoothed out as she went on, "Bert, you do not have to come with us."

"Don't...Madam President."

"I mean it; this is not your duty..."

"Michaela, I said don't," snapped Bert. The sharpness of the rebuke startled Kai. "No matter what, Madam President, I am with you."

Kai nodded in response. She could feel a weight pulling off her chest.

"Well, ain't that just sappy and sweet," muttered Mal. He took the onramp onto I-95 and pushed his speed just below what would get him pulled over, "Let's get to it then. Time to do bad things."

Kai and Bert both looked at him not sure how to comprehend the enigma driving them into the unknown and more violence.

Chapter 25

"This place is a dump," breathed Andrew Otts, each word separated by a gasp for air. "The elevator doesn't even work." He shut the door behind him and look over the fifth-story apartment. Small and cramped, he could hear a train rumbling nearby and the smell of the street seeped in through the closed windows. He shrugged and took the two needed steps into the kitchen and dining space, old dishing filling the sink. He had screwed in worse places. "Hey! Is this your place or something?" he yelled out.

No response.

"Lulu, are you there?" he called out again. "I am good with using your place, but I don't think this means anything. I don't want you getting attached…well attached to part of me is good, but that's all, girl." He flashed his perfect smile even though no one was around to see it.

He heard a rustling noise coming from a door at the far side of the small apartment. "Down to business then," he whispered to himself, a smirk plastered on his face. He moved over to the door and opened it. "You ready for the Otts train?" he chuckled.

The chuckle died away in a choked grasp. Lulu lay on the bed, arms and legs spread out, her clothes torn and ripped open. Her dead eyes looked straight at him, blood soaking the pillow and half the bed. A gash that showed to the bone on her forehead was the source of the blood, though not the fatal wound. A deep purple and blue band of bruises streaked across her throat.

He took another step into the room, disbelief and a bile-lined panic rising in him. *I can't be here. Shi. Shit*, he thought. He took a deep breath, trying to calm himself, *Cash, yes. You always used cash with her. And no way anyone saw you come here,* he tried to convince himself. *You stupid bitch! You are not going to take me down for this.* He turned to leave and came up short as a piece of metal touched the side of his head.

"You shouldn't have kept records or lied to us, Andrew," spoke David Levi in his ever-present neutral tone.

"What…wait…you can'…."

Crack!

Andrew's head rocked away from the gun, the bullet carving a hole through his head and pulling half his skull and a large portion of his brain out onto the far wall. His body crumpled to the ground.

David stepped out from the shadows and stood over Otts's body, the smell of human feces and urine already filled the small room. He tossed the pistol next to the body, in the perfect placement. The whole room in fact was perfect. Murder suicide was what the police report would read. Otts prints were all over the place and on the girl, planted of course, even the gun was covered with them. Several fake text messages would be pulled from the deleted archives, that never truly go away, showing a much more perverted side of Otts and the poor hooker who didn't want anything more to do with his nasty fetishes.

David took one final look over the room before leaving, his eyes resting momentarily on the girl. She had real fire. He appreciated that when he worked. As they said, variety was the spice of life.

○ ○ ○

The smell of greasy fast food filled the small car; even the salt could be smelled in the air. "How in the hell can you two eat this shit?" Kai looked down at the half eaten burger on her lap, a nearly transparent bag of limp French Fries next to it, and a Styrofoam cup of soda in the passenger's cup holder.

Mal didn't respond, his face buried in his second burger. Bert spoke up from the back seat, suit tie long ago tossed on the seat next to him, "Food is food." He shoved another half dozen fries into his mouth.

"Yeah, I have had plenty of those times, but man, I would rather eat an expired MRE than this crap."

"Prissy bitch," said Mal through a mouthful.

"Inbred scruffy prick," snapped back Kai.

"Scruffy?" pseudo whined Mal, finishing his meal by licking his fingers clean.

"You two are meant for each other," Bert shook his head. He cleaned his face off with a sparse napkin. "So, we know diddly crap, well beyond the fact that Frosty here eats like a fat kid just home from fat camp."

The suburban street their car was parked on was manicured and tree lined. A little over a hundred yards away sat the entrance to a massive, immaculate mansion. The driveway of hand fitted stone led to a twelve-foot wrought iron gate, the hinges of which were mortared deep into an even taller stone wall. The wall disappeared out of sight, and they knew it wrapped the entire perimeter of the estate. Only a small portion of the front of the house was visible from where the group sat. A front door was surrounded by marble and stone, a portico stretched into the roundabout, and a stone fountain dominated the center of the circle drive.

"From what we saw on the drive around, the place is covered with CCTV and FLIR cameras, with both passive and active motion detection on top of the wall and, oh, let's not forget the alert guard at the front gate," said Bert. All three looked to the small but clearly reinforced guard booth to the right of the main gate. "We can assume that the security system within the grounds is just as intense and even more so in the house."

"We wait for now," said Kai. "We need more intel. Once Voste comes home, we can see what pattern he sets, and we can find the weak point."

"Great; more time sitting in the car," smirked Bert.

"Yeah, I am no good at waiting," breathed out Mal in a rush. He opened the door and stepped out, both Bert and Kai barking at him to get back in. "Don't worry," he responded. "I'm just going to take a walk. As you said we need more intel."

"Don't go and do anything stupid."

"Me…?"

"You kidnapped the President of the United States. I think stupid is your game," said Bert.

Mal raised a finger. "Successfully kidnapped the President of the United States, please."

Bert flipped him off.

Mal shut the door before Kai could pester him more; he knew she could not follow. His face was still unknown; hers was not. He pulled the collar of his jacket up a little higher to help with the light rain, the clouds were a patchy mix of leaden overcast, broken by chasms of pale blue.

Nearly thirty minutes later, Mal came to a quaint downtown area. The place looked picture perfect; even the trash cans on the sidewalk had been cleaned recently. He considered getting more food but decided against it.

The windows of the shops attracted people who tracked their net wealth, and the sidewalks were alive with people moving around. He saw a middle-aged man and a young girl in a stark white dress and her bright blonde hair in pigtails strolling down the sidewalk. The man stared down at his phone as he walked, the girl trying to get his attention. He batted her hand away. Mal looked at them both from across the street, his first wave of rage replaced in a lightning rush by a palpable sadness that nearly tripped him over his own feet. He could feel his heart racing in his chest and his breath came in short bursts. All he could hear was the singsong voice of a little girl spinning in the sunlight of their backyard, singing at the top of her lungs. The smell of his wife washing over him as she sat down next to him, two cups of fresh lemonade in hand.

The flash of memory fell apart in a practice drill of willpower, as he forced it away. "Focus. Move forward. Never stop," he muttered to himself. He shook the feeling off and had full control over his body again in a few steps. A passing truck caught his attention. A utility tool rack on its sides, a bank of caution lights on the cab rack, and two men wearing high visibility safety vest and hard hats sat in the cab.

An idea formed in Mal's head in a swift stroke. "Well, stupid is as stupid does," he whispered. He continued his walk down the street and soon came to what he was looking for. A mom and pops hardware store straight out of the 1950s, with even the cash register looking like it belonged in a museum.

"Howdy, son, need any help today?" said the old fella behind the counter. A full mop of gray hair and a canvas work apron on.

"You can point me to the hand tools, sir."

"Aisle seven," pointed the man. "Let me know if you need help with anything."

"Will do, thank you."

Mal walked the aisles of the old store, enjoying the collection of tools. He left the store sometime later, a large, canvas, waterproof, work bag filled to bursting. He turned in the direction the work truck had gone and set a brisk pace.

○ ○ ○

Kai and Bert had slipped into an uneasy silence over the last two hours. Early afternoon brought a few more cars on the side street. A white truck with the letters PSEG stenciled on its side and tailgate slowly passed and pulled to the curb halfway between them and Voste's house, blocking most of the view.

"Dammit," snapped Kai, "I can't see crap now."

"We should move," said Bert.

Kai shook her head. "No, we can't. If someone notices the same car parked in two different spots for long periods, it could create suspicion."

They both stared daggers at the workman getting out of the truck, pulling a bag from the truck bed and stepping over to a green power transformer box nestled between a pair of small dogwood trees, completely bare of leaves.

The workman turned and looked directly at the car Kai and Bert sat in, both cursed.

Mal smiled.

He turned his attention back to the transformer box in front of him. He quickly removed the front, his newly purchased canvas bag sitting next to him. The yellow hard hat he wore fit just fine, but the vest he was forced to take was several sizes too big. The two men he took the truck from, one being thin as a stick and the other giving a whale a run for its money did not give him options for a high-visibility safety vest.

With the front of the transform box removed, the hum of electricity grew louder. Mal could see the top and bottom edges of the transformer core. He removed the dead front cover exposing the entire core, plus the primary and secondary windings. The primary winding fed from street power and wrapped around one side of a rectangular steel block with a hole in the center. The secondary winding that headed off to feed several of the nearby houses wrapped the opposite of the steel core, the windings never touched. The core was built of multiple layers of silicone steel.

From the bag, Mal pulled a three-foot piece of wire. A four aught gauge wire of braided copper. He eyeballed the transformer core and cut the wire to length with a hacksaw and heavy-duty wire cutters. He crimped the ends of the wire to flatten it out and create more contact surface. He placed one end of the wire on the 120/240-volt house feed and dumped a bottle of fast-setting epoxy over it. Once set, he held it one handed with extreme care and from his pocket pulled out a small plastic block. He placed the plastic on the street windings, laying the wire onto it. The weight of the wire held the plastic block in place.

The electrical humming filled Mal's ears, but he ignored it, moving briskly, humming his own tune. Next, he carefully placed a kitchen egg timer, one that popped up when the time ended, next to the plastic block. He used a few pieces of tape to secure the egg timer and stood. He looked at his work, feeling very satisfied with himself.

"Let's fry some shit," he said. The last thing he did was use insulated heavy wire cutters to break the wire connected to the grounding rod of the transformer box. He didn't bother putting the dead front back on, but tossed it in the back of the truck and put the face back onto the transformer.

The white truck slowly passed Kai and Bert, Mal waving to them. She flipped him off. Five minutes later he opened the driver's door of the sedan and sat down next to the pissed off Kai and Bert.

"What the hell are you doing?" snapped Kai.

"Something stupid," replied Mal coolly. He looked at his watch, "And five, four, three, two, one." With the last number he looked down and shielded his eyes with his hand. Kai did the same. Bert did not and let out a string of curses when a flash of light nearly blinded him. A deafening, crackling roar exploded from the transformer box. The torrent of arcing electricity lasted for three seconds, then died down in an instant to a smoldering, sparking mess. Both dwarf dogwood trees had burst into flames. Even the surrounding asphalt two feet out from the transformer had turned liquid and started bubbling.

"What the hell was that?," half-yelled Bert, rubbing at his eyes, white starts dancing around his vision.

"That, my cranky friends, is how you fry a state-of-the-art security system," smiled Mal. He pointed to the guard booth. The guard stumbled out of the booth, staring at the burnt transformer, a wisp of smoke coming from his booth. They could see at least one camera with the faintest hint of smoke leaking from it. "I linked the street feed across the step-down core. About 8000 volts, give or take a few, straight into the house feed. Cut the ground too, so there was only one path for the current to travel. Probably burnt the piss out of Voste's main panel and anything connected to it. And the other few houses connected to the same feed." He shrugged off the last part.

"That could have fried you," said Kai.

"Yeah, my personality is too electric for that."

Kai snorted a laugh.

"Now we just have to hope that the house doesn't light on fire and wait for Voste to show."

"Fire?"

"Well, yeah," nodded Mal. "That was a lot of damn power. You do know how electricity works, right?'

"Kiss my ass."

He winked at Kai.
She mimed puking on him.
Bert rolled his eyes.

Chapter 26

A pair of real PSEG trucks showed up within the hour and the three did not have to wait long after that for Voste. Twilight just started brushing the sky when Voste pulled into his driveway, his Aston Martin One-77 gleaming white in the setting sun.

Bert and Mal whistled at the car.

"Men," Kai rolled her eyes.

"Rather have a purse, eh?" prodded Mal.

"No. A gun."

Mal nodded his head in approval.

Voste stepped from his car and started speaking with the guard. From his many hand gestures it was clear the guard was taking a heap of blame for the power surge. Soon Voste left the guard to sulk back into the booth while he walked down the street to the now three power company trucks surrounding the transformer. More hand gestures also made it clear what Voste's words were, not to mention the bird he flipped at what looked to be the lead worker as he walked away. Voste's guard had to manually open the front gate, Voste revving the engine of his Aston Martin, laying on the horn when the guard paused to catch his breath, heaving on the massive gate.

He drove through quickly and the guard much, much slower, closed the gate, shaking his head.

"Okay, phase two," said Mal starting the car and pulling them onto the street.

"Do you mind sharing this elaborate plan with us? Phase two is?" prompted Kai.

"Sure. We go get the work truck. I got a rattle can of white paint to cover up the PSEG markings. We drive up to the front gate, talk or punch our way in, and then we go talk with Voste before he leaves again. I doubt he will stay the night with his house full of crispy electronics."

"That…that plan sucks," muttered Bert.

"Yeah, it really does," nodded Kai. "Do you pull this all out of your ass on the fly?"

"More or less, but we are kind of in fly-by-your-crotch mode." Kai wrinkled her brow at him. Mal went on. "But you give me a month or two and I can make a plan good enough to kidnap the President and kick the Secret Service's ass."

"I'm going to shoot you," said Bert.

Mal shrugged.

A short drive brought them to the work truck Mal had, in his words, "borrowed" from the workers. A short argument started up with both Bert and Mal agreeing that Kai should hide in the bed of the truck under a tarp. Kai protested, but lost before the argument went anywhere. Her face was too recognizable. And the last thing they needed was for someone to see the President of the United States riding shotgun in a random work truck.

○ ○ ○

By the time dusk had rolled in fully, a white truck with barely dried paint, rolled up to the front gate of the Duncan Voste estate. The guard stepped up to the passenger window, Bert rolled it down.

"Evening. We're here to look at the electrical damage to Mr. Voste's house."

The guard shined his light into the cab and quickly over the bed of the truck, the blue tarp in the back reflecting the light. "Who you with?"

"Huntington Electric. Mr. Voste called us, told us there was some mass power surge that trashed everything or something like that."

"Yeah, transformer down the street blew. Like a freaking blow torch. You guys responded fast." He didn't say that last part as a question, but it had the faint tone of being open-ended.

"Yeah, the shop said Mr. Voste was in a little bit of a rush. Rich people, you know."

"I sure do," the guard panned the cab once again with his light, the flashlight beam lingering for the briefest of seconds on Bert's dress shirt under his safety vest.

The guard switched his flashlight to his left hand and let his right-hand fall to his side and out of sight. "So, just electricians. You got a work order? Any paperwork?

Bert opened his mouth to respond, but Mal leaned over and cut him off. "Nope, not really. But we do mean to break into Voste's place, steal some stuff, beat the shit out of him, and ask some pointed questions. Not necessarily in that order though."

The guard just stared at them speechless. So did Bert, a look of shock and rage painted on his face.

"Oh, and sorry. I fried the transformer box. It was pretty cool looking though," nodded Mal like a little boy.

The guard blinked rapidly. "Okay, then. Your paperwork looks in order." He smiled, "Good luck on your work." He stepped away and went to push the front gate open with much more gusto than before.

Mal put the truck in drive and rolled forward. Bert just stared at him, unsure what to think of the man sitting next to him. Mal parked the truck under the terrace, lights glimmered through a few windows. The hum of the generator added to the natural evening sounds.

"You got some balls of steel you know that," said Kai as she stood up in the back of the truck.

"What? Voste is an ass. I took a chance the guard hates him. Not a huge stretch."

"So, now what, hot shot?" asked Bert, tossing his safety vest into the truck.

"Knock and see who's home," replied Mal, merrily taking the front steps two at a time. He hammered his fist on the front door. Kai and Bert moved up next to him, both scanning the area for threats. The front door opened a few minutes later. A middle-aged man in a classic butler uniform opened the front door.

His face betrayed no reaction to seeing three strangers standing in front of him. "Can I help you?" Even his voice had the typical English butler accent to it.

"Yeah we're looking for Voste Man. He still home?" said Mal, a stupid smile painted on his face.

"Is he expecting you? And may I ask your business with *Mr. Voste*?"

"Of course," smiled Mal. "We are here to fuck up his life." The butler barely even saw the fist before he blacked out. Mal stepped forward before the man could collapse and let him slowly to the floor.

"That was subtle," Bert shook his head. "Dumbass." He looked around the marble and gold leafed foyer. "So now how do we find Duncan in a house the size of a small town?"

Mal waved him off. "That's easy." He pointed to an emergency light on the floor; a black cable ran off it and disappeared through a door. "Just follow the power cords from the generator to the lights. I bet Voste has most of them where he's at."

Kai nodded her head and the three set out. A few minutes later, the maze of power lines led them to a large room at the back of the manor. Windows and exotic hardwoods dominated the space. The entire back wall was made of glass and could be opened onto a Japanese garden.

The room shone with emergency lights placed all around and even a portable heater had been powered up to keep the temperature up as night came. A dozen wooden pedestals and a single large table in the center of the room were the only furniture in the space.

Duncan Voste sat on a thick oak chair and leaned over an oak bonsai tree; several soft white lights pointed at it. He wore a large deep violet robe and a thick pair of glasses. He held a handmade pair of Sasuke scissors and a wooden tray which held more custom-made Japanese bonsai tools. He spoke without taking his eyes off the delicate cut he was preforming to the small tree. "Leonel, who was at the door? I hope it was the damn power company with an update."

"Not exactly," spoke out Mal. His voice echoed softly in the sparse room.

Voste turned in his chair, his thick glasses making his face look like an ancient and wrinkled bug. "Who the hell are you?" he snapped. "Where is Leonel?"

"Mr. Voste, that is a question I have been asking him for the last three days and trust me you will get no satisfactory answer," said Michaela as she walked out into the room.

"What is the matter, Duncan? Looks like you've seen a ghost," smiled Mal. He stepped forward while Bert covered him and bound Voste's hands and legs to the chair. He moved away again.

"It's not every day the President of the United States walks into your...whatever this place is," said Bert standing sentry at the doorway. Pistol drawn, scanning the room.

"It is a showroom," Michaela looked around the space again, each pedestal held a perfectly shaped bonsai tree on it. All but one, that being the young one on the worktable next to Voste.

Voste straighten in his chair. "Much more than a showroom. A room of peace... Madam President." He turned to look directly at Mal. "Though I am guessing that peace is about to be shattered."

"Mmm yup," muttered Mal. He took several calming breaths to ease his rage. Voste needed to live long enough to talk, just long enough. He took a step forward and pulled a black five inch, double edged, fixed-blade knife. He tilted his head and stared into Voste's eyes. "It's a simple proposition. You talk and you can keep your old, pudgy body intact."

Voste shook his head, not the motion of a man asking for it to all stop, but a movement of disappointment. "I don't know what you want, but it does not matter. There is nothing you could do to me."

Mal stepped closer to Voste. "You are going to tell me where my daughter is, or I will peel you apart piece by piece."

"Madam President," Bert interjected.

"Go wait outside if you don't have the stomach for it," snapped Mal. "This piece of shit will talk. They always do."

"Madam President, we can't do this!" hissed Bert. "This is not right."

"Right!" screamed Mal. He whipped back and pointed his knife at Voste, still sitting in his chair, the picture of calm. "He knows where my daughter is or knows who knows."

Kai could see Bert's eyes now focused more on Mal and his knife than anything else. His grip on his pistol grew more intense. "Bert, stand down." Before he could contest, she added, "That's a direct order." Kai walked up to Voste and leaned close; she could hear Bert take several more steps into the room. She said in a soft, but clear voice, "Mr. Voste. Let's not pretend that you know nothing. We would not be here if that were the case. In the last twenty-four hours I have had more people than I can count try to kill me. My closest and best friend tried to put a bullet in my head." She leaned to within an inch of his face, their eyes locked. Her voice took on a slow venom. "I want to know what is going on and who is involved. And this man," she nodded over to Mal, only a few paces away. "Will stop at nothing to get the info he needs to find his daughter. So, do we have an understanding, Mr. Voste?"

She continued to look into his eyes. He had barely moved during her talk and his eyes looked calm and collected. She stepped back; a new stress born in the pit of her stomach. "You are not going to talk, are you?"

Voste shook his head slowly and let out a soft laugh. "No, I am not. I applaud your tenacity; and you, sir," he stared at Mal. "Are the epitome of the unexpected. My own personal albatross."

"You will change your tone once we get going," smirked Mal. He moved up within a single step of Voste.

Voste shook his head in a show of pity for Mal. "No. I will not. Because there is nothing you can do to me that would even compare to what *they* would do to me. I am disappointed for it all to end, but I would rather go out like this than at the hands of them."

"Who are *they*?" asked Kai.

Voste sat and looked up at all of them as if he was the one with the upper hand. "You don't understand and truly are not capable of doing so." He tried to smooth the folds of his robe, but his bound hands stopped him. "I am but the tip of it." He looked at each of them in turn "You can work me over for the whole night, peel me apart as you so tastelessly put it. It changes nothing. The people, the group that is above me, could and would keep me alive for years. And have methods of pain that not even your sick little group could understand."

"He is telling the truth," stated Kai. "He won't talk. And we don't have unlimited time here."

The crack of Mal's fist smashing into Voste's face echoed dully in the wood paneled room. He tossed the knife with a flick of the wrist into the wood floor and landed a half dozen punches into Voste's face. He pulled back, blood leaking from lips, nose, and a split on the old man's cheek.

Voste spat out blood and laughed, which turned into a cough as he started talking. "It is pointless. You three are dead and just don't know it yet. I don't give a rat's ass that you are the President, but you will make a *great, dead* President. I have no doubt they have large plans for that."

Kai stood a dozen feet away, her mind racing. Voste was the last of their leads and each time *they* caught up with one, they were coming closer and closer to getting killed. *This is never going to work. Mal can pull that man apart and nothing will come of it. Mal is nothing like I have ever seen, but sometimes it does not matter how strong or downright fucking crazy you are.* She looked around the room. It stood in such dramatic contrast to the man that Mal continued to work over. Bert had a look of cold stone on his face. She could see the whole room had been designed around the simple idea of minimalism and the complex art of bonsai. Then it struck her like an icy slap to the face. She took three quick steps over to the nearest pedestal and bonsai tree. A miniature oak, a beautifully shaped twist in the trunk. The black glaze pot had been stenciled with sand garden swirls.

She pushed it off the stand. The noise cascaded around the room. Bert and Mal both snapped to the noise, but Voste nearly tipped off his chair with a start. She smiled staring straight into Voste's eyes.

She stepped over to the next bonsai tree. A diminutive apple tree, the barest of a fresh apple bud showing on the single branch. She raised her hand to the ivory colored pot.

"No, don…" stuttered Voste, chopping off the sentence halfway through, a true look of panicked terror on his face.

"Well slap me silly and drop me in a bucket," laughed Mal. Bert shot him a confused look. "Guess it's time to do some tree killing."

"My grandfather had a bonsai tree when I was a kid," said Kai. "I remember visiting and looking at it. A beautiful tree. Nothing like the pieces of art you have here, but a good tree none the less. Sometimes my grandmother would joke that he paid more attention to that little tree than her." She looked back at the apple tree. "I have no doubt that my grandfather loved that tree. Loved it like a child." She didn't look back at Voste. "So Duncan. Start talking or I will kill every plant in this place."

"It doesn't matter. Still nothing you can do to me. Just kill me and get it over with," snapped Voste, but all three could see a line of sweat had formed on his brow, mixing with the blood.

Kai pushed the small apple tree to the ground, it smashed with a crack. She followed it up by grinding her boot into the tree, pulping it against the hard floor.

Mal could see the smallest of facial tics on Voste as he watched his eyes betrayed him. Mal pulled his knife out of the floor and walked over to the largest piece in the room. It had the lowest but widest pedestal. The tree stood nearly six-feet tall and had a trunk roughly two feet thick. The leaves formed a flat canopy above the red and brown trunk. He pointed his knife at the tree. "Hey Vossey, what type is this? It's kind of big for a bonsai tree."

Voste cleared his throat doing his best to talk normal. "It is a Sawara Japanese Cypress. It has been handed down from bonsai master to master. It's centuries old. It's a priceless piece of art. It…"

Voste stopped speaking as a thin branch fell from the tree, Mal's knife moving in a blur. "Oops," murmured Mal. "My bad." He nodded his head, "Just twitchy, you know." He stared at Voste and moved his knife hand closer to the tree.

"Don't," half barked, half begged, Voste.

"Talk," replied Mal coolly.

"That is a priceless piece of art. It's 432 years old," tears filled the edges of Voste's eyes.

Mal's knife flashed again, and a half inch deep gouge appeared across the entire face of the trunk. "Then tell me where my daughter is and answer Michaela. Or I swear I will peel the bark off this tree and wipe my ass with it."

"You know that will really hurt," spoke out Bert. "that bark is rough as hell."

Mal looked at the tree and then at Bert and then back at the tree. He raised one finger. "Okay, I didn't think that one through. Talk or I will peel the bark off and wipe your ass with it," he said to Voste.

Bert nodded approval.

"You are all going to die. When they catch you, you will all wish you were never born!" screamed Voste.

Mal took another limb off the ancient tree. Voste's tears had started flowing in earnest. Mal carved a crude image of a penis and balls into the trunk of the tree. Voste bucked against his bonds, nearly toppling over the heavy chair. His face had gone an epileptic crimson.

Kai rolled her eyes. "Real mature." She stepped over to Voste and slapped the man hard across the face. He turned to look back at her. Snot, tears, and blood rolled down his face. "I want names. I want the depth and breadth of how far this thing reaches."

Voste didn't respond. Mal went to work. Within minutes the tree had been reduced to a few spindly branches and an oversized penis carving. He pulled a zippo out of his pocket and looked over to Voste.

Kai stared down at Voste, he shook his head back and forth. *Leverage*, Kai thought. *It comes down to the proper leverage applied in the proper way. We are under his skin, but not deep enough. What brings a man to love these trees with such intensity?* It then hit Kai like a hammer. These trees were Voste's kids. He had never married and had no children. He dealt in murder and other countless crimes. This is the one place he could craft and, more importantly, foster life. She scanned the place again. The architecture of the place was awe inspiring in its simple lines and yet deep feeling of timelessness. The placement of several windows and skylights caught her attention. They were positioned to let in the most light not onto what seemed to be the prize of the room, the tree Mal had just desecrated. It fell onto a small pine tree against the south wall. Even the walls seemed to all point to it, like the whole room had been built to support this one single tree.

She walked over to it. The tree's roots wrapped around several rocks and disappeared into the dark soil of the charcoal vase it was potted in. A small, twisted canopy move away from the bent trunk in an mesmerizing way. A sudden quiet fell over the room. She turned to see Voste staring at her; his sobs gone.

"What is it?"

"A Japanese Black Pine," whispered Voste.

"It's your favorite." She paused for a moment and looked between the fine tree and the broken man. "No, not just your favorite. It was your first, was it not?"

Voste barely nodded his head in acknowledgment of the question.

"Well, hot damn," snapped Mal. "Let's get burning."

Kai raised her hand to stop Mal. She stared at Voste. "How long have you had it?"

His words sounded dead and nearly impossible to hear. "Forty-two years. My fiancée gave it to me a month before she was killed in a car accident."

She stepped over to Voste and matched his soft tone. "Tell us what we want, and I promise I will make sure someone finds it and cares for it."

He looked at her for over a minute and then dropped his head. "I don't know who they are. Really." Kai had to stop Mal from butting in. Voste went on. "That is how it works. I have websites and phone numbers to call to report, but it all changes. Scrambled numbers, masked IPs, no names, not even real voices. All I know is they are very powerful and international."

"You don't have to guess who they are," growled Mal. "That is hard to believe. You've never dug into them?"

"Of course, I did," snapped back Voste. "These are not the type of people who leave traces. All I ever found out is they are imbedded everywhere. They have real power, not some pseudo in the public-light power like you have. These people don't even hate the light, they control it. Focus it away from them to remain where the real power lies, in darkness and shadow," he whispered the last.

Kai butted in, "What was your role then in their plans?"

"It started over thirty years ago. It was small at first, price control on a new pharmaceutical, buy out a certain company, fake test results. The money that came in was good; it helped me grow the company bigger and bigger. Soon, it turned into money laundering."

Mal snorted, "You're a cleaner?"

"I'm businessman, nothing more."

Kai held her hand up to stop Mal once again. "Get on with it," she said.

"We already owned Andrew Otts by then. He worked in the IRS. It was easy with his help to funnel in fake taxes and dozens of other funds into the IRS and then back out as clean as could be. Soon, he became IRS director, and then onto the Senate. With each step he brought new ways to filter the money. It took us from managing only a few hundred-million a year to near a two hundred-and-fifty-billion this last year."

"You are shitting me," spoke up Bert. "That would be noticed."

"America is over twenty trillion in debt and has one of the most complicated tax codes in the world. No one is paying attention," said Voste.

"And my daughter?" asked Mal, a viper like tension in his voice.

Voste became even more uncomfortable. "Intulus Investments owns a hundred smaller companies and dozens of others we are silent partners in. We were approached to create a new drug. One that could target specific groups of DNA."

Kai blinked several times and nearly stuttered, "You created a DNA bio-weapon?"

"No, not quite. The drug can only target groups of DNA, such as the tags that create blue eyes or blonde hair. And it does not do anything by itself. It is only a carrier. Another drug or virus has to be attached to it."

"Why?" asked Kai, her heart rising into her throat.

"To slowly affect the world population. We have hidden anti-fertility, cancer carcinogenic, cardiovascular constrictors, and dozens of others."

"Why the hell would anyone want to do that," questioned Bert.

"Eugenics," whispered Kai.

"Who is the target group?" asked Mal.

"I don't know. The DNA code was given to us…"

Voste jumped in his seat, the bonds making the chair buck, as Mal kicked over the nearest bonsai tree. The entire pedestal ripped from the floor with his massive kick. He bellowed, "Bullshit, who?!"

"Everyone for the most part, yes…yes. I had the DNA sequenced to find out. It focuses predominately on non-Aryan races and anyone with a genetic disorder. It is slow working."

Kai felt like she had just gotten gut punched.

She could tell it had hit Mal hard as well as he whispered, "Where is my daughter? What does she have to do with any of your schemes?" He stepped forward and pulled the photo of his wife and daughter out of his pocket and thrust it into Voste's face. "Your man David put a bullet in my wife's head and took my daughter. He said 'they would take good care of her.' That was before he put two rounds into my chest."

Kai looked at Mal in shock and anger. *That jackass, still hiding info. Like breathing for him,* she thought.

"I don't deal with that portion of the project, but if David took her then most likely it means she is one of the donors."

Mal leaned in and with a voice so cold the room dropped a few degrees said, "You start making sense and talking it all out or I am going over to your child tree," he pointed with his knife to the Japanese Black Pine, "and piss all over it. Then I am going to feed it to you piece by piece."

Voste nodded his head vigorously, more because of the tone of Mal's voice than the threat. "Your daughter must have the enzyme we need. It is a key component in the drug. It is what allows us to attach the secondary virus to the DNA specific group and more importantly, it is what hides the drug. It metabolizes in a person's system in a way that masks it. We can't synthesize it, we've tried. It was the key breakthrough. The mutated enzyme shows up in about a quarter-percent of the world's population and is very hard to detect." Voste let his head fall down until his chin hit his chest. "We have access to hundreds of medical databases. When we find the enzyme, we take measures to make sure we can access it."

"Access it," snapped Kai. "You kidnapped a child and killed her mother for it."

"The mutated enzyme only shows up in children; puberty always changes it."

"You are one sick bastard," said Kai.

"Then my daughter is still alive? You need her to harvest this enzyme. Where is she," the coldness had not left Mal's voice.

"A warehouse in Pittsburg. Just north of the city in an old manufacturing area." He gave them the address.

"Then I got what I need," Mal stepped forward and grabbed a handful of Voste's hair and tugged his head up.

"Wait," barked out Bert. "We can't just kill him," he looked between Kai and Mal. "We have him and a confession let's take him in."

"Are you stupid?" laughed Mal, not a lick of humor in the noise. "Confession! You heard what he said, this goes way beyond him. Do you really think he would face a trial, much less get punished?"

"Madam President," said Bert looking to Kai for guidance.

"Mal…we…we can't stoop to what they are," whispered Kai, little conviction in her voice.

Mal looked at her for a brief second then back to Voste, their eyes locking. "Oh, Madam President, I am already *below* their level." He drove his knife up through the bottom of Voste's jaw, the knife breaking through his mouth and into his brain with ease, cracking bone. Mal never broke eye contact until the light faded from the old man's eyes.

He pulled the blade free and wiped it on Voste's robes. He turned to Kai, then looked at Bert. "Don't be a hypocrite; it doesn't go with that sexy ass of yours… Madam President." He sheathed his knife, "How many people did you kill during your CIA days? How many defenseless people did you murder? And now you're the one giving the orders to kill, so don't stand on a high horse with me."

"And you too, Berty, you dumb ass, smoke stained old man." He looked down at the limp, bleeding man in the chair. "Now, I am headed to Pittsburg to do more killing. So, I think it's time we part. Bert can take the little lady back in and be the hero." With that he walked out of the room.

Kai followed, after grabbing the black pine bonsai tree. Bert followed as well. Mal detoured into the kitchen and a moment later reappeared with two bottles of high proof liquor. He took a drag off the dark brown one, and then let both bottles spill out onto the long hallway towards the front entrance. The butler still lay on the floor next to the main door, but he had started to stir awake. Bert put a stop to that with a boot to the man's face.

Mal looked at him and shrugged in approval. They pulled the butler out onto the lawn and placed the precious bonsai tree next to him. Mal retrieved a road flare from a work box on the truck and tossed the lit flare into the house. A whoosh of fire followed, and the open front door fanned the flames of the main hall into a mini blast furnace.

Chapter 27

"Man, getting to burn two things today. Kick ass," smirked Mal, a lit road flare in his hand, the work truck a few steps in front of him, soaked down with gas. Michaela and Bert stood another several paces back. Mal tossed the flare and turned, striking a pose as the fireball lit up behind him.

Michaela shook her head, "Dumb ass." Though part of her had to admit it did look cool.

"Are you headed straight for Pittsburgh?" asked Michaela, more of a statement than a question.

"Nothing in the world will stop me," replied Mal.

"I have no doubt of that."

Bert dropped his cigarette to the ground with a curse and pocketed his phone, which he had been scrolling. "Senator Otts is dead. Meyers texted me. They found him about an hour ago. First look is murder suicide. He was found at some hooker's place. Hooker was choked to death and self-inflicted gunshot to Otts."

"Yeah, sure," said Michaela. "They are tying up loose ends."

"We should be going, ma'am," Bert said, changing the subject. He looked around the area. A dirt lot, with a few cars, some burned out. The overpass above was painted with the fire light from the truck. New York City, fully dark and fully alive.

Michaela didn't answer, she stood still looking at Mal. Her entire body ached from the lack of sleep, constant danger, and the stress of the last few days. She just wanted to fall into bed and sleep for a week. Part of her knew she never could and that small part of her had always been the strongest voice in her, pushing her forward.

She shook her head, still only looking at Mal. "No. I'm going to Pittsburg." Both Mal's and Bert's eyebrows rose at the statement.

"Madam, you can't do that," said Bert firmly. "We need to get you to safety. Frosty here has the info he needs, and you need to focus on the bigger picture of sorting out the group behind all of this."

"No, I am going to see this through. All the way," said Michaela turning to face Bert. She could see a twitch next to his left eye.

"Madam *President*," he nearly hissed. "You can't go off and put your life in danger just for one little girl. No offense," he nodded to Mal.

"Nah, don't worry about it. I know you're a heartless dick," replied Mal.

"If a little girl is not worth risking my life for, then what is? And beyond that Bert, we can't let them continue to create this drug." Bert looked like he might snap with tension. Michaela went on, "I am going; and you are going back to D.C."

"Oh, like hell. I am not letting you out of my sight. Dammit Michaela, you have a duty as the President of the United States to keep yourself safe."

Michaela's voice broke over his in a crack of anger. "I know exactly what my *duty* is, Agent Renfield. And I will follow it through, no matter what your opinion is." Bert took a step back at the brisk dressing down. She went on, still firm, but with a smoother tone. "Bert, I need you back in D.C. Voste's death is going to come out soon. We barely left there an hour ago. I need you back in D.C. poking around. The next twenty-four hours will be the best to find the people behind this as they scramble to tie up loose ends and do damage control. So, do what you do best, and dig. Like tracking me down, hit the ground and don't let up."

Bert just looked at Michaela not saying a word. Mal broke the brief silence. "We really do need to go." He pointed with his thumb beyond his head, "That fire will be drawing some attention. Not even the amazing NYPD can ignore it."

"Bert, I could order you, but I think we are kind of beyond that at this point," said Michaela. "I need to see this through."

Bert nodded and spoke brusquely. "Twenty-four hours. That's it. If I don't hear from you, I go to the news outlets and break the whole thing. Not that anyone will believe me," he finished shaking his head.

Michaela put her hand out and the two shook. "Good luck then and keep an eye out."

"And you, too. Good hunting."

Bert turned to Mal. "I ain't shaking your hand, man. You're still a dick," said Mal.

A smile tried but failed to come to Bert's lips. "Yeah and you are still a dumb ass. Keep her safe and stay Frosty."

Less than two minutes later, Michaela and Mal were driving away in a freshly stolen car.

"We should make it to Pittsburg about four-am, give or take a little," said Michaela from the passenger seat.

"We have to make a stop first. We need supplies."

Michaela nodded.

A few minutes passed; the New York City streets were busy with the early night life. A new portion of the city just coming out. "Why did you come?" asked Mal.

Michaela continued looking out the window, chewing her bottom lip. Mal had nearly put the question out of mind when she finally answered. "Sometimes duty is not about doing the right thing but about doing the thing that needs doing, no matter how dirty it might be."

Mal nodded and the pair lapsed again into silence. Another thirty minutes brought them to a storage and junkyard on the east-side of the Bronx. A locked gate greeted them, the sound of barking dogs in the distance, a single grim covered streetlight illuminated the gate. The lock fell away with ease under Mal's makeshift lock picks.

The broken asphalt and potholes filled with gravel crunched under their wheels as they slowly rolled down the main drag of the yard. A dozen pole lights stood sentinel in the space, only four of them giving light to the junk and shipping containers dotting the yard. Mal brought the car to a stop and peered out of his window into the near complete darkness, the three-quarter moon giving more light than the grimy pole lights.

"What are we doing here?" No answer. "Hey, Bastard Boy, whatcha looking for?"

"Let's go," said Mal. Turning the car off and stepping out. "Grab the flashlight, but don't turn it on yet."

Michaela shook her head, snagged the light, and followed. Mal walked off into the center of the yard. Paths and alleyways created by the stacked containers, smashed cars, and mounds of assorted junk. He continued to walk, even backtracking several times, then stopping and looking at a blank piece of steel or rusted container with only the shadowed moonlight guiding him.

"Just what a girl wants, a moonlit walk through a dirty junkyard."

"Stuck up snob."

"Redneck asshole."

After twenty minutes of walking the yard Mal came to an abrupt stop in front of a rusted shipping container, a stack of crushed cars on top of it. He stared at the door of the container for a whole minute.

"Light," he held out his hand.

The flashlight flared to life, exposing a pale-blue painted shipping container, more rust than metal. Mal continued staring at it for another minute, then confusing Michaela even more, he walked around the container for several minutes. Even more irritatingly, Mal next spent over five minutes looking and gently running fingers over the front door. He ignored her few attempts to ask what was going on.

"Got ya," he whispered finally, pulling his knife out and wedging it into a rusted seam in the door. He pulled up and then stepped over the main handle and grabbed the lock, a massive hunk of iron with a spin lock holding the door shut. He spun in a code and popped the lock off, the door opening surprisingly smooth for the amount of rust that fell off the hinges.

The light shined into the musty space. "Oh, wow," said Michaela. "Just what we need, dusty, big breasted mannequins." She stepped forward into the space, but stopped with a grunt, held back by Mal's iron muscled arm. He shined his light down a half-foot in front of her. It took less than a second and she saw it. A thin gossamer silver thread. It stretched the width of the space.

"Didn't they teach you better at the CIA of yours?" mocked Mal. He kneeled down, and a few seconds later, rolled up the silver thread, his light falling on the container wall. Facing them, where the thread led into, was a dark green box five inches tall, an inch and half thick, and eight and half inches long. The letters 'Front Towards Enemy' were visible.

"Yeah, they did. Though it's not like I was expecting a freaking claymore."

"That will get you killed then. Always expect it."

"And how is that working for you? Keeping you well-adjusted and happy?"

"Nope, just alive."

Mal moved into the space, pushing the naked and truly large bosomed, mannequins out of his way. He went to the end of the container and started running his hand on the back wall.

"Come on, what the hell are we doing here and what the hell are you looking for now? A hidden bazooka?" said Michaela.

"Just the door handle," he replied as his hand found what he was searching for. Several clicks followed as he pulled hard. The center of the back wall swung open, a wall of pitch dark on the other side. Mal stepped in and florescent lights flickered on with a hum, revealing the hidden room.

Michaela followed, her mouth wide open.

"I know," smiled Mal, looking like a little kid. "It's beautiful."

The small space measured twelve feet long and eight feet wide. The center of the room had a small metal table with task lights, a vice, and tool organized on it. The rest of the space, the walls, racks hung from the ceiling, and piled under the table were guns. A lot of guns.

"All the supplies a fighting man…or woman," he nodded to Michaela, "would need. Well, a small army in fact."

He started moving around the space, opening lockers, exposing tactical clothes and body armor.

"*Who* the hell are *you*?" Michaela watched as Mal started making piles of gear on the table.

Mal stopped and looked up at her for a long second. He abruptly went back to work, but spoke a second later. "My father taught me most of what I know. His name is Victor Frostt." He paused for a moment looking away from Michaela so she could not see him cringe at saying the name and took a deep breath. "As in Major 'Viper' Frostt."

Michaela's eyes went wide, "Shit."

"Yeah, that just about sums it up."

"Your father is Major Viper?"

"Need your hearing checked, aye?"

"He is a *legend* in the special forces and Delta groups. I had to learn tactics he created before I joined the COG team. His work in Bosnia and Desert Storm was ground breaking.

"Yep. Great soldier," he turned to face her. "Great dad…not so much. But I learned a skill. And now it's time to put that to some good use." He field stripped the FN M4A1 carbine he had just pulled out of a wall rack.

"So how does that explain this place?"

"Oh, it doesn't. But I've got to keep some things a mystery. It adds to my irresistible allure," he winked at her.

"Yeah," she replied deadpan. "About as irresistible as a syphilis ridden skunk."

Chapter 28

The pair left the supply room a little after midnight. Both had changed into new clothes. Kai sported charcoal 511 tactical pants and a tight black V-neck, which was covered by a tactical bulletproof vest. A black matte Springfield XD-M 45 ACP pistol sat on her right hip, and she had a Heckler & Kock G36C against her chest, hanging from a chest strap. The H&K G36C was an ultra-compact assault rifle, chambered in 5.56 millimeter rounds. She also had several other weapons on her, a backup pistol, knives, and an assortment of others. A long black coat was draped over her wardrobe.

Frostt walked next to her and painted an equally fierce picture. An F&N M4A1 hanging from his chest, his customized and freshly cleaned H&K P30s 9 millimeter on his hip. He had added another pistol of the same type in a back holster and had at least two backup guns. A tactical Remington 870 TAC-14 compact shotgun was on his back. An assortment of knives and other weapons added to his appearance. A bulletproof tactical vest, all black clothes, a long trench coat, and a duffle bag stuffed with more toys over his left shoulder finished off his intimidating look.

"So, you went with the 45. Make sure that doesn't push you over when you pull the trigger," prodded Frostt as he tossed the bag into the back seat of the sedan.

"Yeah," said Kai, patting the H&K, "I like the feel of a real gun in my hand. Not like some pussy 9 millimeter." She smiled slyly at him.

The pair drove in silence, the night moving past them like an old friend welcoming them home. They both felt an unspoken surrealism as the pavement blurred past them. A sense of moving towards something unbound to this world. They made the drive in record time. A nearly unperceivable pale pink dusted the horizon when Frostt pulled the car to a stop in an alley behind a half-collapsed warehouse, a mile and a half from their target.

Stepping out, the pair retrieved a map from the duffle bag and spread it out on the hood, the edges smudged from being folded too soon after printing in the war room. Mal stocked a small backpack with a variety of explosives while Kai studied the map.

"I say we make ingress at the southeast corner," said Kai, placing her finger down on the map. "It gives the best cover and forces anyone on the roof to step out into the open to see." She looked up at Frostt; she hated the butterflies that leapt into her stomach like some thirteen-year-old girl seeing some hot guy. *Get your head on straight*, she screamed at herself. *He is just another asshole, like all the other men you have worked with*. A hidden part of her knew that statement didn't hold completely true. She went on out loud, "You want to do it hard and loud or slow and quiet?"

"Excuse me?" nearly stuttered Frostt. He had been having a similar teenage feeling, though a wave of guilt and memories of his dead wife were the tools that crushed it down. He recovered without Kai noticing the slip. "Well, I am game for either," he smirked.

"The op, asshole," she shook her head. "Keep your head on the mission. I know that might be hard for the half dozen brain cells you've got."

A huge smile grew across Frostt's face. "Slow and quiet to start. It will get hard and loud soon enough. If they know we are there too soon then they might try to destroy any evidence." Kai nodded at the morbid, but true comment considering by evidence Mal meant his daughter.

They moved off, two killer wraiths in the night.

○ ○ ○

"Do you know why Mr. Creepy Cold is here?" whispered Juan.

"Shut it, man," snapped Jim, the man next to him. The office chair he sat in could barely support his muscle-bound frame.

At that moment, the door to the security operation center, SOC for short, opened and the head of security stepped in, followed by David Levi, or Mr. Creepy Cold as Juan had nicknamed him.

David Levi looked over the small SOC, the security lead standing next to him. Two guards, a hipster-looking Hispanic and a muscle-bound white guy that needed to lay off on the steroids, manned the main monitor bank.

"We are moving the site. Full pack out, code black," said David, as if commenting on the weather.

"What?" piped out Juan. "Why?"

The team lead, a weathered veteran whose face could be summed up completely by his thick gray touched mustache and coffee stained teeth, barked out, "Dammit, Juan, move your ass. Code black, start the hard drive burn outs. There is a chance this location has been blown." He stared cold daggers at both men, more scared that he might appear weak in front of David, Mr. Creepy Cold. "Get your asses in gear," he screamed as both men still had not moved.

The pair of men snapped to work. Another pair of men joined them a few minutes later, paper files being shredded and the scraps loaded into an already burning steel drum.

"Mr. Levi, the other two shifts have arrived. All hands on deck. Do you want the extra men working on the blackout?"

David replied, his soft voice cleanly cutting through the clamor that had filled the SOC. "No, have shift A and B reinforce the perimeter and C group create a secondary perimeter around the housing unit."

"Yes, sir."

"Juan," said David, cutting past the team leader. He had pulled out a pair of silver fingernail clippers and gently smoothed down the side of his left pinky fingernail. "Have all positions check in. I want a full security sweep the second the other shifts get in position. If that is something you can do...unless you want to know why."

Juan looking like a baby seal facing a shark, he stuttered back, "N...no...no, sir. I'm good. Checking all points."

"I am so glad to hear that you are good, Juan."

During the quick exchange, a new man entered the room, making it feel cramped. The new figure didn't fit in with the current crowd in the least. He wore burgundy slacks, a loose fitting button up shirt and tie over his spindly frame, and a white lab coat over it all. The new man pushed his thick glasses up as he addressed David, "What is going on here? I have been told we are evacuating my patients and that I only have an hour to get them prepped." He did not end the statement as a question nor a proper statement, but as a poor mix somewhere in the middle.

"Dr. Harveson, that is correct. I have enacted the Black Protocol. This site may have been compromised," replied David in his neutral voice.

"What? How is that possible?" replied Dr. Harveson with a peevish sneer. "This place is completely safe, and I can't possibly be ready to move my patients in an hour. It takes days of preparation to care for them."

David looked down at his wristwatch; he could hear Juan calling a second time to one of the check points. "Doctor, Mr. Voste has been murdered," Harveson's face flushed white. "I don't know what information was gleaned before his death. So, we are going Black Protocol as directed. You now have forty-nine minutes to prep your patients for transport or put a bullet in them and put them into the incinerator."

"Checkpoint nine. Rick, respond dammit," barked Juan into his headset. "You better not be taking a shit again on your watch."

"What is the problem?" asked David.

"Nothing sir," replied the team lead. "Just a little delay in one of the checkpoints." He knew that a man breaking watch would end badly for him and the watcher.

'Sirs, I am not getting a response out of checkpoint eleven either," interrupted Jim. "I have tried four times." He pushed a switch and overrode Juan's speaker control. "Eleven, check in?" Nothing but static responded.

When David spoke again, the faintest hint of tension ghosted his voice, unnoticed by anyone in the room. "Red Protocol. Full burnout." The room went dead quiet as the words fell to the floor, only the sound of static filled the space.

David turned to Dr. Harveson, "Doctor, you have five minutes to grab your files before we firebomb this entire facility, your patients included."

"You...you can't do this!" yelled the doctor. "It's an outrage. Do you know how many years it has taken us to find these children?"

The crack of the gunshot caused everyone in the room to flinch. Juan completely fell out of his chair. David lowered his Glock G17, the wall behind Dr. Harveson plastered with the man's brain matter. The body crumpled to the ground as David lowered his hand.

"Code Red, people. Four minutes and thirty-four seconds," said David to no one specific, his neutral voice making everyone in the room shiver.

Before anyone could respond, a concussive explosion rattled the walls and tables. The lights and all other power went dark at the same time. Less than a seconds later the UPS system kicked in with the backup generator a second later on its heels.

Team lead shouted into the room, "Sound alarm. Everyone to tactical stations!"

Everyone moved at once, including David, who moved over to a keypad locked cabinet. It opened with a simple code exposing a collection of weapons and body armor. Less than twenty seconds later, David had a bulletproof vest on, a second G17, and a FN SCAR 16 CQC. The latter being a 5.56x45 millimeter rifle with a holographic sight. A handful of mags completed David's kit. He stepped away as the team lead opened a safe located behind the cabinet. He pulled three items from the safe: a black hardened SSD, a thick file of papers, and a grey canvas wrapped pouch.

The team lead pulled the detonating cord on the pouch at the same time the report of automatic gunfire reached the SOC. He looked at David for only a second before tossing the satchel charge into the center of the room and the small strike force moved out, David in the lead.

o o o

The words of Gamba Eze rang in Mal's head; he could picture the six-foot four-inches tall black man towering over him as a child. A laugh that could wake the dead and a smile to calm the soul. A killer of all living things on the planet, including men.

"If I teach you one thing little one," said Gamba, his bald head gleaming in the cold light of the mountain sun and his grey beard freshly trimmed. "It is this. Honor in single combat will always remain the core of what a true warrior is. Honor in war, though, has no place. If an enemy is in your way, you sneak up behind them and cut their throat. The key is understanding the difference between war and combat."

The guard's throat parted as Mal's knife hand dragged silently across it. He lowered the body to the ground, pointing the blood spray away. A half dozen steps later Kai deftly tossed her knife as another guard stepped around a corner, the knife catching the man dead in the right eye.

She whispered to Mal as the pair followed the building power service to the main electrical room. "Sometimes, finesse works better than brute strength. You might want to learn some."

Kai picked the lock on the door as Mal covered the hallway intersection. She stepped into the dull thrum of transformers, the smell of burnt dust and ozone filled the space. She placed two plastic-wrapped packs of C4, with remote detonators stuck into them. A layer of nails added to the lethal packages, one onto the 208 volt and 408 volt gear switches.

She stepped out motioning for Mal to move towards the stair access, when a few feet away an armed guard appeared. His M4 was pointed down, a cherry tipped cigarette between his lips. Before the man could raise his weapon or even make a sound, Mal darted forward, grabbed the M4 by the sight, held it down, and put the man's throat in a one-hand grip of iron. A second and a half later, the man fell to the floor his throat completely crushed and his neck broken.

Kai's eyes went wide at the speed and brutal strength. She had in all her combat career known two men who could have done that, though none that fast or quiet. He grinned back at her, "Finesse by itself is moot and brutality is only a tool. Balance of the two creates something completely new."

Kai just stared at him in response.

The pair moved up the stairs, Mal's M4A1 moving in smooth arcs covering the entire space. Kai acted as rear guard and covered the forward arcs as Mal turkey-peaked around a corner. He moved back, covering the rear so Kai could do the same look around. She pulled a silenced pistol from the holster on the small of her back. Mal placed a pair of claymores in the hallway, with the trip wires strung between them. He then mimicked Kai and pulled his second H&K 9 millimeter with a H&K matching silencer. Kai, using hand gestures, told Mal she would go left.

The two stepped into the long hall, white washed walls and florescent lights reflecting dully off the early 1990s wood paneled office doors. Kai moved like a viper striking, her gun going off in two perfectly placed bursts. The man standing at the far end of the hall and another that just stepped out of an office took two bullets each, half inch grouping, in the chest. Mal did the same to his single target, a burst of three, two in the chest and one in the head. The pair moved in, stepping in unison up the hall. Mal kicked the weapon of the man that peeked out into the hall; he pushed him back into the small room, firing rounds into the man's stomach and chest. He let him fall to the ground and then put three rounds into a man eating at a small table. Mal turned away, placing a round into the man's head on the floor, a half dozen rounds already in his chest. He stepped out of the makeshift lunchroom and took up step with Kai again. The pair reached the end of the hall. A left turn to the north and a door opened to a stairwell going up and down.

"Time to split," said Mal.

"Time to make some confusion then," replied Kai. She pulled the remote detonator from her vest.

"Good hunting."

"Hey, Frostt," said Kai. He looked back at her a step closer to the stairwell. "We'll find her. And watch your six."

"You too, Madam President."

And with that she pressed down on the detonator. A dull thud rattled the building around them, the lights blinking off in an instant. A few seconds later, the emergency lights came on, giving the hall an eerie and foreboding half-light.

Chapter 29

The air smelled of mold, old cardboard, and something astringent. The M4A1's report vibrated the walls as Mal raced forward, sliding behind a set of crates. He flipped out the mag and popped in a new one, the bolt slamming home at the same time Mal pulled the trigger, downing another guard with a three-round burst. He moved forward, a litter of bodies behind him. He went room by room, clearing each one, a mix of abandoned offices, labs, and large storage rooms. He switched between his rifle, pistols, and knives as he cut a bloody path through the building.

He had never felt so focused. No training mission, no other combat had focused him so directly. He felt like a thrown titanium spear, not stopping until he found his goal, or someone cut his beating heart from his chest. He let the battle vigor wash over him. His body working as a mix of instant reactions and a hyper focused combat engine.

He paused, the last few minutes passing in an eidetic vision, not hindering the present inflow of cold data. He leaned his back against a door jam. His mind fractured into three calculated killing machines. One of the past, looking for patterns. One of the present, seeing reactions and causal effects. And the future, working the never-ending mortal chess game. Light poured out of the partially open door; he could hear shouts coming from guards in the room. Orders to spread out. *Just, piss in a bucket. How many assholes do these guys have*? he thought to himself. He pulled a flash bang grenade from his chest and tossed it into the room, following it after it exploded. His rifle found its targets. The space opened into a large lab. The entire place screamed of recent use, the source of the astringent smell lingering in the air. The space had a dozen lab workstations. The ones directly in front of Mal were perpendicular to him, running ran half the width of the room. A new set ran parallel to Mal, stretched the length of the room with several walkways through them. The left wall was floor to ceiling windows, looking down into a large warehouse space. Each bench was covered in medical and scientific tools. Beakers, Bunsen burners, centrifuges, and many more objects Mal didn't recognize.

He did have a very clear understanding of the handful of tactically dressed men in the room and what they wished to do to him. Mal rolled over the first bench, praying none of the glass containers of liquids he broke, or that where broken by the cacophony of bullets, were caustic or poisonous. He dropped the two closest men, letting his M4 drop against him on its tether as he pulled his pistol to square off against the next four attackers barely two feet away, dropping each one. Reloading his pistol, he added bullets to two of the attacker's heads.

He slid behind a lab bench while changing mags on his M4. Glass rained down on him as bullets tried to drill through the stainless-steel lab bench. The sound of gunfire close by, but not directed at him caught his ear and movement in the side of his vision caused him to scan the large warehouse below. He saw Michaela moving from cover to cover, dropping the men who came at her. She moved with an economy of motion and clear combat experience. She had gotten into a hard spot, caught in a triangle of men closing in on her. She did not see the two men moving up on her from the right. Mal took aim through the broken window and dropped both men, Michaela's head whipping up to see him. She didn't give another notice but moved on clearing the space like a one-woman army.

Mal stood again, meeting the three men head on, dropping two and using a broken piece of a glass beaker to tear open the last man's throat. He moved on, trading between all his weapons and makeshift ones littering the floor and work benches. A new trio entered the fray. Mal's focus sharpened further, a quantum drive in overload.

David Levi entered the room, his FN SCAR 16 CQC beating out a dissonant cord to Mal's. David showed more combat instincts than the entire group of men Mal had just killed. He bore the spectral antithesis to Mal's wraithness. His face was cold and cut of ice, the air around him showing his true self, boiling with and corrupted by sadistic hate.

Mal ducked down as a flash bang went off on the other side of a workbench. He stood, his ears ringing, scanning the room for a target. David was nowhere to be seen. He laid down rounds, making the biggest of the three men take cover. He rolled over another workbench, putting another burst of fire at the ox of a man. The third man's eye went wide as half a dozen new holes appeared in his chest. He fell back. Mal spun around, changing mags. A burst of pain exploded in his left side. He turned to see David on the far side of the room, having flanked him. He moved to return fire, his M4A1 coming on point.

The sounds of rending wood and metal snapped Mal's attention away from David, who had just ducked down for cover. The half giant of a man had torn a section of workbench from the ground and with a Herculean feat, tossed it at Mal. The M4A1 was ripped from Mal's hands, who was unable to duck fast enough. The jagged plywood base of the workbench ate into his left shoulder, sending waves of pain down to his fingertips. He rolled with the hit, coming to one knee, the beast of a man right on the heels of the flying workbench.

Mal dodged a face shattering knee, but took a horse kick straight to the chest, rocking back. In one smooth move, he rolled backwards, his chest screaming in pain, and pulled the Remington 870 TAC-14 from his back holster. He landed on his back, his first shot taking the brute coming at him in the right shoulder. He took out the man's left knee next, and then finished the issue with a pump to the face, at a two-foot distance. He dropped the shotgun and kicked hard off the nearest workbench, sliding himself through the detritus of blood and debris on the floor to his rifle.

He calmed his heart and slowed his breath, letting the currents of the space wash over him. The smells, the noise, the soft movement of the air. He heard nothing. He let his eyes scan the area he could see from behind his cover.

He is amazing, thought Mal. *Good. That means I can make him hurt longer.* He quickly checked the wound on his left side; the bullet had clipped the edge of his vest and then into his flesh. The hole poured out blood, but not in a life ending flow of a cut artery. The rent on his shoulder bleed less but worried him more. He could feel bits of plywood and muscle torn and mixed up.

Mal strained with every part of his body. He could hear the soft pop of rifle shots in the distance. A silent part of him hoped Michaela was okay. The smell of gunpowder and blood filled his nose. He then heard noises from three different directions, from a soft clicking to debris shifting. He spun to the axis that had been silent and let out a burst of fire. David ducked and twisted away, dropping his SCAR 16 as metal peeled off it from Mal's bullets. He pulled his pistol, returning fire. The pair moved up and down, over and under benches. Bullets and flying glass filled the space, creating a dichotomy between glittering, shifting lights and bloody death.

What seemed to have lasted minutes in reality only took seconds. The room fell quiet, except for the efficient reloading of pistols and Mal's rifle. Both men could hear the heavy breathing of the other, loud but steady and calm.

"I know you won't tell me who you are," said David in his monotone voice. "But where did you train? I can name maybe a dozen operators in the world at our level."

"My old man taught me, ex-Green Beret and Delta force, for the most part," replied Mal. "As for who I am, you already know that."

"I assume you have a child here and I most likely helped get them here," said David. "But that does not narrow it down much."

"What about you, then? I know Mossad had a hand in you, but as you said, only a few come to our level."

"Oh, yes. Mossad gave me the finishing touches, but it was my time as a child in the Gaza Strip that shaped me. Fire and blood."

"Fire and blood," echoed Mal.

The pair moved out at the same time, Mal using his superior firepower to strafe the top of the workbenches as he moved to flank David. Bullets from David answered back. In a blink of an eye, David was next to him, the M4A1 tossed into the air. Both men, with pistols, out fired in a fury of fists and kicks, both quickly disarming the other. Mal gave a furious flying horse kick to David, picking him off his feet. The recoil from the kick sent Mal crashing back into a bench.

David landed hard against a workbench. He grabbed a still intact beaker full of a pale blue liquid and tossed it at Mal. Mal dodged the beaker, letting it sail past him as he moved in, fists up and light on his feet. Murder and hate in his eyes.

Less than two seconds later and after several landed blows by both men, each hesitated as a roaring crackling sound filled the space, then the smell of burned ozone washed over them. They split apart and jumped for cover a quarter-second before the room went up in a concussive burst of wild chemical reactions and fire. Mal landed hard on the floor and rolled into a ball as the last few remaining windows in the room blew out and a scolding heat licked his exposed skin. A minute later, Mal moved, his body screaming in protest, his ears ringing, and his throat choked with soot and the acrid smell of burnt plastic. David had vanished, but the last place Mal had seen him was by the side door leading out of the room. He quickly retrieved his rifle and checked all his weapons. He had a half dozen more cuts and his lips and cheek were split open. His right forearm was bleeding freely from a gash and his right leg had an inch-wide and six-inch long patch of burnt skin. Half of the blisters had popped and were leaking plasma; bits of his pants had melted into his skin.

He took a deep breath once he stepped out the side door and into fresh air. *Come on. Where are you little girl?* he grimaced. He had barely finished the thought when Michaela came over his radio.

"I found them. Mal, copy, I found them." Distant rifle rounds echoed through the crackling noise that came over the radio. "I am pinned down. I have six tangos closing in."

Mal doubled his pace, scanning and clearing the corners in double speed. "What is your twenty?"

Michaela's voice was garbled with the sounds of gunshots. "Second floor, west by northwe….Dammit! Just follow the gunfire." She bellowed the last and cut out.

He doubled his pace again, recklessly taking corners, even going through a wall when no good path opened for him. The three guards he came across fell dead before they even knew what hit them.

He came to a sliding halt, the sounds of gunfire cascading below him. He stood in a large open area, which looked to once have held cubicles. He stopped moving completely, focusing his body to slow down. In all his life it had never been so difficult, but he pushed with all his will to calm his heart and slow his mind. He let the world around him die down, all but the sounds of gunfire. He let his feet guide him. Two sets of shots: one singular and measured. The second rushed and from multiple shooters. He moved five paces to the left and then two back. One more forward and a little on a right diagonal. He aimed down and unloaded a full mag into the floor. Worn carpet blasted up from the point, followed instantly by pulverized concrete. He dropped the mag and fired another one into the same spot. He reloaded and knelt next to the torn-up spot.

Brushing away the shattered concrete bits and powder, he exposed a small crater several inches wide and roughly two inches deep. He pulled the rest of the C4 charges he had from his pack and placed them into and around the small crater. He then moved over to the pair of heavy metal fire doors leading into the open space. A full mag of bullets later and he was able to tear the two-hundred-pound door off its hinges. He slammed it down on top of the C4 pile. A second later, he leaned against the hallway leading into the room.

"Michaela, blasting hole from on top. Take cover." He got no response. "Michaela, copy!"

He shook his head and pressed the remote detonator.

Chapter 30

Michaela moved away from Mal, catching one last glance of him as he took the stairs up to the third floor. She moved through the warehouse bump door in front of her, her H&K G36C at the ready. "Good going Michaela. Got yourself back in the meat grinder," she whispered to herself. She had sworn after she had gotten out of the CIA that she was done with being in the grime. *I guess some people can't escape what they are good at,* she thought and readied herself for the fight ahead. *Damn, I need a drink.*

She moved through a small warehouse, then into the halls dotted with offices and work labs. Mostly random crates of supplies and empty spaces met her. A pair of guards clearly searching the space dropped with wordless cries as she moved in between them, knife in hand. She moved on. She could hear the distant rumblings of gunfire. *I almost feel sorry for the assholes going up against Mal.*

She rounded a corner, seeing a trio of men sweeping from the other end. The gunfight exploded. Two of the men dropped, one dead and one screaming in pain. Blasts of sheetrock and tacky wood veneered office doors clouded the air. Michaela moved forward, her three-round bursts calm and trained. The men, now having grown to five, could barely respond to her quick and efficient onslaught. They fell back giving ground to her. She took up position at the intersection covering both directions. A flash bang pushed her back and onto her side; she rolled over onto her feet and slammed herself backwards through an office door as a pair of guards rushed her position and filled the air where she had just been with hot metal. She emptied the rest of her mag into the wall next to the open door, both men mowed down as bullets and wall debris tore into them.

A new mag and back into the hall, she didn't give them any time to regroup. She let her own flash bang go down the hallway and moved on. The flash suppressor on her assault rifle smoked with the near constant burst of fire, her hand bringing a new mag to bear before the current one even ran out. She was a machine that dealt death in cold and steady steps.

She did a weapons check as she moved into a massive warehouse area, crates and pallets filled the space. The peaceful welcome she had hoped the room would give her shattered as flashes of lights and pieces of crates ripped apart. She returned fire, moving from crate to crate. A scream of pain exploded from the right and behind her. She spun to see two tangos falling to the ground three bullet holes each, one-inch placement in the chest. She turned to the opposite direction. A second story bank of windows looked down into the space, workbenches filling the room above. Mal gave her a little wave and moved on.

She did the same, checking the windowed room several times. It was like watching something from a movie. She knew she was good, amazing actually by any combat standards. What she was watching was damn inhuman. A mix of gunplay and kungfu. Mal moved like an ethereal wraith not a killer, but death incarnate. A ricocheting bullet slammed the left side of her bullet proof vest. A gut punch and a reminder to pay attention to the death at hand, not the show above. She dropped another guard trying to flank her.

Her body registered the new threat before her mind could even process it. A grenade, an M67 fragmentation grenade to be specific. Michaela was always specific when it came to explosives. The M67 had an injury zone range of roughly fifty feet and a kill zone of sixteen. She hit the ground hard on the other side of the crate she leapt over. She didn't even stand up, rolling to a frog crouch and lunging away. She rolled into the fetal position in midair. The explosion came with a bone- rattling crash as vibrating darkness gripped her.

Her vision danced in and out. A thrumming, high-pitched sound filled her ears. She caught movement out the side of her blurred vision, then her pistol came out of the holster, and she fired twice. The man went down with a scream she could not hear. She moved to the side of a crate, feeling blood on her face and a set of sharp pains from the lower right side of her back. Her pistol fired two round bursts, dropping the group of guards that had moved in. One got close enough to kick her pistol away, but she didn't flinch. With her head spinning and her vision still blurred, she laid into the man, dropping him with a broken knee and snapping two of his ribs before driving them into his own lungs. The next man she jumped using a leg grapple to the man's head. They both fell to the ground, Michaela riding him down and snapping his neck on impact. The last man had more balls than brains, lasting all of three seconds as her knife came out and felled him in a fountain of arterial spray.

She reloaded her guns, checking them and herself in only a few seconds. She ignored the minor cuts and imbedded pieces of wood in her legs and arms. The small gash right above her hair line, was not deep or long, but it bled like all head wounds did. Her hand came away covered in blood from the small of her back, but there was nothing she could do for that but hope. She moved on, her vision back to normal and only a small ringing left in her ears. Only a few guards met her as she moved into a maze of hallways and smaller storage areas. She came across a few sleeping quarters and medical looking rooms. It was through one of those medical rooms, which looked recently used, that she came to a long hallway that led to pair of double doors on the right side at the end of the hall. The hall was dotted with crates, boxes, metal storage cabinets, and medical supplies. She scanned a few of the labels on the cabinets and boxes as she moved along: Fresh Linen, Wash Rags, Body Wash, IV Supplies, Sterile Wipes, Lotion.

She came to the end of the hall and did a speed peek through the small window. The quarter second look stole her breath away. A whitewashed, brightly lit room, much longer than it was wide, was filled with a dozen beds. At least half the beds were filled with children, pipes and wires surrounding each one.

Two bullets from a hailstorm bit into her flesh. One tore a line of fire across her left shoulder and the other one impacted her left side, just inside of the bulletproof vest, cracking a rib. She returned fire without having to think about it. She tried the door, locked. She jumped back, taking cover against a metal cabinet and returning fire. She clicked her mic and yelled into it, "I found them. Mal copy, I found them." She laid down a burst of fire and scanned the far end of the hall. A blast of torn concrete chewed into her face. "I am pinned down. I have six tangos closing in."

"What is your twenty?"

With one hand on her mic and the other reloading her rifle, "Second floor west by northwe- dammit, just follow the gunfire," she screamed in anger and pain. A mix of concrete and ricocheting pieces slammed into her chest and raised hand. She clicked the mic again, but it had gone dead with the damage. She ignored the surging pain in her hand and returned fire, making it five tangos. More fire came her way, the men attacking knew she was pinned down, alternating fire to keep her from getting time to lay down any good fire back on them. A flash bang went off a second after Michaela looked away, covering her head. Her vision and hearing still rocked hard. She returned shots, spraying the hallway on full auto. She dropped out her mag and loaded in her second to last. The entire world slowed down as more bullets tore her metal cover apart and carved into the concrete walls.

She knew the end was only a few seconds away. She had been here before and scraped by the Grim Reaper with only a hair's space to spare. She thought of her father and hoped that this would mean hearing him laugh again.

She felt a cold liquid steel settle in her veins. She took a deep and final breath and stepped out. She would not end like a timid rabbit, but a spitting wolverine making her attackers pay pound for pound for her blood. An unknown part of her whispered hello to the old friend Death. A quarter second later, and two bullets to her vest, the air in the hallway compressed in an explosion so loud her ears rebelled to hear it, but her bones took it full on. She was tossed back, slamming into the wall. The ceiling of the hallway above the attackers blew down, spreading half of them like a pancakes on the floor and walls. The Reaper himself fell from the sky and landed in the pile of broken concrete, sparking wires, ceiling tiles, and torn bodies.

Mal moved forward, the M4A1 rattling fire.
Michaela pulled her pistol, dropping another guard.
Mal let his rifle fall on his chest tether and pulled his
pistol, himself taking three rounds at point blank range
from a guard who bull rushed him with a pistol and
rage on his face. A man who knew death was near.
Mal put two rounds into him, one per eye. He walked
up to Michaela who still sat against the far wall, her
pistol out, her chest and back hurting like hell.

"You look like shit," smirked Michaela as Mal
helped her stand. "I thought you were good at this."

"Yeah, I am having an off day. Getting shot
and blown up does that to a person," muttered Mal,
Michaela nodded. "You aren't looking too peachy
either. Well, except your ass; that is still great."

"Bastard Boy," she said as she reloaded her
H&K. Mal covered the hall as Michaela shot the
door's lock to pieces. The pair stepped into the room,
clearing left and right. A single man in a white coat
stood behind the second to last bed. A half dozen
medical machines stood in front of him.

"On the ground," barked Michaela.

Mal scanned the room, bile jetting up from his
stomach at the sight of the children. In a blink, he saw
her.

His daughter. His life.

Mal's attention was torn from her as the man
pressed a button on the machine he was at and jumped
to the next bed, his hands scrambling over the
machines. Mal dropped him with a bullet to his knee.

The man let out a wailing scream. He tried to push away. Michaela took up guard on the man, who gripped his knee screaming and crying. Mal moved around the long room, medical supplies spread out on tables and around each bed. On the far side of the room, he pushed over a metal cabinet in front of the other door into the space. He moved back to the beds. Five children lay on there, wearing medical gowns. Each had short hair and dozens of tubes and wires in them. Two thin tubes looked to be filled with blood cycling in and out of an unknown machine.

His daughter lay in the middle bed, her hair short and her breath steady. He nearly ripped the wires and pipes off her and picked her up, but he held himself back. A monitor linked to the child at the end of the row started beeping and a few seconds later let out a flatline signal. Mal stepped over to the man on the floor as the next bed started beeping. He picked the man up and spoke clearly and coldly, "You are a doctor." It was not a question, but the man nodded in return.

"My leg," moaned the man. Mal tossed him into the center of the room. He screamed in pain. The next child's bed gave off a flatline noise. Mal stepped up to the man and pushed his rifle barrel against the man's forehead.

"Did you kill those two? Did you get to the middle bed?" The man hesitated for only a breath. Mal screamed, "Did you?!" He gave the man a kick in his shattered knee.

"No, no. I only overdosed the first two. You destroyed my knee before I could move on," the man moaned. "I will never walk the same again."

Mal pushed his rifle harder into the man's head, "I am going to open your head up so don't worry about your knee."

"No, no," begged the doctor. "I was just following orders. I was told to get rid of all evidence."

"You mean, evidence of using these kids to create a super drug," said Michaela. Her attention split between both entrances to the room.

"Yes, yes," said the man. "I was only following orders."

"You just killed two kids and have been helping imprison them. You are doing a bad job of making me think you should live," snapped Mal. "Now, you are going to get up and unhook them."

"I can't stand," bleated out the doctor. He started screaming again as Mal shot him in the left hand. His ring and middle finger disappeared, the pinky only hanging on by some skin.

Mal stepped on the hand and stared directly into the man's eyes. "Get up and unhook those kids. You make one wrong move, and I will take you apart piece by piece. Now move."

"Are you going to kill me as soon as I finish?" whispered the man. His face had gone completely white.

"I will kill you if you don't. You will just have to wait and see once you unhook them," snapped Mal.

"Two seconds, get up or we see what a bullet will do to your elbow joint."

The man scrambled up and half crawled half hopped over to the kids, holding his bloody hand. He started pulling wires and IVs off the children. Mal watched like a hawk. Beyond his daughter, there was one other girl and a little boy. It was hard to tell ages, but he guessed both were younger than eleven years old. Each was skinny, but not emaciated. Their skin was clean and smooth. It was clear that someone had been tending to them. Mal gave the man a swift kick when he slowed even the slightest bit.

"When will the kids regain consciousness?" asked Michaela.

The doctor only answered after another swift kick. "I don't know. At least a few hours if not a day or two. They have been under for some time. We used a very delicate chemical cocktail. I didn't want to hurt them in anyway."

"Because you need them to be healthy to harvest the enzyme," stated Mal.

The doctor finished unhooking Mal's daughter last, a little over two minutes after he started. He collapsed to the ground after finishing. He had gone even paler. "I need to get to a hospital."

"No, you don't," said Mal. The doctor fell back with a bullet hole between his eyes.

"Well, I guess that works," said Michaela.

Mal did not hear her. He leaned his rifle against one of the beds and was bending over his daughter. He whispered, "Daddy's here, baby girl. I knew I'd find you. I knew it." Tears dotted the little girl's white gown as Mal went to pick her up.

A sudden noise snapped both Mal's and Michaela's attention to the doors. Michaela spun to the door they had come through, her H&K let out a blast of fire, a shriek came from the other side of the door. At the same time, Mal did a one-handed leap, using his daughter's bed as a pommel horse. The far door, still barricaded with the metal cabinet, shook violently a something on the other side rammed into it. A half second later, Mal's blood went cold. A hand pushed through the small opening that had been created and tossed a hand grenade into the room. A bullet hole appeared in the hand.

Mal did not notice the cry from the other side of the room. He dropped his pistol and in two massive lunges, shot across the room. First, he grabbed the dead doctor. Then he landed on top of the grenade with the doctor's body under him. The only thought running through his mind: *I was so close. So close.*

Michaela felt the concussive vwoop of the grenade going off. She darted a look over to the other side of the room just in time to see Mal getting tossed into the air, the doctor's body under him spasming up in a spray of blood. A bullet tore into her vest, she let it knock her back rolling to the side. Returning fire, the briefest second of seeing Mal midair just might have cost her everything. She landed on her side bullets flying from her rifle, dropping two of the men who burst through the door, guns blazing.

David darted across the now open door, taking cover behind the concrete wall. Michaela emptied her magazine into the corner, bits of concrete and drywall blasting away. She regained her feet and moved left, trying to get a bead on David. She let out three round bursts at random intervals to keep him wary of stepping through. She risked a glance over at Mal. He was engaged with two men, one on the ground with a shotgun and the other firing point blank with his pistol into Mal's vest. A bullet from her H&K clipped one of the attacking men in the neck. At that same moment, fire exploded across her body, a pair of bullets slamming into her vest, another tearing into the flesh across her ribs, and the last drilling a hole all the way through her left thigh. A pang of fear rushed over her as she turned to see David baring down on her, his next shot lined up for the kill. A blur of sparkling light whipped past her vision and David moved, but too slow as a knife impaled itself into his left forearm, the blade coming out the other side.

The memory of the grenade blast would always be gone from Mal's memory. His next would be looking up from the ground, covered in blood from the doctor, and a bull of a man pointing a twelve-gauge pump action shotgun at him. His muscles responded before his blurred brain could understand. He rolled into a frog pose and lunged forward, the blast from the shotgun burning like molten metal on the back of his right shoulder and impacting the backside of his vest. The lunge worked and Mal's shoulder checked the man away, just in time to find a new attacker slamming into him. The rounds were so loud as they went off point blank into his vest, he couldn't hear them. The man stumbled as a bloody wound appeared on his neck. The split second of a break was enough, the man fell to the ground his neck completely cut open. Mal spun, his heart sinking in his chest, as he saw Michaela rocked back as David put several rounds into her. The knife left his hand without his mind even acting, the blade sinking into David's left forearm. It stopped him from pulling the trigger on the killing shot. The racking of a new shotgun shell broke a new wave of ice to Mal's veins. The bull of a man had Michaela lined up in his sights. The blast hit Mal midair as he leaped in front of it. It felt like a hammer with a pissed off giant behind it.

Michaela's brain worked in overtime, trying to sort out all the things happening at once. The entire room fell into the slow-motion fog of combat. Everything was surreal and beyond burning bright. Mal hitting the floor and sliding away from the shotgun blast he just took, the man pumping the shotgun, the ejected shell spinning through the air; David's rifle bouncing from barrel to stock as it hit the floor. Him dropping it due to a knife now planted solidly in his left forearm. His pistol coming out of its holster. Her gun came up, a bullet leaping out. The shotgun man reeled back as it struck him in the face.

The shotgun went off in a fiery eruption into the ceiling. She pivoted around, dropping low. She could feel the air of David's first shot. She caught the pistol in his hand in a round house kick. It flew from his hand, and he stepped in like a viper, disarming her as well. She parried back, landing strike after strike, but he moved like a cobra and struck like coiled steel. She fell back, her lips split, and a gash above her right eyebrow gushed out blood. He was interrupted in mid-throw by Mal crashing into him.

Mal hit the ground, the world shattering into fractals of infinite color. He screamed with all his will. He could feel it all the way down inside him, a bone marrow ache. A fire so hot he felt it would kill him before any bullet would. The man with the shotgun racked a new shell but fell back with a hole in his face, the shotgun going wide. The fire in Mal burst forward and he knew without a doubt he had to move or it would tear him apart. He spun around, pain raging with an epic dance of long forgotten gods against the fire driven will. The will won. His feet pulled him forward as Michaela fell to the ground. He speared David around his waist and both men went down. They kicked apart and came back onto their feet.

Mal could feel his body, the fire starting to fail against the relentless hatred of pain. It had to end now, or he would fail. He felt terror like he had never known before. The sound of his daughter's laughter rang in his ears. David lunged, a double edge knife now in his right hand. Mal did what any insane father would do. He met the blade straight on, it parted his bulletproof vest and his skin. It pierced to the hilt into his rib cage. He twisted with the blow just enough to cause David to loosen his grip on the knife. He landed a bone crushing head butt, the pain of his own strike shooting down his spine. He pulled his own knife free from David's arm, a guttural grunt coming from the man and brought it up to the bottom of David's jaw. Mal's left hand on the back of his opponent's head, forcing it down.

David let go of his knife and gripped Mal's knife hand and using his injured arm to bind Mal's elbow. The tip of the knife sank a quarter inch into the soft tissue under his jaw. Both men locked eyes, a hate of biblical proportions crossed between their eyes. To predators at the pinnacle of their craft, a battle of wills as much as strength. The fight in Mal was fading, the pain pushing with a hellish power to overcome his will. The knife blade creeped down.

Mal caught the movement out of the far side of his vision. Michaela slid forward, coming up to the side of the men. She delivered a powerhouse punch to David's side. All three could hear a pair of ribs shatter under the blow.

A companionship rushed over Mal, a feeling he had had only a few times in his life. He was not alone in this, in this death and pain. He had a point he could anchor to, a point he could rely on. This man in front of him had taken that from him, but he had found it again. With tears in his eyes and the image of his dead wife in his mind, he surged with power that could only come from a brotherhood forged in fire. The knife plunged up, a cracking noise and a gurgle came from David, and then nothing as the blade stopped in the center of his brain.

David fell to the ground and Mal did the same, stumbling back onto his butt. He looked over at Michaela, her breaths coming just as heavy as his. He stood without a word and without a glance to David. It was finished and it was as simple as that. Both Mal and Michaela found their guns, and Mal limped over to his daughter's bed. With a tenderness only a parent could understand, he picked her up into his arms. She was lighter than he remembered, and much thinner. He turned to look at Michaela. She had put the last two children onto the same bed and took the brakes off the wheels.

"Let's get the hell out of here," whispered Mal, fresh lines of tears cutting through the blood and dirt on his face.

"Let's get you both home," nodded Michaela. They left the room, guns still at the ready. No one was left to stop them.

Chapter 31

"You still look like hammered shit," said Bert as the door closed behind the last makeup artist. He stood in the corner farthest from the door in the small room, the green room next to the Bradly Press Briefing Room in the White House. He was the only Secret Service protection in the room and in fact, the only other person in the room besides President Kai.

"You have a way with the ladies, don't you, Bert," replied Kai, not really putting anything into the jab. Even though she would never admit it, her nerves were on fire. T-minus three minutes until the press conference. Her first national address since getting back to the White House.

The last forty-eight hours had been completely nuts, a blur of questions and doctors pestering her. Bert had set up the cover story even before she had given him a call from Pittsburgh. Her kidnappers were a small domestic terrorist group intent on ransoming her life to have several extremist laws put into place. The Russell Building break-in was their attempt to procure blackmail against several senators, which tied in nicely with the already public suicide and sex-driven murder that Senator Otts was involved in. They then where able to kidnap her again take her north into the wilderness area of northern New York State. Kai escaped and then spent several days playing a game of hunter verse hunter in the woods. Bert had been the one to track her down and showed up to help finish off the last two terrorists.

It explained all her injuries, which were extensive and visible. Bert had even created a false money trail and an entire organization behind the group. He had purposely included dozens of holes and false leads. He told Kai that the devil was in the details, while also keeping it as simple as possible. Make it messy and real, he said.

Mal and Kai had dropped off the two other kids before parting ways at a Pittsburgh Emergency Room. A simple note telling the doctors the kids had been in a chemically induced coma for an unknown amount of time and should have their prints run through NcMEC, the National Center for Missing & Exploited Children. The pair waited long enough in the shadows to make sure the two kids were found. Both still limping, bleeding, and downright broken. They had patched themselves up best they could.

The mirror reflected back a bruised face with several butterfly bandages. Kai stared into it. Only a minute-and-a-half until showtime. She had refused to let the makeup artist cover everything up. She would not hide the wounds she had gotten, as a small tribute to the children she could not save.

This was only the second time she and Bert had had any time alone. They had a little less than ten minutes the day before. His only question about Mal,

"Did dickhead get what he needed?" Kai only nodded in response. He went on to fill her in everything he had learned since parting ways with her and Mal. Nearly nothing had made the news. Otts's death was ruled murder suicide, by D.C. police. Voste's death was a slightly larger deal, but only in the finance news. His death was ruled an accident, a faulty powerline having burnt more than half his house down. As Bert's story went on the depth of the cover up became more and more apparent. The police case for the shootout at the boat had been closed suddenly and the fight with and death of Anna at the hotel hours later never even had a police report started on it. A small single paragraph story about Anna's death, a hit and run car accident, was all he could find in the local paper.

He had dug deeper into Voste's company, Intulus, and into the money trail Mal had started. What he found, was a credit to his amazing detective skills, a web so deep and hidden it put the CIA to shame. He had been able to identify at least two people in the IRS who were involved with the money laundering, but his evidence was not nearly good enough for any DA to press charges. As for Intulus, there was more than enough info for the FBI's white collar division, but all of them were run of the mill corporate crimes. He had sent an anonymous tip to the FBI on all of those.

Something had been nagging at the back of Kai's mind ever since she had gotten a moment of quiet after Mal left. It felt painful just sitting there, wishing to surge forward, but the connections would not form. It drove her nuts.

A knock came at the door and, a second later Chance Gates stepped in, impeccably dressed in a crisp suit and tie. His baby face was completely devoid of expression. "Madam President," he spoke in his lack luster tone. "One minute, then it's time to go on stage."

"Yes, Chance. Thank you." Kai rose and followed Chance, who walked like someone had sewn a board onto his back.

She could hear the murmuring of the press room, packed beyond safe occupancy, before she walked onto the stage. An ear-splitting clapping greeted her appearance with a flurry of camera flashes and hurried murmurs, some very clearly talking about the bruises and bandages on her face and arms.

The White House press secretary had the podium when Kai walked onto the stage and took up her normal spot to the podium's right. The press secretary, Madeline Vento, was a perfect fit for the role. Well spoken, a native Spanish speaker, who spoke flawless English plus six more languages. She stood all of five-foot-two-inches and had the composure of a bull. She handled the press corps like a stern mother. Kai had always liked her.

She saw out of the corner of her eye Bert take up his normal position only a pace away. She also noticed, the only person to, that he paid as much attention to his own Secret Service agents as he did the crowd of reporters. Vice President Cever stood on the left side of the podium, his chief of staff Roger Bliss next to him. His eyes roaming between the crowd and Madeline's ass.

Chance stood next to her, a step back. Anna should have been there as well, but Kai had made sure that would never happen again. The thought of her dead and traitorous friend brought such a wave of mixed emotions, she thought she might be sick. She didn't notice when Madeline gave the podium over to Cever. He spoke in his blue blood voice, "Nearly a week ago, we thought we had lost our President. I thought I had lost a friend." No doubt that sound bite would be running on the nightly news for a week straight. "It has been a time of trial for America. A first for this great nation. A first that we as a people waded through like we have done in countless dark days before. Dark days that I say will strengthen us, as all others have." He struck the perfect strong and somber face, turning it off preciously as he went on. "Then less than two days ago, a bloody and tough as nails young woman came back to us." He turned and led a round of applause for Kai. The words "young woman" grated on Kai's already shot nerves, another great sound bite. He turned back to the crowd. "I am more relieved than anyone," he quipped. "I never want to be President. Let me tell you, it is not an easy job. I prefer to be behind the scenes. The prime spotlight is no place for me." He laughed at his flat joke and stepped aside to give Kai the platform.

Kai stepped forward out of sheer habit. Her entire body felt like it had just been jolted by a lightning bolt. A domino of connections exploded in her mind, making her vision blur. "Where the power is at," she whispered to herself. She heard Chance give a loud cough behind her and she snapped out of the inner fire raging in her mind. The room had fallen into an awkward silence. She looked at the teleprompter and stumbled through the first few words before letting her body fall into a detached rhythm reading the words as they scrolled by. A well worded speech written for her, perfectly political, it said much and meant nothing. Reassuring the general public of the strength of America. She ended the speech and paused for a moment, her mind finally coming to terms with the connections she had made. A resolve of steel formed in her stomach. She looked out at the crowd, hands starting to raise in anticipation of Q&A time.

"There is a corruption in this country. A corruption that led to the formation of the group that kidnapped me. And right here and now, I am giving the American people my promise that we will not rest until we have rooted out and killed this corruption. This is the United States of America and we do not stand timidly before anything," she spoke with a deep passion, leaving several of the reporters in the room with mouths open. The hands shot up like springs, the questions peppering her. She ignored them all and walked off stage.

"Going a little off script at the end, eh?" said Bert taking up his point next to her.

She kept on walking.

○ ○ ○

The desk phone slammed down into its cradle. Michaela could not stop her hands from shaking. The fury in her felt like it might start tearing out of her skin. She brushed her hands through her hair. The urge to rip it out rolling over her. The sky through the windows was pitch black, a heavy bank of clouds blacking out the few stars that broke through the D.C. light pollution.

"That bad," said Bert. The only other person in the oval office. She had ordered everyone to leave her be, even sending the Secret Service agents in the hallway to positions farther down. The team lead for the night protested, but that ended swiftly with a dressing down that the man would never forget. The agents scattered away after that. Over the next few hours, Bert stood waiting quietly outside the Oval Office, the only person in sight. Michaela had called him in a few minutes earlier, but the phone rang as he stepped in, and her mood went from bad to murderous.

"Yeah, bad. Worse than I could have thought," whispered Michaela.

Bert stared at her for a long moment. What he saw was the strangest dichotomy in any president he had ever served. A young girl sitting in a chair of amazing power and at the same time a lioness with more will and fortitude than the last half dozen presidents combined. "So, are you going to just sit there and fret?" asked Bert. "Or are you going to get your ass up and do something the fuck about it?"

Michaela shot him a look that many men had seen, but only a few had survived. She did not respond for nearly a minute and then stood in a snap. "I'm going to do something the fuck about it," she growled back. "Are you with me, Bert?" The question held a hundred questions all at once.

Not missing a single beat, he answered, "Yeah. I am." He had no clue what that meant or what she had found out, but he knew down to his core he would follow her. Something had become beyond rotten in this country and the only person he felt who might have a snowball's chance in hell to sort it out stood in front of him.

"Good. Then let's go find the devil." And with that she walked out of the Oval Office. He took up two steps behind her. The walk did not take long, it ended at an office door. One that Bert would never have expected.

Michaela knocked, but entered before an answer was given. "Evening Michaela," said Vice President Cever from behind his desk, clearly surprised by the brusque entrance of the President.

"Evening Johnathan," replied Michaela as she and Bert stepped into the office. Bert closed the door behind him and took up post a single step to the side of the door. "Burning the midnight oil, I see," said Michaela, her voice a singsong of peppiness.

Cever pulled off his reading glasses and stood. He had noticed her tone; his face showed a mild concern.

"Is there something I can help you with, Michaela?" He had moved to the front of his desk and leaned back against it.

"Yes, there is. And let's stick with Madam President for now," she smiled.

"Okay, Madam President."

"You do know that it was not a domestic terrorist group that kidnapped me. In fact, the man who did is alive and well. He got his daughter back and has gone home."

"What, are you talking about Mich.." he stopped with a hard glare from Michaela. "Madam President?"

"Just what I said," she shrugged, "A single man kidnapped me and then I helped him. We killed a lot of people."

"This is a sick joke."

"No joke, Johnathan."

"We need to go somewhere more secure, and you can debrief me. You killed people? Michaela, this could ruin you, or worse, send you to prison."

"I thought I made it clear to stick with Madam President." Her eyes dropped a level of coldness, her voice still holding the singsong tone. Cever did not respond. "Bert was there as well. Well, not for all of it, but some of the juicy parts."

She moved to only a few paces away from Cever, Bert's nerves jumped to high alert. A small coffee table separated Michaela and Cever, flanked by two leather couches.

"Madam President you can't be telling me this. I will not be an accessory to murder," Cever said a slight quiver in his voice.

"Something has been nagging at me since I got back," Michaela changed gears. "I didn't have time to think about it much before. It was eating at me. Something in the back of my mind. Then it clicked this afternoon during our press conference." She locked eyes with Cever. "True power cannot live in the light. It must exist in the shadows. Those that control the focus of light, control where real power goes." She studied Cever with an unhidden intensity. He didn't show a single twitch as she said the words. She went on, "Voste told that to us. Well, before he took a knife into his brain."

Cever leaned back at her last statement. "Who are you talking about? You killed a man with a knife."

"Oh, no, that one was not me," she smiled back. "Duncan Voste, a name you are very familiar with." Cever was about to protest, but Michaela cut him off, "I had to be sure though. As sure as cloak and dagger games can be. I contacted an old CIA colleague of mine, off the books of course. He specializes in communication analytics, the deep state stuff. The things that the American people would go ape shit over. It was, in his words, 'one of the cleanest and deepest communications he had ever seen.' And he has seen a lot."

"Seen what?" asked Cever, impatience growing in his voice.

"A phone call; well, many phone calls. All from locations you frequent. And to locations that Duncan Voste frequented. No names of course or even recordings captured, but the data is there, deep and hidden," she dropped her voice near a snarl at the end.

Cever looked at her, studying her now in return. "You are one clever bitch. I will give you that. Still stupid, but clever at times."

Bert started to speak but, Michaela cut him off, "Did you think you could organize something this complex and get away with it?"

Cever started laughing, "Oh, little girl. There is nothing to get away with. What you have is not even thin ice, it's water flowing away. Even if you could prove I talked to Mr. Voste, which you can't, due to how you found it, the moment you try to, we will bury you. Metaphorically, of course. Mental break led you to kill your best friend, put a bullet in her head you did. Started drinking again."

"I should have you shot for treason," snapped Michaela.

"Oh, shut up," barked back Cever. "You come into my office on your high horse thinking you've come to cut the head off the snake. There is no head, honey."

Michaela felt the theories in her head start splintering. She had to know more, "Then what is it?" she asked bluntly. "Why kill millions and kidnap kids for some super drug?"

Cever held up a single finger, "One, that is all. One of many endless plans. As for the why. You already said it. It's nothing to do with money, that is only the bonus. The real payment is power. It is the only thing that really matters in the world."

"You get power from killing millions in some eugenics movement?" hissed Michaela.

Cever shook his head, "As I said, clever, but still stupid." He moved away from the desk to stand on the same side of the coffee table as Michaela. Bert tensed and moved forward, "Hey, don't you worry, pit bull," snapped Cever. "I have no intention of hurting Missy President here. We need her." He looked back to Michaela, "As for eugenics, I couldn't care less. The group of people that I am involved with, we don't have any official name, but some have called us the Brokerage. That is what we do. A nut job alt-right neo-Nazi group that wants all the blacks gone and an equally alt-left ecoterrorist group that wants the world population lowered to save Mother Earth." He chuckled at the Mother Earth part. "Add in a few other groups that all hate each other, who never in a million years could work together or even come close to having the resources to see their nutjob dreams come true. That is where we come in. We unite groups unknowingly to each other with the same ultimate goal. We combine the resources of all the groups, take a fair share for ourselves and put their militant plans into action."

He smiled broadly and went on, a gloating smile tinting every word. "You think you became president on your own merit? Some nobody House rep? You are a showpiece girl. Nice body and them Asian looks; America's wet dream."

"Screw you," snapped Michaela.

Cever laughed, "Now, now; be nice. We own you. You go against me and we will have you removed. Please don't though, because I really don't want your seat, but I will take it if needed." He changed his tone, "This does not have to be bad for you, Michaela. You can be the president. The first female President of the United States and go down in the history books. Make changes, work on the country! But keep that pretty little nose out of my and our business. And for your mysterious friend and his daughter. We will find him and take care of that in due time."

Michaela's eyes bore into Cever, a hatred so deep it started scaring her. "Who do you work for? What is every plan and scheme you have going? If you give it all up, I will spare the death penalty for you."

"Ah, shit, girl. That is not how it works. You have no cards to play here. Even if I wanted to, I couldn't tell you. That is the way it works; there is no head to cut off. We are all hidden from each other. We only know the plans that we need to or parts of larger plans to support. It is the perfect set up and we have assets in every part of this government, plus governments abroad."

"So, you're useless then."

"Michaela, I don't want to go down a bad path with you. This is more of an offer than anyone else can give you. Play nice and you will be remembered as one of the best presidents this country has ever seen."

"Have you read my file?" asked Michaela, tossing Cever with the change of subject. "I mean the real one, not the official one. I'm guessing you have with your connections."

"Yes, I have. We know everything about you," replied Cever. "What is the point of this new tangent? I am growing tired of all of this."

"Then you saw the redacted sections from my time at the CIA. I not only worked on the SOG teams but worked solo on deep recon and even assassination work."

"Yes, I know you are some badass. But don't try to threaten me, okay? It will not work. I know you could kick my ass, but are you really going to try to go schoolyard on me?" He laughed.

"One of my tasks was completely off the books. No paper, no trail. Single point compartmentalization, both domestic and foreign high-level assassinations."

"Domestic soil, now that is a new one. Though it's just another scandal we could throw at you."

"I was a natural at it, truly talented. Killing people and making it look like an accident or something completely different."

"So, you're stupid enough to threaten me," snarled Cever.

"No, not threaten..." She moved in a blur. Cever never had a chance to move before she struck. He stumbled back, hitting his desk. his right hand gripping his left armpit. Michaela stepped out of her lunge pose, her right hand relaxing from a two-finger strike.

"You bitch!" his face began to screw up in fury, but half a second later he moved his right hand over his heart.

"How has your heart been lately, Johnathan?" asked Michaela in her singsong voice. Her tone sent a shiver down Bert's spine. He had drawn his gun and stepped to the side to get a clear shot of Cever if he made a move, but the man was looking worse by the second. His face going pale and his breathing coming in grasps.

"I also read your files. Medical history was a good read. Weak heart to say the least. I just struck the basilic vein in your left arm. Your heart is fighting to open it of course, which is raising your blood pressure. For most people it would hurt like hell and then maybe they would pass out, but I doubt your heart is going to take the strain."

She moved closer to him, his breathing becoming even more ragged. His eyes were full of terror. "You should have read my files more closely. I do have to say you are a clever man, but stupid to think you could play me."

Cever's knees started to buckle. He used the last of his strength to lunge at Michaela. A feeble attempt. She sidestepped the lunge and added a slight push for guidance. The side of his head impacted the corner of the ornate coffee table with a loud crack. He rolled off it, blood already welling from a gash in the side of his head. His eyes rolled into the back of their sockets.

She crouched down next to him. His eyes moved around and finally, for a brief moment focused on her, his mouth trying to move. She whispered, "Clever, but not clever enough. Say hi to Voste in hell for me."

She stood and walked out of the room. Bert followed her, speechless. They didn't say a word until they were back in the Oval Office. "That…that…was not, um, not quite what I meant when I said get off your ass and do something."

"He was a traitor, by his own words. You heard them."

"Yeah, but you did just kill the Vice President of the United States."

"No, the Vice President of the United States died from an unexpected heart attack and the nation will grieve for him. A maid will find him in the morning. It will be a major blow to America, especially after everything with me, but it had to be done."

"No way we could have gone public with this?" he asked already knowing the answer.

Michaela only shook her head. A few minutes passed. "It's not over, not by a long shot. Are you still with me?"

"I just watched you kill the Vice President of the United States and did nothing. So, yeah I am still with you."

"We need help. Not like I can go off and take the Brokerage on without everyone in the world finding out. And neither can you."

Bert grimaced, "Ugh, I was hoping you wouldn't say that."

"Can't do this without him," Michaela said as she stood and looked out the window, a rainstorm breaking against the glass.

"You know if he finds that out it will make him even more of a cocky asshole."

"Yeah, it would. But right now, we are going to need that," said Michaela, her thoughts drifting states away to a man and his daughter.

Epilogue

The hills resonated with an echoing crack as the double-bit axe split another piece of wood cleanly in half. Shirtless in the cool April air, Mal kicked the pieces off his chopping block and propped another in its place. Nearly three cords of split wood were piled up next to him, another two yet to meet the axe. He inhaled deeply and swung again. The bruises had faded off his body, though a few tender spots stubbornly remained. The bullet wounds, cracked ribs, knife wounds, and dozens of others still hurt when he moved wrong, but he didn't care. He pushed the pain back with a focused non-stop work.

Avery sat at a picnic table outside of their trailer, her head buried in a book. She had gained just over fifteen pounds over the last ten weeks, still more than a dozen pounds shy of her previous weight. Her fiery red hair still short but coming back in nicely.

Each time Mal looked over at his little girl, his eyes burned with the threat of tears. He still had not truly grieved for Sara, even now that he had Avery back and safe. And beyond that, he had no idea how to care for their little girl, who had been through so much, without the steadfast and wise words of his dead wife.

Avery had thankfully come out of the coma quickly. Mal found them a doctor who didn't ask too many questions. Mal spent nearly the remainder of his money on tests for her: CAT scans, MRIs, EEGs, and a laundry list of blood and lab tests. They all came back normal, minus what would be expected for a nine-year-old girl who had seen little physical activity for near two years. Her mental state on the other hand had Mal worried. She slid back into a normal enough routine, even after being told her mother was gone. She was at a near genius level in all things she studied, though she had been escaping into her math and science books more than she used to. At times, Mal would catch her staring off into space, a dead, untethered look in her eyes. With all of the unresolved corruption, Mal couldn't risk taking her to a psychiatrist and having them be discovered by something Avery revealed. The helpless feeling threatened to tear him apart.

The last weeks were spent tearing down what was left of his burned house. He hoped to have a new one built and livable before the fall rains. He wanted to get things back to some kind of normal for Avery's sake.

The wood continued to rend under Mal's quick and efficient strokes as he pondered their situation. This would have been where Sara stepped in, but he was at a loss. She would have known what to say, what to do next. He was a father floundering in a sea of unknowns.

The sound of a car engine drew his attention, tearing through his troubled thoughts. He watched for the vehicle, leaving his splitting as it headed toward his isolated home. He felt for the pistol at the small of his back and walked over to the trailer as a black SUV became visible a quarter mile down the driveway, dust trailing up from behind it as heavy tires ate up the gravel.

"Hey, Avy, get yourself inside, honey," he told her.

The black SUV came to a stop a hundred feet from him, the midday sun gleaming off the black paint and tinted windows. The passenger door opened, and Mal let out a breath when he saw the woman step out wearing suit pants and a form-fitting blouse with an elegant jacket. Her hair was pulled back in a tight ponytail and the sun bathed her skin, accentuating her Japanese heritage.

Mal felt his heart pick up as she came to a stop in front of him. "Madam President," he said, a smile across his face, "to what do I owe the honor of such a visit?"

"You're healing up nicely," Michaela replied.

He looked down at his chiseled chest, sweat and chips of wood clinging to his tanned skin. "Yeah, nothing but twisted steel and sex appeal," he smirked. He saw Bert exit from the driver seat and take up his normal stick-up-the-butt stance.

Come, on focus, thought Michaela as the light wrapped around Mal's bulky and lithe frame. He truly looked like some Greek statue. His muscles were not gains from a gym, but formed with hard work and a harder life. Deep and corded. *Focus,* she yelled internally again. "How is Avery?" she asked, looking over Mal's shoulder.

Mal did the same and with dismay saw Avery still in her spot at the picnic table, despite his instructions, head still in a book. "Physically, she's okay," he lowered his voice, and the next words came out with obvious emotion, "Mentally... I... I don't know." He looked back at Michaela, "Now why are you here? You are not stupid enough to risk bringing attention here just for a social call."

"Have you kept up with the news at all?" she asked, her tone confirming his conclusion.

"Don't got a TV or nothing, but I take Avery to the local library when I can. Trying to get her interested in anything again. I have checked up on things. I heard about your beloved VP. Super sad that he had a heart attack only days after you returned," he raised one eyebrow.

"No heart attack."

"Oh, that is shocking," he smirked.

"I killed him," she stated without the slightest hesitation.

That made him pause. Mal gave a brief nod of surprise, "Damn. Not what I was expecting, but okay."

"He was the shadow figure behind Voste."

"Okay, now you got me on that one. Piss and a half; are you for real?" he looked truly surprised now.

"Yes," she said softly. She went on to explain all that she had learned from Cever before killing him.

"Well, sounds like you have a full-on infestation on *your* hands. Yet you still are not answering my question as to why you are *here*," his words and emphasis made it clear it was nothing he felt inclined to address, but Michaela ignored it and plowed ahead.

"I need your h-"

"No," he cut her off sharply.

"Mal, we have a duty…,"

"Michaela, the answer is a flat-out no." He looked back at Avery. "I just got my daughter back and I have a house- a *life* to rebuild." Michaela went to speak again, but he put up his hand, "This might be your duty, damnit, but nothing to do with me. I did what I needed and helped you on the way."

"*Helped* me? You selfish bastard," snapped Michaela. The venom in her voice caught Mal off guard. "Like hell you helped me. I had enough on my plate before all of this. What you did was for you and you alone. Don't for a second delude yourself that you cared about anyone else. All you have done is open a can of worms that I now have to clean up." She took a huge breath when she finished, as if the words had been pent up in her too long and she was finally getting a good breath. "I didn't want any of this, but it's here now and someone has to face it. I will not see a group of power-hungry nut jobs ruin my country."

Bert's voice interjected between them. "Five minutes until we need to go. The fundraiser could be missing us even before that."

Michaela stepped forward and pulled a manila envelope from behind her back. "Malcolm, you are the only person in the world I can trust who has the skill and profile to do this." She slapped the envelope against his chest. "It's all here. What you need to get started. A new life in D.C., some basic leads, some ideas for covers, money."

"Did you learn so little about me?" said Mal. "I just got my daughter back. I will not put her back into the shit grinder."

"I have a feeling I might know you better than you know yourself in some ways." Michaela took a step forward, standing only inches away, the smell of him wafting over her. "I am going to do this with or without you, but with you we might… and I mean *might* be able to pull this off and kill the bastards poisoning this country."

"Kai, we've got to go," spoke up Bert again. "I just got a text from Meyers asking how you are and saying that the keynote speaker is wrapping up early."

"Read it," she tapped on the envelope now gripped in his hand against his chest. "Just read it. That is all I am asking. The only way this works is if this guides you to do it." She tapped his chest right over his heart, then turned and walked away.

Mal stood rooted to the ground watching her walk away. He spoke just as she rounded the hood of the SUV.

"Michaela." She stopped and looked at him. "The country is damn lucky to have you as President."

She only nodded in response, her eyes still tense.

He watched the SUV disappear into the woods and continued to watch until the dust from its wheels settled back on the ground. He felt the solidity of the envelope in his hands. Some tumultuous feeling burned in him, anger at the audacity of her request, but also something even deeper at the core of him.

A soft voice broke his inner turmoil, "When do we leave?"

He turned sharply to see Avery standing next to him. He stared down at her thin body, her hair too short and her muscles still much too weak. And her eyes. Looking at her eyes was like looking at Sarah's. Full of fire and life, despite all the world's efforts to quench her.

She said again before he could respond, "So, when do we leave? Best to get to work soon."

"Avy," his voice low and serious, "it's not that simple. I am not putting you back into danger."

"I can handle myself," she snapped, her face transforming in cold rage and hard determination, the most expression she had shown since her return.

"This is not something as simple as handling yourself," he began, but she rushed on.

"I am a Frostt, and I damn well won't sit here knowing those bastards are out there doing God-knows what to others like they did to me, and to Mom." Her eyes flashed like Kai's had when she'd cursed at him. She seemed taller suddenly, older. Too much older. The ancient look on her beautiful face drew pride and grief from Mal in equal measure.

He looked at Avery for a long minute, neither breaking eye contact. He let out the softest of sighs, "We *are* Frostts, aren't we?" He ran his hand through his hair and the growing stubble on his face. "I wish your mother were here. She would have some wisdom for a time like this."

"Me, too," whispered Avery, "but if she were here, she would say without a doubt that if you want an answer, you follow that." She reached up and tapped his chest right above his heart. The echoed words stirred strange emotions in Mal, some he recognized and some he would not name. Avery spoke with the heart of her mother, her eyes held a steel akin to Kai's, and the wisdom of all three women resounded in his mind like a battle cry.

Mal felt the edges of his eyes burn as he looked down at his little girl. "Your mother would be beyond proud of you." He watched tears well in Avery's eyes, the first he had seen since finding her. He pulled her in tight as her tears came in earnest. "You are right. We are Frostts. So, let's do what we Frostts do best."

Avery looked up at him, tears still flowing from her eyes, her chest heaving on a sob. He held her tighter and felt a shared determination. The world would burn before a Frostt gave up.

Frostt & Kai

Kyle T. Davis

Thank you!

Again and always, thank you to Jesus for giving me the faith to keep walking through this life.

I can't thank enough the most important person in my life, my best friend, my editor in chief, my right hand, my favorite person to annoy, my wife. Thank you with all my heart for spending your life with me and making mine better each and every day.

To my kids for always bringing me a smile and opening a whole new world of wonder and joy to me.

To Krista and Vibeke, thank you for your amazing editing skills. Thank you for making my messy words make sense.

Thank you, Melinda, once again for a great and outstanding book cover.

Lastly, and so important, thank you to all my readers. I can't express myself enough the thanks I feel for joining me on this adventure of words and wilds of my mind.

Frostt & Kai